FASHIONABLY FLAWED

BOOK NINE OF THE HOT DAMNED SERIES

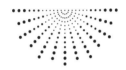

ROBYN PETERMAN

VISIT ROBYN'S WEBSITE

PRAISE FOR ROBYN'S BOOKS

Uproariously witty, deliciously provocative, and just plain fun! No one delivers side-splitting humor and mouth-watering sensuality like Robyn Peterman.

This is entertainment at its absolute finest!

~ Darynda Jones, NY Times Bestselling Author of the *Charley Davidson Series*

ACKNOWLEDGMENTS

This book was incredibly fun to write. It took me on a hilarious ride. I've been waiting a long time to write Satan's book and it was so freakin' satisfying to finally get to the point where it was his turn.

However, writing the story is only part of the journey to getting a book published. There are many people to thank and I'm a lucky girl to have such a talented and wonderful support system.

Rebecca Poole—your covers are brilliant as are you. Thank you.

Meg Weglarz—your editing always makes me look better than I am. Thank you.

Donna McDonald—a gal couldn't ask for tougher, brilliant and more awesome critique partner. Thank you.

Wanda and Susan—you are the best-est beta readers in the world. The journey this time was extremely helpful and a ton of fun. Thank you.

Wanda—you rock hard. Thank you.

My family—none of this would be worth it without you. Thank you for being mine. I adore you.

DEDICATION

For Darynda Jones, Molly Harper, Charlaine Harris and Janet Evanovich. Two of you I know and adore and am proud to call my friends. All four of you I fan-girl over!!

PROLOGUE

THE SUN RISES. THE SUN SETS. AND THE EARTH STILL SPINS IN SHOCK on its tilted axis in reaction to the day that darkness was forever catapulted from the Heavens.

The battle was epic and the craters left behind eventually became the oceans. In its sheer violence, the bloody clash created mind-boggling mountain ranges and lush vistas that would eventually leave man breathless with awe. Beauty created in fury and rage was still beauty.

Or was it…

In the beginning there were two Angels bound by blood. One was created to lord over the light and one the dark. However, Fate had a devastatingly destructive sense of humor and had not made the destiny of these divine beings clear.

The irony of this injustice was not lost on the angelic brothers, but they were connected by a love so great no one believed their fierce loyalty could be severed.

They were wrong—very wrong. For only one was meant for goodness and light.

One brother eventually emerged as the victor. He would be revered and adored. Always.

The other would fall from grace in a spectacular tumble from the Heavens that tore a rift between the brothers for eternity.

So one Angel came to rule the light. He was good, kind, and righteous. This Angel had wings of gold and was beloved by all.

The other lived in the darkness. His wings were as coal black as his soul and he was feared by every living creature. This particular Angel was thought of as evil personified. However, to know true evil, one must have first experienced grace...

Lucifer had known grace. Lucifer knew evil. But most of all, Lucifer knew how to have an outstanding time doing outrageously bad things.

Fate was a bitch, but she usually got it right.

AS THE ORANGE FLAMES DANCED AND LICKED AT MY SKIN, I LET MY head fall back on the marble stone in relief. The intensity of the blaze snarled and bit at me, but I was still far stronger than the glorious weapon of destruction because *I was destruction.*

The weight of the world was indeed burdensome. However, the weight of the most immoral, vile and corrupt part of humanity was at times unbearable. For eons the fire had burned away my sins and pain. I watched in fascination as my skin regenerated as quickly as the billowing flames consumed and seared it from my body.

The solace was only temporary. An inferno couldn't save my soul at this point and I didn't give a damn. My soul wasn't in question. I didn't have one. The bleak future that greeted me daily would never change. And the looming sensation of impending darkness that I couldn't shake off didn't concern me much either. There would always be darkness. Fate had decreed it.

Fate was a first-class bitch.

Fire had always given me a respite from the wickedness of my ways, but it was no longer doing the trick. "Going to have to find something new," I muttered, waving my hand and dousing the flames.

Today was a day like any other. Punishments must be doled out and chaos must be encouraged. A vacation would be lovely, but there was no rest for the weary… or the evil.

Glancing in the mirror at the image of the exquisitely beautiful man staring back at me, I smiled. I was a fucking handsome son of a bitch.

"It's show time, folks."

CHAPTER ONE

"It was a dark and stormy night."

"You've *got* to fucking be kidding me," Astrid muttered, giving me an impressive eye roll that would normally earn any lesser being an agonizing retribution.

My niece was an incredible pain in my evil and very fine ass, but I secretly adored her—not that I'd offer up that tidbit of information freely—I had a reputation to uphold. As Satan, I wasn't supposed to love anyone. That was more my brother God's arena. And since he was a showboating jackass of biblical proportions, I left the touchy feely up to him.

"Hmm, let me think," I said putting my finger to my lusciously full bottom lip and feigning deep thought. "No. Not fucking kidding at all."

"This just isn't going to fly, dude," she mumbled, scrolling through the massive manuscript.

Blackmailing Astrid into writing my autobiography served several purposes. It gave me an excuse to be earth side without drawing suspicion... and I was bored. Being the Prince of Darkness had its perks, but the monotony could be trying. Plus, it was vastly entertaining to drive my slightly unbalanced niece crazy and the venue was outstanding. The office of her mate, Prince Ethan, was a veritable smorgasbord of booty. The Vampyre prince had more office supplies than Staples, which I found absolutely delightful.

"What's the *problem*?" I inquired, tossing my black Armani sport coat on the leather couch and gifting her with an eye roll of my own. Mine was far better. I'd had millions of years of practice.

"You can't start every freakin' chapter of your autobiography plagiarizing Snoopy."

"Why not? And for your information, the original wordsmith who penned the terrible purple prose was Edward Bulwer-Lytton in his novel *Paul Clifford*—not Snoopy."

"Mmmkay," Astrid said, squinting her eyes at me.

I chose to take that as a sign of respect for my prowess with knowledge of obscure writers.

"But still, Uncle Who-shouldn't-be-writing-an-autobiography-at-all," Astrid went on. "Why would you choose to start every single chapter of your memoir with, *It was a dark and stormy night?*"

"Because it was."

"Can't argue with that logic," she muttered and typed it. "Alrighty, so what's next?"

"Should I discuss the month long orgy with the Elizabethan Court or do you think a play by play of when I served up Nero some of his own medicine—you know a little burning, boiling, stabbing and impaling—you get the drift."

"This is the worst damn idea ever," Astrid announced in a grumpy voice, slapping the laptop computer that I'd very graciously provided for our new venture shut with a snap.

"You're attitude is outstanding," I replied easily.

I so enjoyed my niece and her horrific outlook. She was proof that *apples* really didn't fall far from the tree. Astrid could deny her Demon heritage all she wanted. However, she wore it well, much to my amusement.

Vampyres were incredibly ungrateful. Demons were worse. As

Astrid was a combination of the two, it made for some wonderfully trying times. My darling niece had already banged her attractive head against the apparatus six times and expressed herself in a litany of filthy swear words that warmed my cold dead heart—and we still had a few chapters to go.

"We have a deal. The deal is I talk. You type."

"Nope," she shot back. "You blackmailed me into writing your autobiography—which is a fucking oxymoron since you should be writing it yourself."

"Your language appalls me."

"No, it doesn't."

"Touché," I said with a chuckle. "Fine. I can't type."

"You're kidding me. You're the badass of the Underworld. You're supposed to be able to do everything."

"I tried, but it's incredibly boring and not the least bit sexy," I admitted with a careless shrug and a grin. "I did try an online class, but that horrid computer woman, Mavis Beacon, made me have a fit that caused an avalanche. If she were an actual person, I'd treat her to a day in Hell she'd never forget."

"I feel you," Astrid groused. "Mavis Beacon is a total gaping butthole. That finger shit is for the birds. I threw a couple of computers across the room trying to please that hard woman."

"Too bad she's not real," I mused, making myself comfortable on the couch. "I'd like to date someone like that."

"Speaking of…" Astrid started with a smirk. "How's the love life going?"

"First of all," I corrected her. "Love has nothing to do with it. I love no one but myself."

"Liar, liar, Armani pants on fire," she said under her breath.

"I'm going to ignore that since I do find your son amusing and making him an orphan isn't on my agenda today," I shot back with my perfectly arched brow raised high—a look that worked for me —*always*. "Secondly, I tried this *love* you speak of once and it didn't work out very well. Almost ended in the Apocalypse."

"You use the brow thing too much," Astrid informed me ignoring my threat *and* my admission.

"Repeat."

"I *said*, you raise your brow all the time. It's losing its terrifying effect."

Snapping my fingers and conjuring a mirror I examined the evidence. Damn, if I wasn't a good-looking bastard. However, Astrid had a point. The eyebrow wasn't quite doing the trick. First the fire—now the eyebrow. Unacceptable.

"Shall I start blowing things up instead? Or how about I go Genghis Kahn on everyone and pour molten silver into their eyes and ears?" I suggested smoothly.

Astrid blanched and I graced her with a tight smile. It was my job to keep everyone on their toes—keep them guessing at how truly debased I was. I had no intention of filling the orifices of anyone with scalding metal except the bastard Genghis Kahn himself. In fact, over the years I'd treated him to his own medicine too many times to count. Turn about was fair play in my part world. I just happened to enjoy it, which was why I was very good at it. Of course my man Genghis wasn't as keen on the technique when it was done to him—ahhh, the irony.

"Umm, no, the eyebrow will be just fine," Astrid answered slowly, watching me closely to see how much of what I said was true.

The look of uncertainty on her face gave me pause. Damn it to Hell, was I losing my touch? I wanted to console the ungrateful child.

"Look, this book reads like an erotic journey slash some of the most unbelievably violent shit that I couldn't even make up slash a bad acid trip. I don't think it's gonna sell," Astrid stated the obvious, while deftly changing the subject.

"Of course it will." I waved my hand dismissively. "Just put some bullshit happily ever after at the end and we can pawn it off as a romance."

"You're serious?" she asked with a horrified expression.

"Completely."

"But, um... you don't exactly have a happily ever after at the moment," she reminded me cautiously. "You want me to lie?"

"But of course," I replied. "Most of what I've told you is fabricated."

"Are you shitting me?" she yelled with her fingers sparking menacingly. "I've spent a month of my life that I can't get back typing utter bullshit that's been flying from your deceitful lips?"

"I'd have to say that's fairly accurate," I replied with a laugh. Her anger always invigorated me. "However, a month is but a blip when you live forever. You shall see. And lies are *always* more fun that the truth."

"The sex stuff was a lie?" Astrid asked with a wince and a veiled expression of relief.

"No. That's all true."

And the relief disappeared.

"The violence?" she tried again.

"Again, no."

"Then what in the ever loving Hell was made up?" she demanded, running her hands through her wild hair in frustration.

"You're going to set your hair on fire," I commented as I watched a few strands sizzle under her sparking fingers.

"Motherfucker in a miniskirt," she bellowed, slapping at her head. "Do you see what this is doing to me? Are you happy? I almost singed myself bald because you've had more sex than the entire male population quadrupled. I do *not* look good bald."

"Names," I replied, ignoring her outburst. "I made up names. Wouldn't want any lawsuits."

"Shut the front door. Most of the freaks you talk about in the book are dead already and half of the species mentioned don't even exist in human's minds. How can you have lawsuits?"

"You'd be surprised," I replied, pilfering a few Mont Blanc

pens and a calculator. "Just make up a happily ever after and we'll be done."

"For real?" she asked with doubt written all over her lovely face.

"Yes."

"Would you lie to me?"

"Absolutely."

"So we're *not* done, Uncle Fucker?" she asked, narrowing her eyes at me.

Cities on fire, I loved her utter disrespect. "I suppose you didn't read the fine print in the contract," I informed her, biting back my grin with effort.

"I *suppose* I didn't because you didn't give me a *contract*," she snapped.

Pocketing a few more interesting looking gadgets from Ethan's desk, I clapped my hands and produced a thick folder. "Silly me," I chided myself sarcastically. "My apologies. Here it is."

With one last devastating grin at my now swearing and furious niece, I vanished in a cloud of glittering black smoke. Letting her cool down would ensure I didn't have to punish my favorite relative and would also safeguard her compound. Astrid tended to blow up buildings when she got pissed.

She was such a damned delight.

CHAPTER TWO

"HAVE YOU THOUGHT THIS THROUGH?" MY FATHER ASKED IN A concerned tone, pacing my massive office in Hell.

His small feet padded back and forth on the priceless Persian rug and I sighed in annoyance.

My appalling need to hug the small man irked me to no end. He was a Sprite—very rare and unfortunately squishy. My daughters, The Seven Deadly Sins had sent him into traction with their adoration multiple times over the centuries. While he was a good sport about it, he had to want to deck their asses occasionally. Hell knows I certainly did.

"I'm extremely tired of being second guessed on my decisions," I said flatly, playing with anything I could find on my desk.

"You want to hug me," my father stated with a smirk.

"No, I do not want to hug you, Bill. That would connote affection and I feel nothing," I replied.

"You know you want to," he said, moving closer. "And when did you start calling me Bill?"

"Today," I replied, gripping the edge of my desk so tightly my knuckles went white. "If you come one step closer, I *will* hug you and I assure you that *won't* end well."

"Come now, Lucifer," my father said with an impish little grin on his face as he ventured dangerously closer. "Even the Devil needs some love."

"Goddamn it," I bellowed, knocking a few irreplaceable Ming vases off my desk. "You will owe me for this. Is the door locked?"

Nodding and chuckling, my father wrapped his small arms around me and rested his head on my shoulder. This would not have worked if I'd been standing. I was well over six feet tall and Bill came up to my hip.

Growling with displeasure, I fought the need to hug him back. It simply wouldn't do. Getting soft did not go well with my reputation or my sanity. My favorite daughter Dixie and Astrid's son Samuel were the only ones to whom I showed true affection.

"I won't tell," my father whispered as I gave up and rested my head atop his.

"I'll smite your ass if you do," I threatened quietly, closing my eyes and enjoying the moment.

"Doesn't this feel nice?" Bill asked.

"No, it does not," I lied. "Emotion makes one weak. I don't do weak."

Bill tsk'd good-naturedly and backed away, taking a seat in front of my desk. I felt his absence acutely, but ignored it. His *cat who caught the canary* smile made me grind my teeth, but he was correct. It had felt nice. He knew it. I knew it. There was no need to discuss it. Ever.

"For being older than dirt, you still have much to learn, son."

Rolling my neck to shake off any sign of vulnerability, I shot my father a stern glance. "And you, old man, need to remember your place," I snapped.

Nice was not in my wheelhouse. The sooner Bill accepted this— the better off we'd be. Of course secretly, I hoped he'd never give up on me. Hell, he'd been pulling the same lovey dovey ridiculousness for thousands of years. It was doubtful he'd change his ways. And it was doubtful I'd change mine.

An impasse that satisfied us both.

"So as I was saying," my father went on. "This autobiography of yours is causing quite the ruckus in Heaven with your brother."

"Shall I phone him and tell him to fuck off?"

"Umm… no," Bill said with a barely disguised laugh he tried unsuccessfully to cover with a cough.

Bill was *my* father, not God's, and it pleased me that I had someone on my side in my eternity-long feud with my do-gooder brother.

"As interesting as that conversation might be," Bill continued. "I don't think that would go over too well with your mother. She's prone to destruction when annoyed."

"Why is it that everyone in this family blows up countries? Why can't it be something smaller occasionally?" I grumbled.

"Well, you know your mother…"

And as if on cue, flowering trees exploded out of the black marble floor and a flock of colorful wild birds darted around my office, crapping on all of my priceless antiques. Boulders dropped from the sky through the now decimated roof of the Dark Palace and a troop of monkeys appeared in the massive trees. Having my mother show up was always Hell on the architecture.

"Did you invite her?" I hissed, wanting to hide behind my desk from the bane of my existence. Of course, she'd find me easily, and since I'd avoided my weekly call for the past several years, I decided staying put was the wiser way to go.

"No, son, I didn't. I believe your hair brained autobiography prompted this visit," my father yelled over the wind that had whipped up with the entrance of the unwelcome jungle—and my mother.

In a cloud of peach and gold glittering dust she appeared—all red hair, porcelain skin, dressed to the nines, and as batshit insane as ever.

"Hello, Lucifer," my mother trilled as she delicately stepped

13

over a disgusting pile of parrot droppings. "I just thought I'd stop by and kick your ass."

"It's nice to see you too, Mother," I said, trying extremely hard to sound civil.

Which, apparently I failed, if the expression on my father's face was anything to go by.

"Do you really have to make such a goddamned catastrophic entrance, Mother?" I inquired, swatting at a monkey that was trying to steal the items I'd recently stolen from Astrid's mate.

"No, and stop taking your brother's name in vain. It's rude," she replied with a giggle that sounded like tinkling bells. "Anyhoo, knocking is boring. I prefer to make a splash. Come give your mommy a kiss."

"What is it with you people?" I ground out through clenched teeth. "I'm the fucking Prince of Darkness. I don't do…. *pleasantries*."

Her raised brow was terrifying. I needed to copy that.

Standing up and giving her an eye roll that I knew would piss her off, I gave her a brief air kiss and backed off quickly. My mother, *aka Mother Nature*, was prone to electrocution when displeased. Not that it would kill me. Nothing would kill me except the Sword of Death and that was locked safely away.

"To what do we owe this alarming visit?" I inquired.

Mother Nature settled herself on my father's lap and laid a kiss on his lips that was wildly inappropriate in my presence. If it had been anyone other than my parents, I would have enjoyed the lewd public display of affection. However, I didn't care how many thousands of years old a person was… no one wanted to see their parents tangle tongues.

"We do have guest rooms in the Dark Palace," I said, cutting into their appalling foreplay. "I don't have the time or the stomach to view this."

"Too bad, so sad," Mother Nature sang as she obscenely kissed my father once again.

Hopping off his lap and straightening her haute couture pink gossamer gown, she didn't waste any time getting down to business. Her eyes narrowed dangerously as menacing little peach and purple sparks formed a halo around her head. With her red hair blowing in a breeze I was certain she'd manufactured for effect, she pointed a meticulously manicured nail at me.

"*You* are in trouble, young man," she snapped.

"I'd hardly call me young, Mother," I replied with a grin that made her narrowed eyes become slits. "And my being in trouble is nothing new. So if that's all you've got, we're done here."

"You *can't* write an autobiography, you little shit. It's unheard of and we live quietly amongst the humans."

"Again, I beg to differ with your opinion. I'd hardly call the lives of the immortals *quiet*. And why is it that God can write a fucking book and I can't?" I shot back, leaning back in my chair and waiting for her to play favorites in favor of my brother —again.

My mother was the only one in the Universe that could get away with calling me a little shit and live to speak of it. The only reason I let it go was because I'd heard her call God the same thing. I knew the bastard phoned her on a regular basis. It chafed my ass that my brother had racked up more brownie points with our certifiable matriarch than I had. God was the ultimate kiss ass and I was the ultimate bad boy.

"God didn't write a tell all," Mother Nature said, confused.

"Lucifer's referring to the bible," my father explained, fondly patting her bottom.

"Oh for the love of everything good, evil, and somewhere in between," my mother groused and stamped her tiny Jimmy Choo clad foot causing a small tremble in Hell. "God wrote a *history* book."

"And I did as well," I said, defending my life story. "At least my book wasn't passed down by word of mouth for hundreds of years and then written in a dead language only to be translated innumerable times and interpreted by halfwits. Mine is straight from the guilty bastard's mouth."

"Little harsh on your brother there—not to mention yourself," Bill muttered.

"Yes, well the truth hurts," I informed him, doing my best imitation of my mother's raised brow. "This is why lies are so much more fun."

"He does have an interesting point," Mother Nature said to my father before looking back at me. "But do not tell your brother I said that. I'll deny it and set off an earthquake in Hell that will make the Valdivia quake look like a burp."

"So noted."

"So you're telling me your book is full of lies?" she questioned, petting a monkey that had dropped from a tree and landed on her shoulder.

"Not exactly," I hedged. As much as I enjoyed stretching the truth till it popped, it wasn't good form to lie to Mother Nature. "However, all the names have been changed for protection."

"Protection of the innocent?" she inquired.

My harsh laugh echoed though the destroyed room and I slammed my hands down on my desk causing both my parents to sit up and pay attention. "For *my* protection. I could care less about the innocent. That's God's territory. I just punish the evil ones."

"Tut, tut," she chided, pointing at me again. "You make yourself sound like such a bad person, darling."

With an exasperated sigh, I banged my head on my desk. "I *am* a bad person, Mother. I'm the fucking Devil—*the* Fallen Angel— the baddest of the bad guys."

"Sweetie, you simply punish the evil doers," she explained as if I didn't know what the Hell I did. "You didn't create evil, you simply penalize those who choose that path."

"Semantics, Mother. I enjoy it and I do it well. However, while we're on the subject… it was that sanctimonious shit up above that gave man free will. I'd like to go on record saying that evil is technically his fault."

"Little bit of a stretch there," my father muttered.

"Not at all," I replied with a shrug.

We all sat in uncomfortable silence for a moment and digested my theory—uncomfortable for them. I was quite fine with my assessment.

"He's actually a really, really, really good boy," my mother commented as my traitor of a father nodded in agreement.

"Fine," I snapped and crushed my new stolen calculator with my fist. Damn it, I liked that calculator. "God's good. I'm bad. I wrote my autobiography to clear up some misconceptions and you all can go fuck yourselves. Anything else?"

"Your brother has requested to read the tome before it goes out into the world," Mother informed me.

"Why? So he can make sure I depicted him in a glowing light? Like I was able to approve his description of me in the bible?" I shouted. "The answer is no. You can tell him he can shove his self-righteous bullshit up his pious ass. He's barely in the book at all anyway, Gaia."

The silence was long and awkward—exactly the way I liked them.

"How about this?" my mother suggested with an eye roll that I almost congratulated her on. "We tell your brother it's going out as fiction and you'll use a pen name. You do realize as nice as your brother is, he's awfully good at causing epic floods. And when did you start calling me by my first name?"

"Today," Bill offered, patting her hand so she wouldn't use it to electrocute me.

"You may tell my brother anything you'd like to tell him. I don't care," I said, waving my hand and repairing the calculator. "And I had planned to use a pen name. No one is going to buy a book by *Satan*."

"Fine point. Well made," my father said with a nod.

"I didn't ask for your opinion."

"My bad," he replied with a grin.

My mother blew out an exasperated and overly dramatic sigh. This of course caused a minor tornado that blew down several of the trees she'd brought with her. "Why are you doing this, Lucifer? Do you need money?"

"That is an utterly ridiculous question." I stood to signal our somewhat hostile meeting was over. "I've stolen more money than I know what to do with. I'm simply bored and the book amuses me."

"Can't you find a hobby that won't reveal us?" she countered in a whiny tone, not one to give in easily. Ever. "You do realize if humans think the actual Devil wrote it, the sale of Ouija boards will go up exponentially. You'll be summoned constantly."

"Which will give me something to do on Friday nights," I shot back thinking I should buy some stock in Ouija boards.

"Would you like to know what I think?" she inquired silkily in a tone that made me want to either hide or throw something at her.

My family was annoying and certifiable—all of them. Normally, I would accept that as a badge of honor except when I had to deal with them. Today I had no time for this. Something evil and dark was brewing that needed my attention and it would take a few hours to repair the damage to my office.

"Is this a trick question?" I asked, knowing full well that I had no choice in the matter.

"I think you need to find a nice girl and settle down."

Again with the awkward silence... except this time I was uncomfortable and pissed.

Waving my hand in a swift motion, I burnt all the trees to the ground in a flash of red lightening. I spared the monkeys, because I actually liked monkeys. However, a few of the birds might have gone up in flames. I didn't take kindly to my abode being crapped on.

"I tried that once, Mother," I growled. "It didn't turn out well, now did it?"

Mother Nature stood, leaned forward and placed her hands on my desk. A rainbow of sparks glittered around her signifying an explosion was imminent. "You didn't love her. You only wanted her because your brother did and the same goes for him. Eve was not meant for either of you."

"She's the mother of my child," I ground out, annoyed because my mother had made some fine points that hit home.

"You have eight daughters by *eight different women*. You didn't stay with any of them," she reminded me as if I didn't know that already.

"Your point?"

"My point is that a good—or in your case, *evil* —woman might keep you from writing autobiographies," she announced, quite pleased with herself for solving my problem that I didn't think I had.

"While this may be true, Eve was a decent woman who is now simply a husk of who she was," I said flatly. "And I don't do monogamy."

Regret was something I didn't enjoy. My mother was correct. What I'd thought was love was simply the need to best my brother and in the end we'd destroyed the first human woman created. My love always ended with collateral damage. The Devil didn't get a happily ever after. On the rare occasions I'd tried, it had ended horribly.

"Eve will be fine—or a loose definition of fine. She'll never be quite normal, but then again she was always one apple short of a bushel," my mother said with a shrug of her slim shoulders and a delighted giggle at her pun. "She'll go on and be useful at some point, but not as a mate to you or to God. Fate is a bitch and she has decreed that little nugget."

"Is that all?" I yawned just because it was rude and sat back in my chair. "I have business to take care of."

"I'm done," my mother hissed as she clapped her hands and gestured to her monkeys to gather. "I will tell you this though... if you make me look bad in that book, I'll move to Hell and terrorize you for all eternity. Am I clear?"

"Quite," I replied with a laugh and a shudder. "I only mentioned you once."

"Really?" she asked with another giggle. "What did you say?"

What I was about to tell her could go one of two ways—her being happy or Hell exploding. I was no idiot. I'd lie. "I spoke of your prowess in the kitchen and your love of pole dancing."

My father's eyes grew wide in terror. Mother Nature couldn't cook to save her life. Pompeii had been buried in mountains of ash and lava because someone had insulted her cake at a horrifying family picnic. And the pole dancing? That was nightmare inducing.

"Wonderful," she squealed and gifted us with a hip grind that made me throw up in my mouth a bit. "Did you use my name?"

"Absolutely not. I changed all the names so you couldn't sue me."

Mother Nature paused and took that in, playing with her red curls as her monkeys danced around her. "Wise choice, Lucifer," she replied taking my father by the hand. "Bill, I need you in Nirvana. My dishwasher is broken."

With a snap of his small fingers, my father produced a toolbox loaded with things I was quite sure he'd never used in his life. In his incredibly old age, the Sprite had taking to doing manual labor as a hobby. He'd destroyed more appliances in Heaven and Hell than could be counted on a thousand hands. However, no one really seemed to mind since the bastard was so damned charming. I even ignored the ten flat screen TVs he'd *fixed* in the Dark Palace. Things were replaceable. My overly affectionate father was not.

"Call me, darling," Mother Nature said with her fabulously raised brow high as a pale peach glitter storm whipped up and surrounded my demented parents.

"Will do," I replied with a wave.

"Liar," she shot back with a wide grin. "Just remember, son of mine, this autobiography will get you into far more trouble than you bargained for."

"I certainly hope so."

"Beware of what you wish for, Lucifer. I will so enjoy saying I told you so."

And on that cryptic and quite amusing note, they disappeared.

More trouble than I bargained for? My mother may have thought she'd put fear in me but she'd done the exact opposite. I lived for trouble.

With an evil little smile of anticipation, I clapped my hands and repaired enough of my office so it was usable. My staff would take care of the rest later. Unfortunately for them, they were well used to my mother's visits.

All sorts of trouble was brewing.

It was turning into very fine day.

CHAPTER THREE

"Repeat," I demanded, pressing the bridge of my nose while holding my temper—and laughter—with effort.

"I'm going by Dino now, my liege," the formerly named Skuolonu explained as he bowed deeply before me.

Three of my finest Demon warriors stood in front of the desk in my still slightly demolished office to apprise me of a disturbance on Earth. I stared at them silently as each lowered his eyes in deference to me—or more likely fear. I tried so hard to let them find themselves creatively. Happy Demons—*a relative term*—were more productive Demons. However, this changing names game was going to grind my nerves quickly.

But then again, when one lived for thousands of years, it was difficult to begrudge them some amusement. I was fortunate. I went by many names—Lucifer, Satan, Beelzebub, Prince of Darkness, Divine Asshole, Uncle Fucker…

Sighing, I leaned back in my chair and eyed the deadly idiots. "And the rest of you? Have you changed your names as well?"

"Yes, your excellency," the one I'd forever known as Bealsahm informed me in his harsh voice that I'd always found strangely calming. "I'd like to be called Darby."

"*Seriously?*" I asked. Who in the Hell would choose Darby?

He nodded as Gamunoch stepped forward. "And I now answer to Dagwood."

"And is there a reason you're all choosing D names?" I inquired expecting them to tell me they were pulling my leg.

"Coincidence," Darby said without a trace of humor in his tone.

They were clearly *not* pulling my leg. For such stoic and vicious killers, they'd certainly chosen some appallingly wimpy names.

"Coincidence?" I repeated slowly, still searching for the joke.

"Absolutely," Dino confirmed. "We thought the names had a nice ring with Demon tagged onto the end... as a surname, since we don't actually have one... as you know."

"Also far easier to pronounce than our old names, therefore easier to get laid," Dagwood added with a thumbs up.

The correlation escaped me and there was no joke to be found. Squinting my eyes at them, I wondered if I'd chosen the correct right hand men. They were never going to get laid *or* instill fear with names like that. They were much better off with their former names. Far be it from me to point that out. The names were ridiculous—Dino Demon, Dagwood Demon and Darby Demon. Of course they were handsome men—all Demons were beautiful in their human form. It made it far easier to get away with all sorts of unsavory things if one was pretty.

The Demons from nightmares existed as well and it was part of my job to control them. Living forever did things to the mind and spirit. Eventually, most of my kind went bad—another relative term—at some point. The otherworldly beauty faded quickly once a Demon descended too far into the darkness. Sadly, destroying them had become easy over the years. I had very little feeling about it at all.

"What do you think?" Darby inquired as his eyes went red with excitement.

"Of what?" I asked, not following.

"Our names," Dino supplied as excited as the others.

"I think that I shall reserve my opinion for the time being. However, did any of you consider the name Dick? Seems to me that one gets straight to the point if getting laid is the reasoning behind this strange new hobby," I replied, not wanting to break their alarmingly strange creative leanings.

Nodding collectively they gave each other dirty looks.

"We all wanted Dick," Darby hissed, glaring at Dino. "We fought for it."

Oh there were so many ways to reply to that one…

"But since Darby lost his leg, right arm and left hand in that minor altercation, we decided none of us could be Dick," Dagwood, ever the peacemaker, volunteered with a wide grin. "Even though Dino *is* a dick."

"At least I *have* a dick," Dino snarled and went at Dagwood with his fangs bared.

"Enough," Darby bellowed and tackled both his fellow Demons to the ground while brandishing an impressively large dagger. "We all have dicks. No one *is* a dick. And no one can have the name Dick. Am I clear? Cause if I'm not, I'd be happy to remove both of your dicks, you stupid Dicks."

"How about this?" I suggested sarcastically. "Why don't each of you take the middle name Dick? Darby Dick Demon. Dagwood Dick Demon. Dino Dick Demon. And then you can all be dicks."

They were silent as they pondered my proposal. Of course they were supposed to laugh, since it had been a fucking joke, but I always seemed to forget how literal most of my Demons were.

"I was kidding, boys," I said with an eye roll and a put upon sigh.

"I don't know," Darby said thoughtfully. "I kind of like it. The monogram would be outstanding."

"Sounds kind of gay—you know like we're dick Demons," Dino pointed out.

"But I am gay," Darby reminded him.

"I'll pop anything so it doesn't bother me," Dagwood announced.

"Settled," Darby grunted with delight. "Henceforth, we shall be known as the triple D's. The Devil's Dick Demons."

I was almost rendered mute by this bizarre exchange. The conversation had definitely taken a woefully wrong turn somewhere. Unsure how I would be able to address my deadliest *Dick* Demons with a straight face, I simply shrugged and gave up. As long as they obeyed me without question, their names were of little consequence.

"All right then, umm... Darby. Report on the disturbance."

"Can you use my full name, sire?" he inquired.

"No. No I can't," I replied as my fingers began to shoot red jagged sparks. "It's taking all I have to address you as *Darby*."

"Roger that, my liege."

Darby, Dagwood and Dino eyed each other cautiously. After an entertaining and frantic moment of silent communication, the most vicious of the three stepped forward. I believe it was Dagwood... or Dino... or Dick. Whatever.

"There's a woman selling souls on Earth," he began.

"Well, that's certainly a big fucking no-no. Is she a Demon?" I inquired.

Full-blooded Demons were permitted to roam the Earth. Keeping an eye on them was trying at times, but we needed chaos to survive and the humans were full of it. I wanted to get to the bottom of this soul seller quickly. I couldn't shake the unsettling looming darkness that was beginning to consume me.

"Umm... no. We're not exactly sure what she is. However, her rack is truly outstanding," Darby said, joining his comrade.

"You like dick," Dino snapped. "What do you know about racks?"

"I know a good rack when I see one, dick face," Darby shot back with a vicious right jab to Dino's jaw.

It was an outstanding punch and the blood sprayed

everywhere. However, I didn't have the time to enjoy a fistfight. I had things to do.

Expelling a long sigh, I placed my hands on my desk in full view of my men. This was a sign that I was doing my best not to smite them where they stood. Half answers, vague hints, the name Dick, and arguing about the quality of racks of soul sellers displeased me. Greatly.

"How old are you?" I asked Darby in the most polite tone I could muster.

"Five thousand," he replied uneasily, keeping his eyes glued to my hands.

"And you?" I inquired of Dagwood.

"Eight thousand and twelve."

"And you, *Dino*?" I questioned with a raised brow that made all three of them back away.

Astrid was gravely mistaken. My eyebrow move still worked beautifully.

"Seven thousand five hundred," Dino whispered.

"Interesting. So explain to me how three Demons with over twenty thousand years of debauchery between them can't tell the species of a woman selling souls?" I bellowed. "I don't pay you to be indecisive. I pay you to know what the Hell you're doing."

The bravest or the stupidest of the three went to his knees and raised his eyes to mine. "We've never seen anything like her before. We sent twenty of our best to access the situation and end it, but they came back broken men. They're all in a coma-like states and have been quarantined to the infirmary in Purgatory."

"Why Purgatory?" I questioned their judgment.

"If they wake up violent, it's so damned beige and boring there we figured it would lull them back to sleep. That shitty elevator music alone is enough to put most into a coma," Dino explained the odd course of action.

"While that was somewhat thought out, I want them put in the Sub-Basement and confined. If they wake up sexually aroused—as

Demons are wont to do after battle—that could cause problems in Purgatory. I have no time to deal with that right now. God has as much jurisdiction over Purgatory as I do and a surprise orgy is not something I see going over well," I instructed with an evil little grin and a shrug.

Hell was divided into levels. Not Dante's version of levels, of course—*my* version. That arrogant bastard was unhappily surprised he hadn't gotten it right. Such a stupid man. He thought he could best me and lost his soul. Too bad, so sad.

Purgatory was Purgatory—bland, beige and boring. I hardly ever visited.

The Basement was one of my favorites. The lowest level had crude stone walls and uneven rock floors illuminated by enormous iron torches. The odor was exactly what most would think Hell would smell like—absolutely putrid. The Basement housed the worst of the worst souls and there was no way out. A huge wall of gorgeous fire and lava blasted out of a crevasse in the floor that was ten feet wide and spanned the entirety of the area which was the length of approximately fifty football fields. The Soul Lights of those damned to Hell darted in and out of the flames screaming in agony and paying for sins so vile they even gave me pause.

The Sub-Basement was for *lesser* evil souls. There was an exquisite inferno there as well, but not quite as hot. The unlucky bastards that resided there weren't quite wicked enough for the Basement, but not quite good enough for Purgatory.

The Rehab room was a place I liked to ignore. I was *forced* into providing an area where souls had the choice to do penance so they could one day leave Hell and ascend to Purgatory... then possibly to Heaven. It was a rare occurrence for this to happen, but on the unlikely occasion it did, my brother gloated and sent flowers. To be fair, I sent him poison ivy every time an Angel fell.

However, the loveliest part of Hell was the Main Floor. The Main Floor was as big as the continental United States but far more beautiful. The Dark Palace was in the northeast corner in an area about the size of Washington DC—green and lush with more exotic plants and flowers than Earth twenty times over. All of my Demons lived on the Main Floor and I kept track of every single one.

One didn't become a Demon. One was born a Demon and one would die a Demon. There was no way around our fate. It was also a misnomer to label a Demon as evil. We were by no stretch of the imagination good, but we didn't cause evil even though we thrived on it. God created free will. Man was inherently naughty— and could be very, very *bad*. This was very, very *good* for my people and kept me in business.

"This woman, did she try to kill our men?" I asked, far more interested now than I was moments ago. Any woman who could best twenty of my Demons was a woman I wanted to know.

"There was no sign of injury other than higher than normal body temperature," Darby confirmed carefully. "We were able to debrief two before they fell into unconsciousness and they were euphorically happy and very sexually aroused."

"So you're telling me they got laid by a mystery soul seller and are now in a vegetative state? Little far-fetched, Darby," I said flatly.

Darby cleared his throat uncomfortably and stepped back with a deep bow.

"No sign of sexual intercourse," Dagwood said with a confused shrug. "If I were to guess, I'd have to say we have a rogue Siren on our hands."

Now my interest was piqued. It was a possibility, but a very slim one. Sirens had been extinct for thousands of years. I would have known if any were left.

"Not likely," I said, standing up and rounding my desk. "Where was this woman last seen?"

"Earth," Dino volunteered.

"A little more specific would be helpful," I said, again pressing the bridge of my nose. "Earth is large. Do you feel me, Dino?"

"Sorry sire," Dino said with a curt nod of embarrassment. "Chicago. She's posing as a photographer."

"What do you mean *posing*?" I snapped in exasperation. "Does she take pictures?"

The Demons nodded.

"Does she have a studio? A fucking camera?"

Again they nodded. I really needed to find better help.

"And does this dangerous woman have a name?"

"Adrielle Rinoa—goes by Elle."

"Never heard of her," I mused aloud. "And we're quite positive she's not a Demon?"

"Quite," Dagwood replied. "Shall we send another unit after her?"

"No. We shall not," I said, speaking as I formed a plan in my head. "Does anyone know where Fate is residing at the moment?"

All three Demons shuddered at the mention of Fate. I shuddered as well, but internally. Never good to show your army any fear—or hatred. It weakened authority. Going to Fate was a calculated risk, but she owed me. The bitch would owe me till the end of time. I knew it and she knew it. I'd very rarely called in favors from her over the centuries. Her price was usually too steep, but time was of the essence. This Elle woman needed to be taken care of and then I needed to find the source of the darkness that was haunting me.

"Vegas. Fate's in Vegas," Dino informed me.

"Of course she is," I replied with an eye roll. "At one of my casinos?"

Since I owned most of them—albeit as a silent partner—there was a fine chance she was in one of my establishments. That would work to my advantage as I could watch what the Hell she was up to over the video feed before I cornered her.

"No, my Prince. She's at the Royal Castleton Northeast."

"Never heard of it. Is it near the Bellagio?"

"Not exactly," Dino said with a chuckle.

"No matter. Order one of my limos up and have it ready in an hour. We'll transport to Vegas but then we'll move around like the humans do—less conspicuous. You three will come with me, but get several units in Hell ready to go. Once I find this Elle woman, I might need a hand with something else."

"May I be so bold as to ask you what you're referring to?" Dagwood asked.

The question was legitimate. It was protocol to know what we were sending our Demons into. However, I had no idea what was brewing. All I knew was that it was dark and it had the ability to consume me. And if something happened to me, the end of the world was quite near.

"You may," I replied slowly. The truth was I had no damned clue, but that simply wouldn't do. "You'll know when you need to."

"Very well, my liege," Dagwood said with a respectful nod. "We will alert the troops regardless. They will be available at your command."

"Get yourselves ready boys," I said dryly. "We're going to Vegas to see what fate has in store."

The play on words amused me, but the reality of meeting with someone I despised turned my stomach. So be it. Fate could be kind occasionally. However, *occasionally* rarely happened when I was involved.

CHAPTER FOUR

"M<small>MMKAY, SO CORRECT ME IF</small> I'<small>M WRONG</small>," A<small>STRID GROWLED AS SHE</small> shoved Dino to the side, crawled over him and got up in my face. "Not only have I been writing your eye bleeding and gas inducing autobiography for the past month, which has *really* screwed with my sex life by the way. It's seriously hard to be horny when burned into my brain are images of The Prince of Darkness himself, humping toothless, blind, albino, banshee witches. You feel me, Uncle Fucker? And now I'm sitting in a *white* stretch *Hummer* outside of a skeevy casino in Vegas with the Devil and three Demons who have identical middle names glorifying their skin flutes. *And it's three o'fucking clock in the morning.*"

"It's Dick, not skin flute," Darby offered weakly from the driver's seat.

Practically every Demon in Hell was terrified of my profane and insanely powerful niece—emphasis on the insane part. And if I were being honest—which was never —I'd have to admit the wild child even unnerved me at times. I was counting on Astrid throwing Fate off her nefarious game.

"That's what I said, *Dick*," Astrid snapped at Darby.

"Umm... actually," Dagwood corrected her in a whisper. "You said skin flute."

"My bad," Astrid said as her hands and arms began to spark ominously. "I meant pork sword—teeny tiny eeny weeny pork sword. Better?"

Silence ensued. Hell on fire, Astrid was a delight.

"They weren't toothless," I said with a grin.

"Who wasn't toothless, for the love of Cousin Jesus in a thong," Astrid shouted so loudly I was certain the entire Strip could hear her.

"The banshee witches. They all had full sets of teeth. I would never bed someone missing their pearly whites."

"Well, that's certainly a fucking relief. The image is so much less offensive now," she said in a tone dripping with so much sarcasm I almost applauded. "So this shit had better be good. I was freakin' sleeping next to the love of my undead life and then I was all of a sudden I was here. Spill it, Uncle Fucker, or I'm gone."

"I need a favor," I said easily.

"And what do I get in return?" Astrid shot back with narrowed eyes and the beginnings of a devious little smile pulling at her lips.

Astrid was a piece of work. No one played me like she did and got away with it. No one. And what a joy it was. "What do you want?" I asked.

She pretended to think hard, but I knew her game. She was a horribly wonderful little Vampyre slash Demon. She knew as well as I did that favors from the Devil were difficult to come by and therefore extremely valuable.

However, Astrid was far more than a half Vampyre-half Demon. She was a True Immortal—like myself and nine others. We were virtually unkillable—a very lovely insurance policy.

There were ten of us roaming the planes of existence. We had jobs or rather the jobs had us. I, of course, was the harbinger of Evil, and my sanctimonious shit of a brother, God, represented all that was Good. My father was Wisdom, and my unbalanced mother, Mother Nature, was Emotion. My favorite of my eight daughters, Dixie, was Balance, and her mate, The Angel of Death, was... well, Death. Not my first choice for a son-in-law, but as long as the shit treated her well, I'd leave him alone.

Lucy, the daughter of Eve—the woman my brother and I had fought over—was Temptation. And the idiot that currently pined after Temptation—the Angel of Light—represented Life.

And then there was Astrid. The half Vampyre-half Demon was Compassion. Interesting choice for one of her heritage, but I had to admit the insane woman was a perfect fit.

However, the most powerful immortal of all was still a small child. Yes, the miracle child born of Astrid and her mate Ethan represented all of our powers combined as one—he was Utopia. The child, Samuel, had the most precarious road to travel of all the True Immortals. His future would be something I would watch very closely and with great interest.

"State your favor, Astrid. What is it that your undead heart desires?" I pressed my niece.

"I'll get back to you on that," Astrid replied, using one of my own lines on me. "And you'd better have left some kind of note for Ethan because if he wakes up and I'm missing there's gonna be a massive can of Master Vampyre whoop ass headed your way."

With a wave of my hand and a wide grin, I allayed her fears. Her mate was the Vampyre Prince of the North American Dominion—very strong—very possessive. "Yesssss, I left the Vampyre a note and returned a few of the Mont Blanc pens I borrowed," I assured her.

"You mean stole," she corrected me.

"I prefer *pilfered*—more poetic," I shot back.

With an eye roll that should have ensured she could see her own backside, Astrid laughed. "Fine, why am I here? I would think you and the three Pocket Rockets should be able to handle any issues up here on Earth."

The huffing and puffing from Dino, Dagwood and Darby made

me chuckle. Astrid had a creatively profane way with words that would hopefully make my Demons rethink their middle name choice.

"Darling child," I said. "You know as well as I do that Hell isn't below and Heaven isn't above. We're all simply on different planes. We share the same sun, moon and sky."

"Dude," Astrid snapped, completely exasperated. "If I came here for a freakin' immortal geography lesson, I'm gonna go ape shit on all of you. And *no one* wants me to go ape shit."

"She makes a fine point," Darby volunteered, and then shut his trap when I shot him a look that was just short of deadly—literally.

"I need you to throw Fate off her game so I can get what I need from the bitch," I explained. No need to beat around the bush. If you don't ask, you don't receive, and I very much liked receiving.

"Shut the front mother humpin' door," Astrid shouted, making me wince. "Fate's an actual person?"

"Unfortunately, yes," I replied curtly as I waved my hand and dressed my niece in a vintage red Chanel cocktail dress. It perfectly matched the devilish red streak in her mahogany hair. Adding a pair of silver stilettos and a diamond choker that was clearly priceless, I grinned and waited for her reaction.

She didn't disappoint.

Glancing down at her new attire, Astrid gasped with delight. She was such a materialistic little Vampyre—and such a girl. Her nightclothes wouldn't do when meeting with Fate, so I treated her to a little upgrade.

"Oh my Hell, I look hot," she squealed, fingering the choker and smoothing out the dress. "Can I keep it?"

"Will you screw with Fate?" I shot back.

"What has she done to you?" Astrid wisely asked.

"What hasn't she done?" I shot back.

Astrid eyed me for a long moment and then let her head fall back on the seat. "You're in trouble, aren't you?" she inquired softly. "Something is very wrong. I can feel it."

I said nothing. Her astute guess was exactly why I needed her at the moment. She watched me and waited. As my silence continued, her eyes narrowed to slits.

"Plug your ears, you Baloney Ponies, or you're going to lose your middle names—pun violently intended," she ordered the Demons, waiting until they did as she asked.

Astrid turned and faced me with an expression that I hated. I recognized it. It was her compassionate face. When was my family going to realize I was the Harbinger of fucking Evil? All this emotional namby pamby ridiculousness was wearing me out.

"Whether you like it or not, I love you and I know you love me even though you're too much of a jackhole to admit it," she said with her own brows appropriately raised. "I will help you—no favor required. However, I want the dress, choker and shoes," she added with a grin.

"They're yours," I said, happy that there was least a small modicum of blackmail involved. "So you'll mess with Fate for me?"

"For diamonds and Chanel from my Uncle Fucker who secretly loves me? Absolutely."

"That's my girl," I said approvingly. I wasn't entirely sure what love meant, but if the definition included killing for someone, then I supposed I *might* love my niece. I would incinerate to dust anything that threatened her. "Let's go have some fun."

"*Fun* being a *relative* word?" she questioned with a smirk.

"Absolutely."

"YOU CAN'T BE SERIOUS," I MUTTERED AS I TOOK IN THE DILAPIDATED interior of what barely passed as a casino. "Fate must be slumming it."

It was small as far as gambling establishments went and clearly hadn't been remodeled since the 1970s. The stale smell of stale alcohol, cigarettes and desperation permeated the air. The colors were faded and the tables were shoddy. I couldn't begin to imagine why Fate had chosen this place to frequent. But then one never knew why Fate did what she did.

"This place is a dump," Astrid agreed, trying not to touch anything as we made our way inside. "There are no humans here. It's all Vamps, Demons, and I don't even know what else."

"Shifters, Fairies, and a few Gargoyles," Darby said quietly as he and my two other Demons flanked us protectively.

It was more for show than safeguarding. I was a walking weapon of destruction and Astrid wasn't far behind. However, pomp and circumstance was the way I liked to roll.

Darby was correct as far as the lineage of the patrons went. Clearly my men were excellent at detecting species. Why couldn't they place the soul seller in Chicago? Pushing that thought aside, I focused on the matter at hand—it was unsavory and needed to move along quickly.

Would I leave with the information I sought? No fucking clue.

Our entrance caused quite the stir, as I'd expected. The sheer amount of magic Astrid and I possessed together was jaw dropping and my three Demons were no slouches. Several lowlifes whom I was quite sure were on the invite list to Hell slipped out the back door and several others got under the filthy gaming tables.

"Gargoyles are real?" Astrid asked in shock. "I need a dang species list. This is getting out of control."

"They exist and you don't want to engage them—very difficult to kill and their blood stains your hands for months—forget about your clothes. They have to be trashed," I said as I scanned the room for the sorry excuse of a woman I was searching for.

"Are you shitting me?" she asked with a scrunched nose.

I gave her the raised brow and she backed up a step. "I'm not shitting you. Just stay with me and follow my lead. Clear?"

"As mud," she mumbled. "What do you want from Fate?"

"Information."

"And she's going to give it to you?"

"Probably not."

Astrid groaned and elbowed me. "So this is just a middle of the night exercise in bullshit and futility?"

"Possibly, but it will be fun." I winked and pulled her along to the back of the casino.

Fate was not in the main area, which meant she was most likely hidden in the back. Hell, she probably knew I was coming. She was Fate after all.

"Define *fun*," Astrid hissed as I kicked in the locked door at the far end of the room.

Ignoring my obnoxious niece, I gave a curt nod to my men. They immediately spread out and blocked all the exits. I recognized four others of my own in the room and gave silent communication for them to go outside and surround the dilapidated building. Didn't want Fate to slip through my fingers. She might not give me what I wanted, but she was going to see me.

"Will she try to kill us?" Astrid asked as she before we entered the darkened back room.

"She can't. We're un-killable."

"Didn't ask if she would succeed," Astrid pointed out correctly. "Asked if she'd try."

"That's not how Fate works. She doesn't have to lift a finger to instill terror. She controls destiny," I said flatly.

"Did I forget to say *thank you* for possibly fucking up my life?" Astrid inquired with so much sarcasm it was scathing.

"I believe you did forget," I replied with a grin.

"You are gonna owe me so big, Uncle Butthole," she muttered as she shoved me out of the way and marched into the room with her horrifying attitude displayed beautifully.

"I know," I said. My niece didn't hear me as she was already in the room. "I just hope I'll be around to repay."

CHAPTER FIVE

"Well, this is an interesting *surprise*," an alluring female voice purred from the darkness.

"Interesting good or interesting bad?" Astrid asked cautiously, peering into the darkened corner where Fate sat or stood or floated.

One never knew what form the old bat would choose.

I was having a difficult time spotting her as well. I was quite capable of seeing clearly in the dark as was Astrid, but Fate had cast some sort of spell that made seeing her murky at best.

"Interesting in neither fashion," the voice said with a derisive chuckle. "And it's hardly a surprise."

"So Fate, how are you doing? Busy fucking up lives?" I asked in an attempt at my most charming.

The silence lasted about three seconds too long and the look Astrid shot me confirmed my greeting wasn't very charming —at all.

"Do you care, Lucifer?" Fate inquired archly as the shadows began to slither away and a feeling of foreboding flooded the small dank room.

"I don't," I replied smoothly. "But then again you already know that."

As the darkness faded, my nemesis appeared. It took all I had not to gasp or look away from her haggard appearance, but Astrid wasn't nearly as collected.

"Sweet mother of Buddha on a bender," Astrid shouted and plastered herself against the wall. "I was not expecting *this*. You look, um… like, you know… not what I thought," she petered off weakly as Fate hissed.

"And you are?" Fate snapped as she stepped into the light and eyed Astrid with displeasure.

Astrid was correct. Fate looked like the Basement of Hell on a bad day. If this was a façade she'd chosen, she was losing her mind. Her normally thick wavy blonde hair was gray and sparse and her eyes appeared sunken into her gaunt face. Normally bright and arresting purple, her eyes were now flat and lifeless. Her body was hunched over and her hands gnarled. I hadn't seen the old witch in centuries, but she couldn't have possibly aged this much.

"You don't know who I am?" Astrid asked, not quite sure how to proceed.

"Of course, I know," Fate said flatly. "A few manners every now and then would be a nice change."

"Right. Sorry," Astrid apologized and gave a rather clumsy half curtsy slash half bow to the hag. "I'm Astrid."

"Make sure you tell her your deepest desires so she can shit on them," I added amiably.

"Dude, you're not helping your cause whatever it is," Astrid chided me.

"The child is wise, Lucifer. You should listen to her," Fate said with a cackle that made my skin crawl.

"What has happened to you?" I demanded.

A diaphanous silver dust blew around the room as Fate snapped her fingers and closed her eyes. The temperature went from moderately warm to frigid. As immortals, Astrid and I were impervious to the chill, but it was unnerving and unnecessary.

"Umm… what's going on here?" Astrid whispered.

"She's stopped time," I said under my breath.

"Why?"

"Because she can."

If Fate was on her last legs, it didn't bode well for anyone. As much as I despised the woman, her death was unacceptable. Who knew what would replace her—if anything.

"It's bothersome to have the weight of the Universe on one's shoulders," Fate announced curtly. "You should completely *understand* that, Fallen Angel."

Ignoring the jab, I shrugged and approached her. She backed away and re-shrouded herself in the darkness. It was visual and physical. The insane old woman had barricaded herself from me.

"Tell me what I've come for," I insisted as I admired the intricate spell she surrounded herself with. There were holes in the carefully woven sorcery. I knew I could break through with a flick of my wrist, but for now I'd play her game.

"And why would you think I would tell *you* anything? You're the scum beneath my shoe," she growled menacingly.

Rolling my eyes, I grinned at Astrid's indignant gasp. I was used to Fate's rude diversionary tactics. Piss off the Devil so he does something heinous and she gets to leave. Not going to happen this time.

"Yes, well it's been *lovely* to be stepped on by such a sub-par and certifiable immortal as yourself for thousands of years," I told her with a large yawn that I knew would infuriate her.

"You have deserved everything you've received, Evil One. I've no time for you or your requests."

"You owe me," I snapped as I felt my eyes go red with resentment.

"I owe you nothing. You made your bed, stupid man. And now you lie in it."

"I beg to differ," I argued in an icy tone, my cracks of fury and rage beginning to simmer to the surface. Fate was a hardened bitch and knew how to pour acid into wounds. "You played with us. You destroyed an unbreakable bond. You damned me to Hell. Do you sleep well at night, old woman?"

"I sleep just fine, Despicable One. You are nothing and you will remember that. Be gone," she shrieked.

The magic infused wind grew stronger and the temperature dropped to deadly for a human.

"Hold the fuck on for a second here," Astrid snarled as she shoved me out of the way and slapped at the darkness surrounding Fate. "You are way out of line, you old bag."

"Astrid, enough," I said, pulling her back. "I can handle this. You stay out of it."

"No can do, Uncle Fucker," she said, shrugging me off and placing her sparking hands on the wall of inky black. "You brought my sleeping undead butt here to help you and that's exactly what I'm going to do."

"You are more a fool than the Devil," Fate hissed.

"Yep, you stanky wanker. You've got that right. But I'm a fool who actually *cares*. I don't know who gave you this job, but I gotta say your people skills suck ass. Just because Lucifer has a bad reputation doesn't mean you can be such an assmonkey. It's not fair."

"And what do you know of *fair*?" Fate demanded. "You've had but thirty years in this realm."

"True," Astrid shot right back. "However, I know what kindness and common courtesy are. I know how *not* to act like a douchecanoe manager from a fast food restaurant who has gone giddy with power and makes all the high school kids work through their breaks and scrub the disgusting bathrooms while he sits on his fat ass and eats the all the fries."

"Is she right in the head?" Fate asked, confused.

"Absolutely not," I confirmed with delight.

"I'm not right in the head and it might be because I had to scrub the *men's* bathroom which is way more vomit inducing than the women's bathroom—bastards can't aim right with a gun to their heads—pun intended," Astrid shouted, clearly still on a roll. "So unless you want me to leave here and tell everyone who will listen that you're nothing but a fast food manager wank from the smelliest part of Hell who eats all the fries and doesn't give a flying fuck about the world or high school kids who just want some mother humpin' spending money, just keep going."

"You're as deluded as your uncle," Fate's voice boomed from behind the wall of black.

"And you're just mean. My uncle might be a badass asshole, but he's also good... in a vague definition of the term, and if you can't see that you're blind *and* toothless" Astrid paused her tirade and turned to me with pursed lips. "I'm gonna guess you haven't popped her?"

My expression was wide eyed, shocked, completely appalled and wildly amused. I'd expected Astrid to throw Fate off her game, but I didn't quite expect this. "Correct. I have never *popped* Fate."

"Thank God for that," she muttered with relief. "I figured since she has no teeth you wouldn't have tapped that ass. Anyhoo," she went on as if Fate were just some random woman—not the controller of destiny. "You want common courtesy, Miss High and Mighty? Well, then you're gonna have to tamp back the bitch act. Satan isn't evil. He *punishes* evil. Yes, fine... he does cheat, steal and fornicate like a damned rabbit in springtime hopped up on a vat of Viagra, but he doesn't *create* evil. You should know this, you big butthole."

"Did you just call me a *butthole*?" Fate demanded, flabbergasted.

"You bet your flat ass I did. It's four in the freakin' morning now. I'm exhausted, and trust me, *butthole* was kind considering my potty mouth—which I'm working on because of my son. But obviously my son isn't here so your mean ass is very lucky right now."

"Umm… Astrid," I tried to cut in.

"Not done here yet, Uncle Fucker. All Lucifer wants is some information and you're being a heinous shitass about it. Something is happening and it's bad. The least you can do is cough up some news that might help."

"Are you done?" Fate inquired.

"Probably not, but if you've got something to add, go for it."

Fate laughed with sheer delight and the spell she'd woven broke into thousands of tiny glittering pieces and shattered on the filthy floor at her feet. She also dropped the façade and was exactly how I remembered her—otherworldly gorgeous, but far more dangerous than beautiful.

"I can't say I've ever been called a butthole before. It's quite refreshing," she said to a slack jawed Astrid.

"You have teeth," Astrid said, confused.

"I do," Fate admitted. "And I bite."

Astrid quickly backed away. I stepped in front of her to shield her just in case Fate had taken up cannibalism in her insanity and old age. Killing Fate would be an enormous faux pas, but one I'd make if she went for my niece.

"Very interesting," Fate said, examining my stance in front of Astrid. "I was joking about biting."

"With you, one never knows," I commented. "How about resuming time?"

She paused and snapped her slim fingers. The room went from dank and freezing to opulent and warm.

"Not yet," she said. "It's of the essence for you, so you can thank me for hitting the pause button."

"Explain," I said tightly.

"Wait," Astrid interrupted. "Are you a good witch or a bad witch?"

"I'm not a witch at all, child," she replied smoothly, taking a seat on a golden brocade covered divan. "I'm simply cursed with knowing *all*. It sucks."

"Doesn't mean you have to be a raging bee-otch," Astrid pointed out.

Fate shrugged and produced a bottle of extremely rare scotch and three crystal tumblers. "Join me for a drink?"

"I'm dead. Can't drink," Astrid announced as she made herself comfortable on a velvet couch adjacent to the divan.

I was the last one standing and I was going to stay that way.

"Lucifer?" Fate inquired.

"I'll pass. Enjoying libations with you is not why I'm here—and it would hardly be enjoyable. I need a hint about what's happening."

Fate smiled and poured herself a hefty scotch and threw it back in one long swallow. She poured herself a second and proceeded to sip it like a lady. She was no lady.

"The darkness is coming for you, Lucifer. You will need to embrace it when she arrives," she said in the same bland tone one would talk about the weather.

"More specific," I demanded.

"No, that's not how it works. You know that," she replied coldly, gleefully observing me hold in my rage.

"If I die, the world ends," I stated and watched for even the tiniest reaction to gauge how much she truly knew.

"Holy shit," Astrid gasped out. "Can that really happen?"

"Which one?" Fate asked. "The world ending or Lucifer dying?"

"It's one in the same, so if you have anything else to share, say it now. Otherwise we'll be on our way," I said through clenched teeth.

"I rarely get amusing company anymore. No one likes to hang out with me," Fate pouted. "Are you quite sure you won't have a drink?"

"Quite. Information?"

"Drink?" she shot back, knowing full well she had the upper hand.

"Fine," I hissed as I watched her pour my scotch and top off her own.

Grabbing the glass rudely from her outstretched arm, I threw it back and dropped the expensive glass to the floor. The shattered crystal joined the jagged pieces of the sparkling black darkness she'd protected herself with.

"I drank. You talk."

"So much anger," she tsked. "You should lighten up." Laughing at her tasteless joke she went on. "The winds of change are blowing hard and your own fire no longer purges your soul."

She paused and closed her eyes.

"I know this," I growled. "Tell me something I don't know."

"The price is high." Her eyes snapped open and she looked me up and down like I was a piece of meat.

It repulsed me.

"Name your price," I ground out, taking the bottle of scotch and finishing it off in one long swallow. The liquid slid down my throat and burned in a way that made me feel alive. It wasn't fire, but it was the closest thing available at the moment.

"There's fire in the darkness, Lucifer. A fire that will weaken you, yet make you stronger. A fire… that could restore your soul."

"Stop talking nonsense, old woman," I roared as the building trembled in reaction to my ire. She was fucking with me and I wanted to end her with my bare hands. "I have no soul. It was obliterated when I fell."

"Is that what you think, Lucifer?" she questioned, examining me with pity.

"It's what I know. We're done here. As usual, you've been useless. I'd say thank you, but I'd be lying. I enjoy lying, so that's too great a gift to give to the likes of you."

Fate tilted her head and laughed. "You may despise me, but you should still listen to my words carefully. I don't create karma.

Hell, even *I* don't know exactly what is going to happen. It's already set by magic far stronger than mine. I'm simply one of the reporters."

"One of?" I questioned with suspicion. Hell, hopefully there weren't more of her.

"Turn of a phrase," she replied. "I'm *the* reporter."

"Whatever helps you live with yourself," I said rudely. "You're a better liar than I am."

"No, Lucifer, you're the best of them all... but even the best can be bested."

"Is that supposed to mean something to me? I was hoping to keep the dumbfuckery to a minimum this evening," I said in a voice so devoid of any emotion Fate glanced at me in surprise.

She took a long slow sip of her scotch and eyed me over the rim of her glass.

"Good things can happen to bad people," she said cryptically. "And bad things can happen to the good."

"You done?" I inquired, feeling weary.

"Never," she stated, equally as weary. "However, you will be done unless you find what is searching for you."

"Is that a threat?" I demanded, beginning to regret the visit.

"I don't make threats—don't have to," Fate said with a shrug and a shrill giggle that made me slightly ill. "I just call them like I see them. It will be fun to watch the darkness own you, Lucifer. It's long past time."

"You're a really sick piece of work," Astrid ground out, standing up and aligning herself next to me. "And I'd have to say you're lying like an ugly puke green shag rug about sleeping at night. I would think your heartless cruelty would keep you up for eternity."

"Take care of your business, Lucifer. I hear some immortal is breaking the law—selling souls no less."

"I know how to do my job," I snapped.

Fate shrugged again and leaned back on the divan. She graced us with a smile so beautiful, one could almost forget and forgive her viciousness. And then she disappeared in a blast of glittering silver smoke and dust.

Astrid and I stood in silence for a long moment and stared at the spot the provider of providence, luck and devastation had just sat. I locked everything the old woman had said into my brain. I would decipher the information as needed.

"Dude, that was deep, and I didn't understand most of what she meant. Did you?" Astrid asked, staring at me with concern.

"Not much, but fate has a strange way of revealing itself. Not always pleasant, but at least I have something to go on."

"What?" Astrid asked.

"First, I have to find the damned soul seller and then I'm looking for the fire in the darkness. If I don't find it, everything ends."

"Define *end*?" she prodded.

"No fucking clue, but I'll win. I always do."

"Want some help?"

Astrid's question took me by surprise. No one had my back. The Devil needed no one. I was feared and reviled. It was a foreign concept to be offered assistance. However, she'd been outstanding in the meeting with Fate—slightly confusing, but that was her talent.

"It could be quite dangerous," I said, slowly still trying to discern if she was simply being polite.

"Un-killable immortal here," she stated with a grin.

Astrid wasn't being polite. She was genuine. She was also clearly insane. Helping the Harbinger of Evil was never a good idea. Ever. However, I was a selfish man—very selfish.

"Ethan will be furious," I commented, referring to her mate.

"This is true," she agreed. "But I have a few tricks up my sleeve that will make him very, very happy."

"You're serious?" I asked.

"About my blow job skills or the fact that I'm coming with you to beat the shit out of the fire in the darkness?"

"The latter," I replied dryly. "I want to know nothing about your *skills*. Ever."

"Didn't take you for a *prude*, Uncle Fucker," she said with a laugh.

"I'm not. Orgy should be my middle name. I just don't want to hear about the sex life of someone I think of as a daughter," I replied.

"Oh. My. Hell," Astrid shouted. "That is the nicest thing you've ever said to me. You *do* love me."

With a long put upon sigh, I grinned as I shook my head in defeat. "I do not love you. I *like* you enough to tolerate your bizarre eccentricities. Nothing more."

"Liar," she mumbled with delight, as she turned to leave the room.

She was correct. I was a liar. I was the best of the liars. And I would continue until the day I was no more. With luck, that day would not be coming any time soon.

CHAPTER SIX

"IT'S A VERY, *VERY* BAD IDEA," ETHAN GROWLED.

His arms were crossed over his chest and a look of utter fury was directed my way. If looks could kill, I'd be ash. Delightful. Vampyres were such wonderfully rude company.

Sitting down on the couch in his grand office at the Cressida House, I made myself comfortable and waited for the sparks to fly —or the room to go up in flames. A lovely start to a new day. This one in particular had dawned bright and sunny. I far preferred dark and cloudy with a chance of natural disaster. But the weather was my mother's department and Mother Nature didn't take kindly to criticism.

Neither Astrid nor I had slept a wink after the irritating and foreboding meeting with Fate. And clearly Astrid's mate hadn't either, if the tone of his voice was anything to go by. Normally I adored discord, but this time I actually agreed with the obnoxious Vampyre. It *was* a very bad idea.

"Ethan," Astrid said, narrowing her eyes at him. "You're supposed to *support* me in my job. Have you ever heard me complain when you have to go behead a bunch of bad bloodsuckers? Never. I even helped. Your alpha hole is showing."

"Your *job*," he ground out, "doesn't include helping Satan get out of messes. If he's capable of getting himself into them, he can get himself out. Your job is Compassion and defending our people."

"That's not really very nice," I chimed in with a nicely perfected fake pout.

"Wasn't supposed to be," Ethan shot back, holding his fists clenched at his sides. "Astrid will under no circumstances die for you."

"I can't die," Astrid reminded him with an eye roll.

"There are many forms of death," Ethan said quietly. "Not just physical."

His words hit me in an unpleasant place—*the feels*—as my daughter Dixie would call it. Clearly lack of sleep was affecting my bad judgment. I never had a difficult time making horrible decisions. It was my calling card, damn it.

Astrid, quite unhappy with the direction of the conversation, started to glow—never a good sign if you valued your surroundings or property. Her hair began to float around her head and her fingers began to spark ominously. It was utterly delightful, but...

As much as I would have enjoyed watching my niece blow a few walls out of their mansion, I felt the need to say something. Not my usual style at all.

Wait one goddamned minute...

A warm unfamiliar feeling inside my chest made me wonder if the darkness had come and killed me when I wasn't looking. Quickly producing a mirror, I heaved a sigh of relief. I was alive and as good-looking as ever. Then what the Hell was happening to me? This simply wasn't right.

Did I suddenly have a conscience? Was the darkness chasing me making me a good guy? Unacceptable. Jiminy Fucking Cricket was not going to invade my despicable moral standards.

And then the horrifying feeling got warmer and cozier.

"What in the ever loving Hell?" I shouted and clutched at my chest.

"Ohmygodohmygodohmygod, what's wrong with you?" Astrid screeched. She sprinted over and placed her hand on my forehead.

"Is he all right?" Ethan asked skeptically, joining his mate and examining me.

"I had a twinge of sound ethical standards. It was absolutely horrible," I hissed. "I feel so dirty."

"Don't you see?" Astrid demanded of Ethan waving her hands in the air and blowing up the coffee table by accident. "*Something* is making the Devil *nice*. This is awful. The heinous fast food restaurant manager said the world would end if Satan didn't kick some dark fiery butt soon. Toothless assbuckets who don't care about high school kids having to clean bathrooms on their breaks should not be making big decisions about the world possibly coming to an end. I'm just sayin'."

"I am so lost right now," Ethan said, running his hands through his hair.

"The Vampyre is correct," I said, raising a hand before Astrid could debate me. "This is not your problem. It's mine."

"Still confused here," Ethan announced. "You people went to a fast food restaurant with high school humans?"

"Kind of," Astrid said. "What it boils down to is that Uncle Fucker needs my help."

"For the love of everything illegal and foul, in the presence of others you're going to have to put a kibosh on the Uncle Fucker endearment," I informed my niece. "It's not dignified. I'm fucking Satan. And your Vampyre is correct. You're not coming with me."

"Wait," Astrid gasped out with a horrified expression. "You can fuck yourself?"

"Only figuratively. I'm not that talented," I replied flatly. "More importantly, you will not be joining me on this excursion."

"But you need my help and you didn't do anything *wrong*," Astrid protested, much to Ethan's growing displeasure.

"Define wrong," Ethan muttered under his breath.

"Okay, fine," she conceded with a grin. "I don't think he did anything wrong to have caused Fate to be such a wanking bitch-sicle."

"Back up," Ethan growled as his fangs descended and his eyes went green. "Lucifer took you to meet *Fate*?"

"Umm… yes?" Astrid confirmed in a whisper.

Ethan paced the room in a fury—his power bounced off the walls like bullets. The room vibrated and the floor trembled beneath his feet. It was wildly impressive. If the Vampyre ever wanted to hop over to the bad side, I'd take him in a hot second. His killing skills outrivaled my most fierce and demented Demons.

"If your death wouldn't end the world, I'd kill you with my bare hands right now," the Vampyre hissed at me with the veins in his neck bulging. "Astrid doesn't need to be on Fate's radar. That woman is batshit crazy."

"Exactly," Astrid yelled, hopping up and down like a child. "Fate—who by the way does have teeth and might bite—said if Satan doesn't kick the ass of the fire and darkness and stop the renegade soul seller, we're all gonna bite it in a big fat hairy way."

"And this involves you how?" Ethan demanded, placing his hands on either side of Astrid's face and pressing his lips to her forehead.

Hugging him back, she laid her head on his chest and closed her eyes. It was sickening—like watching a chick flick. Love made me itchy. Happiness gave me hives. Who had I screwed over that I had to witness this? It was far better when there was the potential of Astrid blowing up her own home.

"Something bad is happening and Uncle Fu…Lucifer can't find the answer alone. He would have completely screwed up the meeting in the skanky Vegas club with Fate if I hadn't been there to save the day," she told Ethan.

"Now that's stretching the truth a bit," I said with an eye roll.

"First off, it's not," Astrid retorted with an eye roll that almost beat mine. "And you like lies, half-truths and all that shit. However, I'm not lying. If you'd gone in there with only your three thuggy beef thermometers, there's no telling what would have happened."

"Thuggy beef thermometers?" Ethan inquired with a wince.

"Demons," Astrid explained. "They've all changed their names to Dick, so I feel no remorse at having a little fun at their expense. You feel me?"

"I do," Ethan said with a laugh, taking her in his arms again.

"If you dead people continue to insist on showing affection, I'm going to have to incinerate something," I said, staring at the ceiling. "Lust I can handle. This love nonsense gives me a rash."

Ignoring me, Astrid brushed Ethan's hair from his brow and kissed him sweetly. "This is no joke and it's not a game. I know in my gut he needs me," she whispered.

Ethan paused and stared hard at me. "You could truly be ended?"

Shrugging off the feeling of unease that skittered up my spine, I smiled. "Eventually, all of us come to an end. However, my demise holds enormous consequence for humanity."

Gently pushing Astrid away, he moved and stood before me. He didn't kneel, but he wasn't under my jurisdiction. He had one of his own. Paltry compared to mine, but he was revered in his own right.

"What did Fate say to you?" he asked.

"Oh you know... this and that. Oh, and that I should embrace the darkness coming for me," I quipped.

"Is she implying you should walk willingly to your death?" Ethan voiced the very same thoughts I was having.

"I've considered that. The only way to permanently end me is with the Sword of Death and I have to be agreeable to it or it won't work. I'm not agreeable."

"Well, I would sure as Hell hope not," Astrid snapped. "I mean, I wanted to kill you when you destroyed Christmas, but I wouldn't have really done it."

"Thank you," I replied with an arched brow.

"Welcome."

"So I'm still invited back?" I inquired innocently.

"Are you going to destroy all the new Baby Jesuses I had to buy online because you blew up my collection?" she asked with arms crossed over her chest and eyes narrowed dangerously.

"Umm… well, ah… this is very difficult," I complained. "Can I lie?"

Astrid's laugh made me grin.

"Sure. Go for it."

"Excellent. I will not blow up Baby Jesus."

"Or give all the Nut Crackers boners," she continued extorting me.

"Come on now, seriously?" I choked out trying not to laugh. "That was hilarious."

"Okay, fine, you butthole," she conceded ungraciously with a giggle. "One Nut Cracker can have a woody. But if you even look at my Baby Jesuses, you have to go to church every day for a month."

"You're a horribly evil child and you drive a devastating bargain," I replied with a grunt of approval.

"Learned from the best," Astrid shot back with a thumbs up and then turned her focus back to Ethan. "I would very much like your blessing because I love and respect you more than anyone in the world, but I'll go regardless."

Nodding his head and taking her hands in his, Ethan gave her a resigned smile. "You are my world. You drive me to the heights and to absolute distraction. Astrid, you have my blessing and I have your back. I'm not happy about this at all, but I trust you. Always."

"I love you, you sexy, hot Vamp." She threw her arms around her mate and held him tight.

Ethan then shot me a look that wasn't loving at all. It was vicious. I needed to copy that one. It was excellent.

"Astrid will accompany you," he conceded tightly. "But you will also take Tiara. Her power is astronomical and I'll feel better if Astrid had a Demon with her that I *trust*. She's of your bloodline and is also undead. Her loyalty is to both races."

"Tiara's a Fairy too," Astrid reminded everyone. "With a voice that could lead to the need for new eardrums."

And that was the understatement of the morning. Tiara was the newly discovered half-sister of Astrid—a lesbian Demon-Fairy-Vampire who spoke at a decibel that could call up the Hell Hounds from a three hundred mile radius. Both women were the daughters of my very dead and very despicable Demon half-brother—killed by Astrid's own hand. It was a favor I would owe her for always.

While I had no issues destroying Demons that had gone too far to the dark side, offing my own half-brother was slightly complicated. Thankfully the job had been done for me. However, as truly heinous as the Demon had been, he'd sired two incredibly strong immortals—profane, violent, inappropriate and beautiful. As far as I was concerned, they were mine now. I simply ignored the other parts of their lineage because Demon blood was far superior to any other species.

"I will take Tiara as well as Darby, Dino and Dagwood. I shall have my army awaiting my instructions in Hell and would greatly appreciate any backup you can provide," I told Ethan in a curt tone. It seriously sucked to have to express gratitude.

"That almost killed you didn't it?" Astrid asked with glee.

"I have no idea what you're talking about."

"Saying thank you to Ethan," she gloated. "I think I see a few hives popping up."

Breathing in through my nose and blowing the breath slowly from my lips, I shook my head. "Yessssss, it sucked. However, as evil as I may be, I'm not stupid. Stupid would never have survived as long as I have."

"Darby, Dino and Dagwood?" Ethan questioned with a perplexed expression.

"My top Demons," I confirmed with a slight wince. The names were truly going to have to go. I was losing respect even uttering them.

"Same ones who changed their middle names to Dick," Astrid added with a laugh. "Dino Dick, Darby Dick and Dagwood Dick."

"And they've all taken the surname Demon," I added morosely.

"Not gonna touch that," Ethan said with a laugh.

Astrid hopped up into Ethan's arms and snuggled close. It made me long for... nothing. Their road was not one I would ever travel.

"Wise choice, mate of mine," she said. "I want to go kiss my baby and I'll bring Tiara back with me. We're gonna find this shit and end it. Fast."

"Where will you begin?" Ethan questioned.

It was a good question and the answer was that I was unsure. However, fate had a way of revealing itself as you went along with your daily life.

"We will resume normal activity," I said. "If we go about business as usual, whatever fate intended will find us."

"Fate's a bitch," Ethan said.

"You took the words from my mouth."

CHAPTER SEVEN

"LET ME GET THIS SHIT STRAIGHT," TIARA SAID IN AN OCTAVE THAT should be reserved for shattering glass. "The darkness and fire—whatever the effing Hell *that* means—is gunning for Uncle Fucker. We need to make it our bitch so the world doesn't end. Buuuuut, instead of looking for it, we're gonna go find some female soul seller that puts Demons into comas. Then as if that's not a bizarre enough field trip, we're gonna get Uncle Fucker's questionably truthful autobiography published and go to a Romance Readers convention so he can possibly get a movie option on his life story?"

"Sounds about right," Astrid said, dragging two enormous suitcases into Ethan's office.

"That's one tall, seriously fucked up order," Tiara commented as she helped Astrid stack the suitcases.

"God did it with his insufferably *long* book multiple times," I reminded them. "He's made a fortune. It's my turn."

"He does have a point," Astrid conceded.

"So Uncle Fucker, your autobiography is a *romance*?" Tiara inquired with an expression of utter confusion on her lovely face.

Before I had a chance to answer, Astrid confirmed the anomaly

—or as I liked to call it … poetic license.

"Yep, I just slapped a bullshit happy ending on it and called it a day. Uncle Fucker is getting a happily ever after," Astrid announced making me curious to read the fabrications her artful yet insane mind had wrought.

My nieces were polar opposites in the looks department, but equally as stunning. Tiara was blonde and statuesque with gold eyes. Her multiple heritage was evident when her eyes changed due to her mood. One became red and the other silver—very unusual and wonderfully disconcerting. Astrid's hair was as dark as Tiara's was light, however they shared the same golden eyes, bad attitude, outstanding killing skills and love of filthy language. At least the unforeseen near future would be amusing with my girls at my side.

"We're going to work on eliminating the moniker *Uncle Fucker* from your vocabularies," I informed them in an icy tone so they would know I meant business. Secretly, I enjoyed being called *Uncle Fucker*. It was every kind of wrong and profane. "Besides I need to use a pen name. You will address me accordingly."

"Did you pick one?" Astrid inquired, pretending to busy herself with the locks on her suitcases.

She was up to something. The lack of eye contact was an undead giveaway, plus there were no locks on her luggage. Ethan had gone to confer with his top generals to make contingency plans in case my Demon army needed back up. I was quite sure I would need none of them. Fate hadn't mentioned anyone but me in the unfolding drama with the impending darkness.

"Do you have something in mind?" I asked giving her the eyebrow she'd so recently insulted.

Her laugh rang through the room and even I had to grin. It was liberating to be with people who weren't completely terrified of me. Of course her choice of name was sure to be horrifying, but I was curious to hear what debased moniker Astrid thought appropriate.

"You really don't want to let her do this," Tiara warned with an evil little grin pulling at her lips.

"I'm offended," Astrid shouted in mock rage. "I read romance novels, for the love of everything bodice ripping and fabulous. I *know* what the ladies want."

"Let's hear it then," Tiara said with a bark of laughter.

"Dirk," Astrid said with wide eyes, waggling brows and an even wider grin. "Dirk D. Deemonee!"

I was quite sure the expression on my face looked like I'd swallowed a lemon. The name was appalling. There was no way in Hell I was going to answer to Dirk. I'd go with Uncle Fucker before I went with Dirk D. Deemonee.

"What does the middle D stand for?" Tiara asked, attempting to hold back her squeal of laughter.

"Dick!" Astrid bellowed and fell to the floor in giggles.

Tiara lost her valiant battle with her composure and landed in a heap next to her sister.

"While I find your bonding over my emasculation amusing, I will *not* go by that name. Even you can't utter the abomination without guffawing like a common peasant."

"How about Sam Sinessssster?" Tiara suggested between unladylike grunts of glee.

"Or Vinnie Villanilicious?" Astrid squealed.

"Or Nardel Nefariouso?" Tiara shouted as three windows in the room burst and shattered to dust.

"Or Lou Sy?" Astrid took another appalling turn.

"Or Abe Bominable?"

"Or Dizzy Greeable?"

"Or Wick Edest?"

Closing my eyes, I leaned back on the couch and let the imbeciles wear themselves out. When there appeared to be no end in sight, I stepped in. Clearly, they could go on for days. And I was fairly sure the Vampyres of the Cressida House would be annoyed if all the windows and glass in the large compound got destroyed by Tiara's earsplitting cackling.

"I shall be known as Blade," I announced. "Just Blade."

"Like Beyoncé or Cher?" Astrid questioned, pushing a still laughing Tiara off of her.

"Yes. Except I'm sexier."

"Hmm, it's not bad," she mused, considering it. "But you really *should* have a last name. Sounds less like a male stripper that way."

"She's right," Tiara agreed. "What do you love? What makes you happy?"

Interesting point. I certainly didn't want to come off as a stripper—not that there was anything wrong with being a stripper. I had many lovely and busty stripper friends...

"I enjoy sex."

"Blade Fornicate or Blade Boink doesn't work for me," Tiara said, thinking aloud. "How about Blade Boffmeister?"

"No too literal," Astrid said. "What about something more obscure like Blade Nooner?"

"That's better, but I like alliteration. How 'bout Blade Baller or Blade Bugger."

"How about no fucking way," I inserted just to make them stop.

"What else do you like besides bumping uglies?" Astrid asked.

"For the record, mine's not ugly. And the answer is fire. I adore fire," I said with confidence. It was nice not to have to lie every now and then. However, I wasn't going to make a practice of it.

"*Blade Inferno,*" Tiara said, her mismatched eyes wide with excitement. "It's hot and dangerous. It's very memorable—I mean not as memorable as Satan, Lucifer, Mother Humpin' Prince of Darkness, Blade Boink or Uncle Fucker, but I think it will work."

"It's perfect," Astrid agreed with a clap of her hands.

I wasn't quite as certain, but it beat all the other names they'd so helpfully suggested. I *was* hot and dangerous. Blade Inferno could work.

"Blade Inferno it is," I said, relieved we were done with renaming the Devil. "Now we need to get the book published and take this party to Chicago."

"Is that where the Romance Convention is?" Tiara inquired.

"No clue," I admitted. "However, I have a little soul seller there that needs to be stopped. We can get rid of her and then go make me more famous than I already am."

"Like that's not gonna go to his head," Astrid muttered and then froze. "Wait. Pretty sure we can't just tell a publisher to publish your book. Don't think it works that way."

"No worries, I own all of the Big Eight New York Publishers. I'll have my people call their people and it shall be done."

"Dude, you are one slippery mother humper," Astrid said with admiration.

"Thank you."

"Umm... this soul seller..." Tiara got back to the prior subject. "Is she a Demon?"

"She's a photographer," I supplied. "And we have no clue on the species. It was reported back to me that she might possibly be a Siren."

"No. Fucking. Way," Tiara gasped out, disintegrating the glass on Ethan's massive desktop computer. "They don't exist anymore."

"Exactly," I agreed. "She's most likely something far less, like a Mermaid."

"Mermaids are real?" Astrid shouted with joy. "Like in the movie *Splash*?"

Hell's bells, these girls were loud and destructive.

Tiara and I both shuddered. Mermaids were nothing like the way they were depicted in fairy tales and Disney movies.

"No," I replied curtly. "They are cannibalistic sex fiends."

"Holy shitballs on fire," Astrid swore. "This is going to be fun."

"You say she's a photographer?" Tiara questioned.

Nodding, I waited for something good—or nonsensical. I

wasn't disappointed.

"You're an author," she started.

"Loose definition of an author," Astrid chimed in and earned an impressive glare from me.

"Authors need headshots for the flap on the inside of the book. Right?" Tiara went on.

"They do," I said with a grin, following her train of thought. Tiara's thought process was far easier to understand than Astrid's non sequitur ramblings about fast food managers.

"Bingo," she shouted as Astrid and I slapped our hands over our ears in self-preservation.

Eardrums would grow back. I just didn't want to get blood on my custom Armani suit—especially if I was going to be photographed in it.

"You are brilliant, sister of mine," Astrid congratulated her half-sibling with a back slap that sent Tiara flying across the room. "It will be a two for one. We get Blade Inferno's head shot and we stop the man-eating soul seller."

"And then we find the darkness and fire?" Tiara asked.

"Trust me. We probably won't have to look. Once Fate is involved, the prophecy will find us—or rather me," I replied.

"Us," Tiara and Astrid insisted in unison.

"It will find us," Astrid continued. "You're not flying solo this time. You have two slightly insane and very well dressed killing machines with you."

"We've got your back, Uncle Fucker," Tiara added and then slapped her hand over her mouth. "Sorry. I mean... *Blade Inferno,* we have your back. Always," my gratingly voiced niece corrected herself.

I was certain my eyes were watering because of her piercing pitch—not because these ridiculous girls were repeatedly hitting me in the *feels.*

I'm Satan. I feel nothing for anyone.

And if you're buying that, I have a bridge to sell you...

CHAPTER EIGHT

"WHAT THE HELL ARE WE DOING IN NIRVANA?" I BELLOWED. I stamped my foot in fury causing a flock of purple parrots to explode from the flowering trees and dive bomb us. "I'm supposed to be in Chicago decapitating a soul selling Mermaid. Mother, you have some explaining to do."

One minute I was soaring above the clouds with my raven wings glistening in the sun and the wind ruffling my feathers. The next minute I was sucked violently into a vortex and unceremoniously dumped into my mother's neck of the Universe. Not to mention, I was being attacked by fucking birds. Astrid and Tiara were taking the unexpected detour with far more grace than I was.

"Dude, relax," Astrid said as she squatted down and scratched the belly of something that was a colorful mix between a dog and a rabbit with small horns. "Obviously Gigi has something to tell you or she wouldn't have yanked our asses out of the sky and brought us here."

"Ohmyfreakinwheelsonamonstertruck," Tiara shouted as she darted around the lush gardens and touched everything. "This is my first time in Nirvana—totally mother humpin' awesome!"

"Thank you, darling," Mother Nature said, appearing in a blast of enough peach glitter to supply ten thousand beauty pageants. "Would you girls mind walking the monkeys over to the diving pool? It's time for their scuba lesson."

"Or in other words, you want a moment alone with Blade Inferno," Astrid said with a knowing grin. "We're on it, Gigi. Just call out when it's safe to come back."

"Can I scuba dive with the monkeys?" Tiara asked Mother Nature *aka Gigi* to her grandchildren.

"Of course, my sweet. Just watch out for the Loch Ness Monster. She's here on vacation."

"Will do!" Tiara hooted as she took off at a sprint.

I watched them leave and then turned on my mother. "This had better be good. I'm working under a time crunch at the moment and a visit to Narnia wasn't on the schedule."

"It's Nirvana, young man. Narnia is fiction. And you will watch your tone with me," Mother Nature hissed.

With an annoyed sigh and a few mumbled curses, I took a seat on a trillion year old log surrounded by ferns sprouting blossoming pink daisies and waited. I was here. I would hear what the nut bag had to say and then resume my mission. However, my attitude would stay shitty. Period.

"Who is Blade Inferno?" she inquired as she sat on an intricately carved log across from me and clasped her dainty hands in her lap.

"I am," I snapped, moodily. "It's my pen name."

"I like it." She nodded and smiled. "Very fitting—sharp and hot blooded."

"Clearly I'm not here to discuss how desirable and good looking I am. What gives?"

Mother Nature stared at me long and hard. "Fate dropped by. She said she had a little meeting with you and you were incredibly rude."

"And your point?" I ground out.

"Well, I was just wondering what she had to say. It's not often you would seek her out. I mean no one wants her as a dinner guest anymore, not after that time she got drunk and started sharing all sorts of ghastly sexual secrets about everyone. I was certain Catherine the Great was going to positively explode. I mean, her horse was there and everything."

"While I find that comical in a disgusting sort of way, I have no time for gossip. I have things to do."

"Tell me what Fate said. Let me help you," my mother insisted, all of her usual posturing gone.

Why in the Hell was everyone wanting to help me lately? It was unacceptable and made me think my demise was far closer than I'd originally thought. Goddamn it, I was seriously close to a panic attack. The last time I had one of those Mount St. Helens exploded.

"I don't need help," I hissed. "I need to figure out what the old hag meant."

"She always means far more than she actually says," my mother reminded me. "Damned pain in the ass talks in riddles— total nightmare."

My mother's eyes were warm and her smile made me feel like a total shit. Could she shed any light on my impending doom? Only one way to find out…

"Fate said darkness is coming for me and I have to embrace it," I said tonelessly.

"What in the Hell does *that* mean?" my mother screeched as mini explosions rocked her gardens. "I swear on my grandson Jesus, I'm going to kick Fate's interfering ass into a realm with no alcohol. That will show her not to mess with my baby."

"While the sentiment is lovely and alarming, do you have any clue what she meant?" I asked.

Mother Nature stood and began to pace. With every step she took, flowers in rainbows of color appeared, making the garden look like it was on steroids… or acid. She paced circles until I felt dizzy. Why did I think she could help me? My mother had a zoo and stripper poles all over her property.

"The darkness represents something—but doesn't necessarily mean death—although it could. However, I would think the drunken old cow might have warned a few more of us if the world was coming to an end."

"She didn't warn me, mother," I reminded her. "I went to her. I've felt the darkness for a while. And my fire doesn't purge me anymore."

"Your fire doesn't cleanse your sins and pain anymore?" she asked, shocked.

"No. It doesn't," I replied tersely.

"That's a rather huge problem. Why don't I know any of this?" she demanded in a shrill voice. "When you were a little boy you told me everything. If you'd return my calls once every few decades, I'd know what's going on in your life. I would have made you a cake, damn it."

"A cake solves nothing." I tried not to gag at the thought of her cooking anything for me. I wasn't sure how my father did it. Maybe Sprites had no taste buds. "I'm just going to plow on and when the darkness shows, I'll destroy it. I'm quite adept at destroying bad things," I added with pride and no humility whatsoever.

"Is that why the girls are with you?"

I paused and attempted to figure out why I had let them come. I suppose it boiled down to wanting company. Very selfish and very typical of me. However, this time my actions didn't sit well. If the end was coming, they should be with those they cared most about—not with me.

Easily solvable. After the soul-selling Mermaid was headless and gone, our field trip was over. I would send the girls on their way and deal with the rest on my own... just as I'd always done. I was a fucking island.

"Yes, that's why... but you've made me rethink the wisdom of it," I told a surprised Mother Nature. "It was their decision, but it's a bad one."

"Are you sure it wasn't fated?" she asked wisely, giving me pause.

Was it? I didn't know. Hell, I didn't know much at the moment. I only knew I wanted to leave here immediately. It was not good for my attitude to get maudlin or sentimental. Being on my game was of utmost importance right now. Weakness could be used against me.

"Do you believe in pre-destiny, Mother?"

"Interesting you should ask," she said. "Your brother gave man free will, so I believe the humans can shape and reshape their own destinies. However, for us? I have no answer for that one. We were in existence before rules were made. We made our own and we have to live by them."

"That's the most lucid thing I've ever heard you say," I muttered with a chuckle and a shake of my head. "So our futures really are in the hands of Fate?"

"Possibly," she nodded and gave me a small smile. "However, knowing that what lies ahead of us is determined by that inebriated raging alcoholic bitch is a bit disconcerting."

"Do you really blame her?" I asked.

"For being a bitch? Yes."

"No, for blurring the pain of knowing all."

My mother sat down next to me and took my large hand into her smaller one. Tracing the lines on my palm with her slim finger, she sighed. "Yes, I blame her for drinking on the job. Our positions are monumental and the responsibility can overwhelm and create irreparable holes in our psyche, but we were chosen for a reason."

"If someone had given you the choice—the actual choice— would you have taken it?" I inquired.

Without missing a beat, she giggled and laid her bouncy red curls on my shoulder. "Absolutely. There is no one better than me.

I'm practically perfect. Heaven and Hell forbid if someone else had gotten my job."

"And your ego is large," I said with a laugh.

"As is yours, my child. Would you have taken the job if you'd been offered a say?" she asked, turning the tables right back on me.

I nodded slowly as a smile pulled at my lips and relief washed over me. "There have been days during the millions I've been alive that I might have answered differently. But when you've been in existence as long as I have, days are mere blips. What I do is as important as what your *other son* does—maybe more. Without me, there is no him. We're two sides of the very same fucked up coin. Without me, there is anarchy. Ultimately, I may be the reason for peace—not that I would share that tidbit—might ruin my reputation."

"You're pushing it a little," she said dryly.

"Not at all," I said with total and well-deserved conceit as far as I was concerned. "I'm fucking Satan."

"Oh my! Can you do that?" she asked shocked and possibly the slightest bit impressed.

Letting my head fall to my hands, I barked out a laugh. "I really have to stop using that line. And no, I can't fuck myself… literally speaking."

"That's probably a good thing. You'd never come out of Hell if you could," she said with a sage nod that made my laughter increase. However, she was correct.

"You're the badass sheriff," she insisted with a delighted grin. "Nothing exists in its purity—not good and not evil. There are shades of gray and blinding color everywhere and that can only be because you and your brother are doing the very best you can."

"Sometimes the best isn't good enough."

"Sometimes the best is all we have," she pointed out.

Circles. Eternity was made up of unending circles. Occasionally, I was envious of the humans. Live for a small stretch, choose your own destiny, and then pay for it in the afterlife. Mostly, however, I was delighted to be me. I mean who wouldn't be? Envy was a trait that I enjoyed on a fairly regular basis. I'd even named one of my daughters Envy. Of course she was a royal pain in my ass, but that was exactly how I liked it.

"This talk is over," I said, standing up and stretching my long legs. With a slight tilt of my head I called to my wings.

In an eerie whisper on the wind the black magic roared through my body and my wings burst from my back in all their mystical glory. Glittering black mist floated through the gardens sparkling like death. It was gorgeous. I felt free and evil and pretty damned fantastic. It was good to be me. I simply now needed to make sure I could still go on doing it.

"Thank you for your time, Mother. I actually enjoyed it, much to my surprise."

Her opened mouth shock and inability to speak amused me. Maybe I'd stop by more than once every century... Nah. Once every hundred years or so was enough. I certainly didn't need her crazy rubbing off on me. I was unbalanced enough as it was.

"Astrid. Tiara," I called to my nieces. "It's time to go. We have a Mermaid to drown."

"Coming," they yelled.

I air kissed Mother Nature and gave her one of my patented devastating grins.

"Goodness, you're such a beautiful man. I feel so inspired. I want to pole dance. Would you like to join me?"

"Umm... no. Never, actually, but... ah... thank you for asking. I have a Mermaid to behead and some nieces to get home. And then I shall meet my fated destiny and obliterate it. Lots to do."

"You'll be great," she trilled as all the flowers in the garden burst into song.

This was far too much happy for me to deal with. I needed to leave before I broke out in a rash. I couldn't risk it. I needed to look good for my headshot.

"Remember," Mother Nature called out as I took to the sky. "There is usually more than one meaning to a word. Pay close attention to the words, I think that's the key."

"Good talk?" Astrid inquired as she floated in the air next to me. My Vampyre-Demon niece didn't need wings to fly. Her power was indeed rare.

Tiara's wings were black, red and silver—very impressive. However, mine were better.

"Good is a relative term," I said with a shrug. "Informative? Possibly."

"Sometimes mothers know best," Tiara said, sounding far older that her years.

"Not mine," Astrid said with a grunt of disgust.

"Or mine," Tiara added with a shudder that made her wings flap wildly in the wind. "But that doesn't mean Mama Nature doesn't know a few things."

"Chicago. Now," I commanded, effectively ending the conversation. But they gave me something to think about.

Maybe... on very, very rare occasions, mothers did know best. I was about to find out.

I would listen for the words. The double meanings in the words.

CHAPTER NINE

"ABSOLUTE BULLSHIT," I SHOUTED AS I HURLED MY CELL PHONE AT the brick wall and watched it shatter into pieces. "Those bastards are trying to screw me over. No one screws the Devil and lives to tell."

Standing atop a tall building in the blinding Chicago morning sun, I did everything I could to keep from blowing up the Windy City. The bad day kept getting worse. Throwing my cell phone wasn't going to solve anything, but it had certainly felt good.

"No wonder you can't keep a girlfriend," Astrid commented dryly, smoothing out her clothing from our midmorning flight. "If the price of playing hide the salami with Satan is death, I can see how that might not appeal to the ladies."

"For the love of everything reprehensible, if you keep purposely misunderstanding me I will incinerate every ceramic Baby Jesus you own," I grumbled. With a wave of my hand I repaired my shattered phone so I could throw it again. Destruction was so therapeutic.

"I'll buy more Baby Jesuses," she threatened disrespectfully with a shrug and a wide grin.

"Fine," I shouted, still trying to get a grip on my itchy trigger finger. Blowing off steam over ridiculous Christmas ornaments was actually relaxing. It kept me from leveling a city, another point for Astrid. "I'll put permanent erections on all your nut crackers and oozing warts all over your truly frightening life sized Santa."

"You will *not* defile Santa," she shouted beginning to spark like a firework.

"And I'll give all your cute little elves size triple F bosoms—enormous bosoms with tassels."

"Oh my Hell in August," Astrid choked out, bent over with laughter.

She was no longer sparking menacingly—she was laughing at me. What in the ever-loving Hell was happening here? Whatever it was, I did *not* like it.

"No one says *bosom*. Only losers say bosom," she choked out through her giggling.

"She's right," Tiara agreed. "And I'm a lesbian. I would know."

Was this correct? I'd used the term bosom constantly over the centuries—never had a problem with it. Damn it, maybe they had a point. It was an odd word.

"How did this even start?" I demanded, completely thrown off my game and trying to regain some ground to be the Devil in charge again. Hurling my repaired phone at the wall did the trick. And just for good measure, I called on a wake of buzzards to swarm the city. That would definitely make the evening news.

"Umm... not sure," Astrid said, squinting her eyes in thought and hiding her own cell phone. "You threatened my Baby Jesuses and then..."

"And then he threatened to give your nutcrackers chubbies and freely admitted that banging Beelzebub ends in loss of life—total buzz kill," Tiara offered, laughing through the entire explanation while also covertly tucking her phone away.

"I do not know why I thought bringing you two was a good idea," I muttered. I ran my hands through my hair while watching the screaming people on the street dodge the dive- bombing buzzards. Delightful.

Glancing around the barren gravel roof of the skyscraper, I considered blowing a hole in it for fun, but decided against it. Not knowing what was below gave me pause.

"Who is screwing you over? Santa?" Tiara asked as she fiddled with the sunglasses I'd made her wear so she appeared to be blind.

Not knowing the species of the soul seller was dangerous—not for Astrid or me, as we were True Immortals. However, Tiara could be vulnerable to Sirens, Mermaids and several other unsavory species, hence the glasses that would protect her eyes—the window to the soul and favorite place for Mermaids and Sirens to draw victims in. The chance that the soul seller was a Siren was next to nil. They'd been extinct for several thousand years, but I refused to take chances with my nieces—even ones that made my ears bleed. Tiara was a blind woman walking, but she wouldn't be a dead one on my clock.

"No, *Santa* didn't screw me over. He doesn't even exist. However, if you rearrange the letters in the fat fictional bastard's name you get Satan. I find that very interesting… What the Hell am I talking about?" I shouted. Being with these girls confused the Hell out of me.

"Umm… you were going to tell us who screwed you over," Astrid reminded me.

"Oh, right," I said, happily regaining a modicum of composure. "The New York publishing industry is trying screw me over. Did you know that a woman named Janis Evenwitch got an eighty-nine million dollar advance for her book and those cheapskates only want to offer me a paltry fifty million?"

"Janet Evanovich," Astrid corrected me with an expertly delivered mini eye roll that was almost more effective than the one where I was sure she could see her backside.

"No, I'm sure my agent said Janis Evenwitch," I replied, trying her eye roll on for size.

"Then you need a new agent," she shot back, clearly unimpressed with my attempt. "Janet Evanovich is a freakin' goddess. I've read everything she's ever written, twice. I'd read the mother humpin' phone book if she wrote it. Who in the ever loving Hell is your agent if he doesn't know who's the highest paid romance writer in the world?"

"He's fired. That's who he is," I snapped, wondering why I'd thought having a Gnome for an agent was a good idea. They were clearly hard of hearing and tended to be violent in negotiations. Normally a bit of bloodshed was helpful, but maybe not in the book world. Humans were such babies.

"What will you do?" Tiara asked as she ran into a large air vent.

Pausing for a brief moment, I thought it through. Thankfully something heinous and unethical came to me immediately.

"I'll simply funnel the money for my advance into the hands of the correct person who will put it right back in my pocket," I explained as I conjured up a new phone and texted my soon to be dismissed representative. "Then I'll have it called into all the financial news organizations and Blade Inferno will soon be known as the highest paid romance author in the world."

"Dude," Astrid gasped, grabbing Tiara before she walked off the edge of the building we'd landed on. "The book sucks ass. You *really* shouldn't do that."

"The book does *not* suck ass," I told her in a clipped tone. "My life story is riveting."

"That's one way to put it," Astrid conceded with extreme hesitation. "But it's not edited or anything. I mean, I just typed exactly what you said. I never went back over it. It's filled with more fucking cuss words than I've ever heard of in a book."

"No worries," I assured her. "That son of a bitch, Hemingway owes me. He's editing as we speak."

"*Ernest Hemingway* is editing your semi-autobiographical *romance*?" Tiara asked, slack-jawed. "Hemingway lives in Hell?"

"No, he doesn't," I snapped, annoyed at such lack of faith from my nieces. "However, he comes for poker night every Thursday. He lost ten weeks in a row so he's editing. Are we done with this conversation? We have a Mermaid beheading to attend to."

"Did you cheat at cards?" Astrid inquired.

"Of course. Your point?"

"No point," she replied with a grin.

"Are we ready?" I asked.

The girls nodded, still somewhat speechless. Damn it, had I made a mistake having the drunken bastard edit my tome? I'd considered Jane Austin, but she wasn't as partial to Hell as Ernest was—not to mention I hadn't called her back after our tryst fifty years ago. Whatever. I had far bigger problems at the moment than if Hemingway was going to add a few bullfights into my life story.

"Can I ask a question?" Tiara inquired, still adjusting the sunglasses I'd conjured for her.

Crossing my arms over my chest, I eyed her. While I enjoyed the irreverence of the girls, I was getting tired of the back talk. "Just one?"

"Umm… sure."

"You may," I replied, tapping my Armani clad toe and wondering where in the Hell my trio of Demons had gotten to. I needed a little respect and I certainly wasn't getting it from Astrid and Tiara.

"Why am I wearing sunglasses? I can barely see out of them. If you want me to kill stuff, this could be a potential shitshow waiting to happen."

With a sigh and flick of my wrist I destroyed my cell phone one more time for good measure and then shook my head. "If the soul seller isn't a Mermaid and is indeed a Siren, you'll be susceptible to her deadly charms. The glasses will prevent you from falling under her spell."

"What about me?" Astrid demanded, looking a bit worried.

"You and I are not vulnerable to the magic of the man eaters."

"Because?" she prompted.

"Because we're True Immortals. Besides the chances of the woman being a Siren are slim to none, but the glasses will also protect Tiara from a Mermaid," I explained as Dino, Darby and Dagwood appeared in a blast of glittering black mist.

"Sire," they said in unison and dropped to their knees.

Finally… some goddamned respect.

"Have you cased the building?" I inquired, indicating with a curt nod they could rise.

"We have," Dagwood confirmed. "The soul seller is on the thirteenth floor. Only one passenger elevator in the building. Seems odd, but we checked thoroughly. The service elevator is out of order because we loaded it with rabid, horny porcupines and cadavers. We also made an appointment to have your picture taken for three weeks from next Tuesday."

"There are so many things wrong with what you just said, I'm not quite sure where to begin," I replied flatly making the idiots take a few steps back. "First of all, buildings do not have thirteenth floors—bad luck. The second blunder you made was that I don't make appointments. I don't need to. I'm the fucking Devil," I bellowed, causing a small windstorm that blew my Demons off their feet and into a pile on the ground.

"You're okay with amorous porcupines and dead bodies?" Astrid inquired with a wince.

"I'm not touching that one," I replied, pressing the bridge of my nose and considering sending all of them back to Hell.

"Well, at least you're *the* fucking Devil and not *fucking* the Devil anymore," Tiara pointed out gleefully to the delight of her sister and the Demons.

"Enough," I hissed at all of the imbeciles on the roof. The darkness was looming closer and I wasn't pleased. Was Chicago going to be the location I met my fate? I was so hoping for Paris or Milan—much more decadent—and the food was better. But, if it was Chicago, so be it. I watched my three Demons get back on their feet and eye me warily. "What else did you find?"

"Eunuchs," Dino said. "There are Eunuchs guarding the thirteenth floor. And this building has a thirteenth floor."

"Actually all buildings have a thirteenth floor, they just don't label them," Tiara announced at an octave that made my deadliest Demon warriors look like they wanted to cry. "Some say that the reason is triskaidekaphobia."

And that certainly put a confused wedge in the conversation.

"Are you making shit up?" Astrid demanded with her hands on her hips.

"Nope, triskaidekaphobia is an intense fear of the number thirteen," Tiara informed the still perplexed group.

"I call bullshit," Astrid said with a grin.

Tiara laughed and adjusted her sunglasses. "Triskaidekaphobia causes acute anxiety when people come across the number thirteen. Symptoms can include nausea, vomiting, difficulty breathing, rapid heartbeat, sweating and excessive use of the word shit-titty."

"Shit-titty?" Dagwood asked, clearly impressed.

Tiara cackled with glee and we all winced in tremendous pain. "Nah, I was bullshitting you with shit-titty, but the rest is true. Anyhoo, a bunch of brainiacs think the fear of the number thirteen dates back to one of the earliest written texts—the Code of Hammurabi. Story goes that the dumbass writers left out the thirteenth law on the list, but get a load of this bizarre bullshit... they didn't even number the fucking list. A douchehole set off a goddang panic that's lasted for thousands of years for nothing."

"Are we done here?" I asked getting annoyed.

"Is she fibbing?" Astrid asked me while poking her sister.

"She is not," I replied. "The laws were entertaining. The punishment for robbery is death. Kidnapping—death. Designing a house that collapses on someone's head—death. As I said... amusing."

81

"You're shitting me," Astrid said.

"I shit you not," I replied, mentally cataloguing the information my Demons had just imparted. Eunuchs. Interesting. "How many Eunuchs?"

"I counted twelve," Dino said. "But the strangest thing is that the soul seller seems to be human."

"And hot," Dagwood added.

"Tremendous rack," Darby finished off.

"Impossible," I muttered.

"Seriously," Darby countered. "Never seen a rack like it—perky and bouncy at the same time."

With a sigh slash hiss that caused alarm from my rag tag squad, I began to pace the roof and think. "I wasn't speaking of the soul seller's bosom," I replied to snickers from the crowd.

"*What?*" I demanded.

"My liege, no one says bosom anymore," Dagwood informed me with an enormous smile. "Very old school."

"And losery," Dino added.

"I *told* you," Astrid chimed in giving Dino a high five that sent him flying across the roof. "Sorry, dude."

"No worries," he grunted in embarrassment, quickly getting to his feet and jogging back over.

Again, I deeply regretted my choice of company. These people were driving me nuts. Deciding to ignore the bosom comment, I went on. However, I made a vow to drop the word from my vocabulary.

"I will no longer use the term bosom. Apparently, I'm dating myself," I announced, putting an end to the amusement at my expense—or so I thought.

"Well, dating yourself is better than fucking yourself," Tiara announced with a grin so wide I almost laughed.

Almost.

Instead, I shot her a look so evil she could see it through the darkness of the sunglasses. That was sufficient for ending the insulting wordplay—at least for the moment. Quite honestly, I planned to have Tiara attend the next poker game in Hell. She'd wreak havoc with her voice and her horrifying observations.

With a glance at all of the idiots on the roof, I sighed and continued. "Astrid, Tiara and I will enter from the ground floor. Darby, Dino and Dagwood you will jam the elevators and block all emergency exits after Astrid, Tiara and I hit the thirteenth floor. Darby, you will then come back to the roof. Dino and Dagwood stay in the lobby."

"I think we should have used horny honey badgers," Dino announced. "They're quite disgusting."

"What in the bloody Hell are you talking about?" I bellowed as I gave up on my good intentions and zapped a nearby cell tower with an explosive shot of red lightning. The blast was outstanding. It was either the tower or the Demon. I was proud of my choice.

Trembling like a leaf, Dino shrugged and gave me a weak grin. "Don't think anyone will go near an elevator filled with fornicating honey badgers. Those fuckers don't give a shit. They'll eat anything—might have been better than the porcupines and dead guys."

Pressing the bridge of my nose, I wondered if the darkness that was after me wasn't such a bad option. Dealing with halfwits was getting tiresome.

Forgoing a response was a mature and responsible approach and I could do mature and responsible… occasionally. Chicago was a nice city—lots of crime and mischief. It would be a damned shame to blow it off the map. "Are we clear on the plan?"

"Nope," Tiara said. "Not a bit."

"You two are with me. You will kill anything that tries to stop me from getting to the soul seller, including the Eunuchs. Decapitation works best, but any kind of dismembering will do. They fight dirty and racking them is useless as they have no balls. Dino, Darby and Dagwood will kill anyone suspicious that tries to leave or enter the building. I'll have my picture taken then I'll kill the soul seller. Clear?"

"So we're just gonna kill a bunch of shit?"

"Yes."

"Sounds good to me," Tiara said as the three Demons nodded their agreement.

"Mmmkay," Astrid said, clearly taking issue with my plan. "But are all of these dudes bad guys?"

"Does it really matter?" I shouted, exasperated. "I have a few more pressing issues to deal with after the soul seller—potentially *world ending* ones. A few casualties are an acceptable loss. You feel me?"

"I do not," Astrid shot back, stepping up and going toe to toe with me.

"You either have a death wish or you've lost your mind," I growled as my eyes went red and a black mist began to slither over the city.

"My mind has been questionable my entire life," she replied, not backing down an inch. "As far as a death wish—no. And I'm awfully hard to kill,' she added with a grin. "You don't randomly kill for sport. You punish evil."

"Your point?" I demanded.

"My point is… don't bring on the damn darkness before it arrives on its own."

"What if this is what Fate has decreed?" I questioned her harshly.

She shrugged and placed a kiss on my cheek. "Fate's a bitch. I don't give a horny porcupine's ass what she's decreed. We're gonna make our own ending and it's going to be a happily ever after."

"Isn't that pushing it a bit—don't think anyone will buy that," I quipped with a raised brow and the beginnings of a smile pulling at my lips.

"You think people are gonna buy your piece of shit autobiography vaguely disguised as a romance?"

"But of course," I told her.

"Then they're gonna buy this and so are we," she stated and then stepped back.

I was quiet for a moment while I digested the fact that I'd almost just leveled Chicago because I didn't like what Astrid had to say. Goddamn it, the truth was far stranger than fiction and it tended to hurt. Whatever, I enjoyed a little pain. It made me feel alive. Maybe Fate had chosen my present company for a reason—or maybe not.

"How are we going to get in without an appointment?" Tiara inquired, checking her arsenal of weapons that she'd hidden all over her body.

"Watch and learn. I always get what I want," I replied. "On three, everyone transport. Ready?"

"Nope, but that's never stopped me," Astrid said.

"Let's kick some ass," Tiara shouted.

"Yes. Let's."

CHAPTER TEN

"WITHOUT AN APPOINTMENT, YOU *CAN'T* SEE MISS RINOA. SHE'S *VERY* busy. You can leave now," a horrid, mousey little woman snapped at me from behind a large ornate black desk. Her glasses were tinted an odd shade of grayish brown. I was curious for a brief moment what awful color the world must be from behind those lenses.

"I'm sorry," I replied with a tight smile through gritted teeth. "I don't think you understood me. I'm here to see Miss Rinoa. *Now.*"

"Here's a thought, *little mister,*" she informed me in a pleasant tone that belied her insulting words. With a tilt of her head she sized me up dismissively and clearly didn't like what she saw. "While I'd really like to see your point of view, I'm not sure I can wedge my head that far up my ass."

Holy Hell, she was outstandingly rude, but I was better. "My, my… a thought crossed your mind? Must have been a long and lonely journey."

"Trust me, it wasn't," she said with a delightfully evil sneer. "However, your family tree must be a cactus because you're most certainly a prick," she parried, pushing her ridiculous glasses up her nose and leaning forward aggressively.

Did she seriously think she could insult me out of the room? Laughable. I was fucking Satan. Wait. No, damn it. I wasn't fucking *myself*. Now *I* was misinterpreting my own words. This old bag was throwing me off my game. Unacceptable.

"Shock me," I purred and winked at her, which made her hiss. "Say something intelligent."

"Umm… don't think this is going to help you get an appointment," Astrid whispered while elbowing me in the stomach.

"Hush now," I admonished my niece. "I'm having fun."

"I have a problem," the mousey woman said, slapping her hands down on her desk and glaring at me.

"And what would that be, darling?" I asked, enjoying myself immensely.

"Your face. I can see it."

While I appreciated the elaborately decorated office complete with flashy crystal chandeliers and questionably appropriate nude statues, I didn't appreciate the tone or the words from the *receptionist*. My *face* happened to be a work of art. Normally, I'd find her appalling behavior amusing—even offer her a job in Hell. Truly ill-mannered help with a good dose of sarcasm was difficult to come by. However, today she was just pissing me off.

"Dude… guess she just told you," Astrid muttered under her breath.

I was fairly certain my charm wasn't going to work on the atrocity now staring daggers at me, but it was worth a try. While the insults were invigorating, I had business to attend to.

My new impertinent friend simply scowled at me with the tiniest hint of a victorious smile pulling at her mouth. It was admirably annoying.

I had half a mind to zap her bespectacled ass into oblivion, but the waiting area was filled with humans—underfed models waiting to have their photos taken by the infamous, soul selling Miss Rinoa, to be more accurate. God would be pissed if I started messing with his pets without provocation and I didn't need to get my brother involved. He would tell our mother and all Hell would break loose—literally.

"I don't think you understand who I am, *darling,*" I said in a smooth voice I reserved for seduction.

Every human woman and man in the waiting area was affected by my tone—orgasmic sighs and giggles permeated the air and lust wafted thickly around the room. However, the old bag seemed unmoved by my skill and watched with disinterest as the humans began writhing and touching each other.

"And I don't care, *darling.* No one sees Miss Rinoa without an appointment," she shot back.

"Now listen," I started only to be cut off by the smack-talking mess behind the desk.

"Save your breath, big boy. You'll need it to blow up your latex date later."

Point to the mousey old woman. I'd have to use that one.

Squinting my eyes, I wondered what she was—definitely not human—however, I couldn't place her. Odd. Possibly an ancient witch? An extremely ugly ancient witch…

"Do you know who I am?" I demanded.

"Should I care?" she asked, rudely.

"Actually, you *should,*" I replied flatly as my eyes blazed red and my fingers began to spark.

"Tamp it back, dude," Astrid said, grabbing my hands in hers and hiding the flames.

"You're speaking to Blade Inferno—*the* Blade Inferno," Tiara announced, stepping in front of me before I turned the disrespectful freak show into a pile of dust. "The highest paid romance author in the mother humpin' world—gets paid more than Jenny Ebonobitch."

"Oh my Uncle God," Astrid grumbled. "It's *Janet Evanovich.* He's paid more than *Janet Evanovich.*"

"Whoops, my bad. Janet Evanovich," Tiara corrected herself

with an apologetic shriek as the entire room groaned and slapped their hands over their ears.

"I should say so," Astrid said.

"I don't read romance," Tiara defended herself. "I read comics and cookbooks."

Astrid let go of my hands and narrowed her eyes at her sister. "Why in the Hell do you read cookbooks? You can't eat. Right? I mean that would be totally unfucking fair."

"Umm..." Tiara hesitated at the expression on Astrid's face.

"Are you telling me you *can* eat?" Astrid demanded as the humans paused their orgy and watched the bizarre conversation with rapt fascination and a healthy dose of fear.

"On full moons, I can eat," Tiara admitted in a whisper, darting behind me for cover.

Astrid was still royally pissed that, as a Vampyre, she couldn't eat food. We heard about it constantly. Her ability to consume chips and salsa along with black raspberry chip ice cream had been stolen from her when she died. My guess was that Tiara's strangely mixed heritage enabled her to eat occasionally.

Stomping her foot and walking in tight little circles around the now naked group of models, Astrid tried to work off her fury. If I'd had time on my hands, I would have enjoyed her fit, the orgy, and the churlish receptionist, but I didn't have that luxury at the moment.

"Your grandmother can give you a reprieve and you can eat for a day," I hissed in her ear as I grabbed the collar of her shirt and yanked her back in line. "Right now you shall behave."

"Sorry," she mumbled. "And I'll pass. If Gigi grants me a concession, I'll have to eat her cooking. I'd rather die."

"You're already dead," I pointed out.

"Touché." Astrid's eyes stayed narrowed, but the corners of her mouth tilted up. "My apologies," she announced to the room of startled good-looking people. "My diet makes me cranky."

"I hear you, sis-tah," a human blonde gal called out

disengaging herself from the sexual debauchery. "I've eaten nothing but celery for a month straight so I'd be skinny enough for my photo shoot today."

Astrid's eyes grew wide with horror and she approached the emaciated model. "Listen to me, Blondie," she insisted. "One of these days you're gonna try to stop smoking and get hypnotized at a seedy strip mall by a fucking Russian whack job who may or may not be distantly related to you in a totally farked up way. This is going to seem like an excellent idea until you wake up dead and can never eat again. Ever. And to make matters worse, you'll have to drink blood—totally skeeved me out in the beginning, but you get used to it. So seriously, celery is bullshit—tastes like butt—not that I know what butt tastes like, but it smells like butt so you do the math. Don't eat that crap. Eat pizza and tacos for the love of everything unholy, holy and all the stuff in between," Astrid shouted at the terrified woman. "I mean being dead has its advantages, but for real, eat everything while you still can. You feel me?"

"Umm... sure," the woman stuttered as she stood up and sprinted out of the waiting room in her birthday suit followed by a few others.

With a wide smile at my niece's inadvertent, albeit hard to follow help, I turned back to the nasty piece of work, leaned on the desk and grinned at my nemesis. "Looks to me like Miss Rinoa now has a few opens for today. I'll take one."

"You will do no such thing," the newest bane of my existence contradicted me with a finger pointed at my face.

It was a surprisingly appealing finger considering how heinous the rest of her was. Normally I'd incinerate someone as rude as the woman, but she held the key to what I wanted at the moment and she amused me. After I got to the soul seller, the old bag would receive a one-way ticket to Hell. She'd fit right in.

With clap of her hands three Eunuchs walked through the door and flanked the desk, leering at me menacingly. This new development was fantastic as I was itching for a bloody fight. However, I needed to remove the collateral damage from the room so Astrid wouldn't crawl up my ass.

With a wave of my hand the humans disappeared. The old woman looked surprised for a brief second, but schooled her unattractive features quickly.

"Umm, where are the starving models?" Astrid asked as she sized up our burly opponents.

"Purgatory."

"Seriously?" Tiara questioned my choice as she pulled a mean looking dagger from her designer purse. "You just sent hungry, horny, naked models to Purgatory?"

I paused a moment, considered my actions and then shrugged.

"I see your point," I said. "My persnickety brother hates surprise orgies in Purgatory, but I thought my neck of the woods might be a little off-putting. I was trying to be *nice*."

"You really should stop that," Astrid advised.

"Point taken," I replied, and then turned my attention back to the matter at hand. "I'd like to see Miss Rinoa *now*."

"Or?" the woman asked, eyebrows high.

"Or the Eunuchs die and you shall follow," I told her with my most charming smile as the Eunuchs growled with displeasure. "Your choice."

"Honestly, if I wanted to die I'd simply climb your ego and jump to your IQ," she said in a fabulously bored tone and then went back to her work.

For the first time in a few million years, I was speechless. No one spoke to me like this deranged old hag... and I loved it.

"I think a beheading would be a little quicker," I shot back. "Far less painful considering that my ego—along with other parts of me—are *enormous*."

The shocked expressions on my niece's faces gave me pause. What the Hell was I doing? Was I flirting with the heinous woman? I do believe I was. The end of time must be very near. It had to be.

"You think you can take *my* men?" the woman demanded, ignoring my sexual innuendo and leaning back in her chair with the ease of someone who wasn't just threatened with death or an enormous dick. The challenge of her insolence was invigorating. She was a hateful piece of work.

The woman's choice of words were interesting, but she clearly was crazy. The Eunuchs were hers? I didn't believe that for a second. Crazy people didn't always make sense and this one was certifiable.

"I believe I can handle a few immortals without balls," I replied, rolling my neck and cracking my knuckles with a nasty smirk on my lips.

"Why do you want to see Elle?" she demanded, standing up.

She was surprisingly tall for a woman so mousy and there was something strangely off about her. She had seemed small and meek, but it was clear that whatever kind of old witch she was, she had power.

"Well... since I am the fucking highest paid romance author in the world, I want my picture taken for my book," I explained slowly as if English was her second language. Hell, if she was as old as I assumed she was, English was probably her twentieth language. "And then the rest of what I want is between me and your boss."

Her cackle went through me like shards of ice and the Eunuchs simply chuckled at her glee.

"My *boss* doesn't talk to Angels," the woman said flatly.

"You speak for your boss?" I demanded, growing frustrated with the ridiculous banter.

"I absolutely speak for my boss—my word is her word."

"And you think I'm an *Angel*?" I asked in a voice so deadly quiet, she startled for a second.

"Don't think. Know," she hissed with disdain. "You people

have come before and you will come again. Elle will have nothing to do with you."

"Do you have a death wish, old woman?" I snapped. She was no longer amusing—at all. "Because I could help you with that."

"Be gone," she snarled. "Celestial beings are not welcome here."

"Lady," Tiara piped in. "You've got Blade Inferno all wrong. He's definitely not an Angel—not even close. He's a Demon."

"You're a Demon?" she asked, eyeing me with doubt as she walked from behind the desk and examined me.

"Demon by birth or by design?" I asked in a silky tone, still curious about her breeding. What was she?

"I sense Angel—not Demon." She circled me as the Eunuchs watched carefully, ready to attack at any moment.

They didn't stand a chance, but a fight would be quite relaxing right now. The old witch's senses were keen. Very rarely was I recognized for my true being.

"Does it really matter? Is an adopted child any less of a child?" I shot back.

"No."

"All right then, next question."

"You didn't answer my first," she said, stepping away from me.

I felt the loss of her heat immediately. Had she tried to put a spell of sorts on me? Interesting.

"You didn't ask one. You only made assumptions."

"I don't make assumptions. I speak truth—and I use words that make sense."

She did. However, my lineage was none of her business. I had half a mind to show her exactly who I was, but blowing my cover at the moment didn't seem prudent.

"I shall give you one more chance," I ground out through clenched teeth as a menacing wind began to blow through the room. "Tell Miss Rinoa that Blade Inferno is coming back to have his picture made."

The old woman shrugged and laughed. "Go. Go tell her yourself. I know for certain she'll be appalled to meet you. She and I think very much alike."

"We shall see about that," I growled.

"Yes, we shall," she replied with another chilling cackle.

Storming away from the laughing fool, I waved my hand and blasted the door that I assumed to be the studio with an explosion of red fire. Astrid and Tiara were on my heels as I strode angrily into the room—only to find it empty. No camera. No equipment. No Adrielle Rinoa.

No fucking way.

I use words that make sense. My men. She and I think very much alike. I absolutely speak for my boss—my word is her word.

Words. I didn't listen to the words. Damn it, my mother was correct. The words had meaning, I just wasn't listening. The old woman wasn't the receptionist for Adrielle Rinoa. She *was* Adreille Rinoa.

With a furious curse and a massive explosion, I transported myself right back to the desk in a blast of glittering black magic. I'd been made a fool of and I was not pleased—at all.

As the smoke cleared, I was met by a sight that would be burned into my mind for the rest of time. I gripped the edge of the desk to stay on my feet. Suddenly breathless, I stared at the vision before me.

"Amazing," I murmured, taking in the glorious evil beauty.

Behind the desk now stood the most exquisite woman I'd witnessed in my eternity—masses of honey blonde hair framed her perfect face and her body would make the Angels on high weep.

She was surrounded by twelve Eunuchs and literally glowed in a sparkling amethyst light. Her eyes were a deep purple ringed with gold and they glared straight into my soul with fury and displeasure. Her wild blonde hair blew around her head as strong gusts of sensual magic darted around the room.

I knew what she was now. Adrielle Rinoa was most definitely a

Siren. They were clearly not extinct. I was shocked, intrigued and wildly aroused.

"Did you find her?" Adrielle, aka *Elle*, aka the *soul seller*, inquired as she tossed the grayish brown spectacles to the floor.

"I do believe I did. You've been a very bad girl, Adrielle Rinoa," I shot back, bending slightly forward to release the pressure of the most painful erection I'd had to date.

"Tell me something I don't know."

"All right," I said smoothly, regaining my composure—if not control of my dick. "I know that you're going to have to answer to me about your little soul selling venture."

"I don't answer to anyone," she replied breezily in a sexually charged musical voice, eyeing me curiously as I didn't fall to my knees in front of her.

Most men would be lost by now with the way she was throwing her deadly carnal power around.

I was not most men.

"You *will* answer to me," I replied, throwing some of her own hedonistic spell right back at her.

My Siren grew uncomfortable quickly and tilted her head as she examined me like an experiment gone wrong.

"What are you?" she whispered.

"I'm your worst fucking nightmare, my love. Now that I've found you, I do believe I might keep you."

"You *really* think you've found me?" she asked, narrowing her purple gaze dangerously.

"Don't think... *know*."

"Finders keepers. Losers weepers. Start weeping, big boy," she said as she slowly raised her arms and disappeared along with her henchmen in a raging gust of amethyst magic.

"What the hey-hey?" Tiara shouted as she reentered the room, diving at the desk and trying to stop the exodus with brute strength.

Astrid was right behind her and they landed in a tangled heap on the floor. Not only had the Siren disappeared, but all the furniture down to the chandeliers and nude statues had accompanied her.

"She got away," Astrid gasped, crawling to her feet and examining the now empty room. "What the Hell was that?"

"It might have been my fate," I replied absently as I bent down and picked up the only evidence that she had even been here.

Holding the ugly glasses in my hand, I examined them closely. She'd hidden those amethyst eyes behind them. She was hiding much more—of that I was certain.

Only one species in the Universe had eyes like hers and I was sure they'd been gone for centuries. I was wrong. The soul seller might have hidden from me once, but she would never be as successful again.

"Where did she go?" Tiara asked as she sprinted around the room searching for clues.

"Don't know."

"Do you think she has something to do with the darkness coming?" Astrid asked, watching me pocket the glasses.

"Do you believe in accidents?" I inquired.

"Is there a correct answer to that question?" Astrid countered.

"Yes, there is. There are *no* accidents," I replied. "I don't know if this Elle woman is bringing on the darkness, but I will bet my immortal life that she will lead me to it."

"But if you follow her, you could be walking straight to your death," Tiara pointed out.

"And how in the mother humpin' Hell can you follow her? She disappeared with everything except the kitchen sink."

"Not to worry, my sweets. I'm Satan. I can find anyone."

"Seriously?" Tiara asked, impressed.

"But of course. And I do think my Siren wants to be found."

"Umm... could have fooled me. Why do you think that?" Astrid asked as she stowed her weapons and straightened her sister's wild hair.

"Because she left me a gift to track her with." I held them in the air. "I have her glasses."

"So we're just gonna go get her?" Tiara questioned.

"Nope, we're going to go about normal business. It will lead us right back to her."

Astrid wrinkled her nose and gave me a look. "Sounds a little wonky to me."

"How old are you?" I asked.

"Thirty."

"How old am I?" I continued.

"Umm... older than dirt?" Astrid replied with a grin.

"Correct. Trust me on this. I know what I'm doing."

Or at least I hoped I did... Only time would tell. I might not have much left, but it would certainly be interesting.

Fate was a bitch, but at this juncture I found her antics entertaining.

Very entertaining.

CHAPTER ELEVEN

"WHAT FRESH HELL IS THIS?" I DEMANDED, STEPPING QUICKLY BEHIND my nieces to avoid all the grabby hands of the overly excited women.

The large ballroom of the hotel Astrid had insisted we go to was filled to the brim with insane and aggressive women. I loved women—a lot—but this was a bit much even for me. There was very little rhyme or reason to the madness. They reminded me of hungry piranhas and I was clearly on the menu.

"It's the Romance Readers Anonymous Convention—acronym RRAC—kind of what it looks like all these women are going to do to you—so cover your jewels, Uncle Hot Pants. Apparently, your book is a smash hit, dude," she replied, blocking a particularly pushy trio of women.

And that's when I noticed the books—piles and piles of them set out at tables with formerly smiling authors sitting behind them. They were no longer smiling as the crowd had now set about tackling me, or racking me if Astrid was correct in her assessment.

Damn it to Hell. What had I been thinking? No one had explained this clusterfuck to me. This was utterly debased insanity.

"What do they want?" I shouted over the rising hysteria as I noticed the twenty foot posters of me plastered all over the room looking incredibly sexy, if I did say so myself. They were a tad bit out of date since I was fairly sure they'd been snapped in the 1970's, but I hadn't aged in millions of years. I was a handsome bastard.

"You," Tiara shouted causing a chandelier to crack and fall to the ground. "They want you!"

"Of course they do," I said with an eye roll. "I'm Satan. Everyone wants a piece of this, but..."

"Oh my God," a woman who stood no more than four feet tall and had a mop of blue and pink hair screamed at the top of her lungs. "It's Blade Inferno. The highest paid romance author in the world."

She waved a newspaper high above her head with an outstanding picture of me on the front page which was definitely more recent. My agent must have had a few good shots sent over from Hell for the press release. Maybe I'd keep him after all. Normally, seeing my smiling face was delightful. Right at this very moment—not so much.

At least three hundred rabid women were now gunning for me. It would be horrible form to incinerate them so I did what any sane leader of everything evil would do. I froze them. All of them.

It was amusing in a nightmarish way. Hundreds of women in mid-step or mid-grab—mouths open in silent screams of excitement. Eyes bulging and hands extended.

"I really hope this isn't permanent," Astrid said, staring in shock at the now silent and immobile room.

"It's not," I replied as I stepped out from behind my nieces and took a look around. "What exactly is happening here? Is this some type of subculture I'm unaware of?"

"It's on the itinerary your idiot agent had messengered to us by a freakin' three headed pigeon," Astrid said with a laugh and a shake of her head. "Doesn't the douchebail have a phone or a computer?"

"When did this happen?" I asked, taking the paper from Astrid's hand.

"Hmm... let me see," Tiara said with her finger to her lip, mocking deep thought. "I believe it was when we were walking down Michigan Avenue while you were checking yourself out in every single window we passed."

"What can I say?" I inquired with a shrug. "It's a sunny day and I'm gorgeous."

"Right," Tiara said with a snort. "You didn't even notice when the deformed pigeon attacked what was left of the buzzards you let loose on the city. It was a bloody damned mess."

"Who won?" I asked, perusing the itinerary.

"Astrid did," Tiara informed me, picking up a book and checking out the back cover. "She sent the remaining buzzards and the three headed monstrosity to your bedroom in Hell."

"Is that a horrid joke?" I asked, glancing up in alarm from the paper.

"Guess you're gonna have to wait and see," Astrid replied with a wink.

"Payback's a bitch," I reminded her.

"That *was* payback, my dear uncle."

"Touché." My niece was a wonderfully heinous young woman. That was a dreadful thing to do. I wondered how she was going to enjoy the rabid, horny honey badgers I was going to have delivered to her... or was it porcupines? No matter. Either would suffice.

"So... are we just going to leave them frozen?" Astrid asked as she too started reading the book jackets. "Sweet mother humper on a bender," she gasped. "I've been waiting for this book! You're gonna have to lift the spell—at least off of Darynda Jones. I want to get it signed and she's kind of rigid at the moment."

"Does she make more money than me?" I asked, looking at the

sweet face of this Darynda woman Astrid seemed so enamored with.

"Dude, no one makes more money than you," Tiara reminded me. "You make more than Joanie Elompostitch."

"I'm going to stab you in the head if you fuck her name up one more time," Astrid threatened her sister and then jerked to a halt in front of a table. "Oh my Hell, you've paralyzed Charlaine Harris and Molly Harper—I *love* their books. This is just not right."

"Well, what do you want me to do?" I demanded, stomping my foot and throwing my hands in the air. "I stand a fine chance of being castrated if I lift the enchantment. Do you care more about getting a book signed than my testicles?"

"You will be punished for putting an image of your privates in my head. Do you understand me, Uncle Fucker? That was uncalled for and I don't even have the luxury of puking."

"I can puke on a full moon," Tiara announced and then sprinted away as Astrid screamed and lunged for her.

As they beat the living Hell out of each other, I continued my observations of this bizarre human ritual. Was this fun? How could attacking and dismembering authors be fun? I mean... I enjoyed attacking and dismembering Trolls, Dark Fairies and rogue Vamps, but *authors*? All they did was spout bullshit onto paper for the pleasure of the masses. I'd quite enjoyed spouting bullshit and lies and turning it into a book. My brother had certainly done it to great success. It was my turn.

"Stop trying to kill each other," I reprimanded my nieces. "Your demise is not on the schedule for today."

Walking over with torn clothes and a few gashes, my nieces were grinning from ear to ear.

"You have *insane* moves," Astrid congratulated Tiara with a pat on her back.

"You're a deranged fighting machine," Tiara replied, hugging her sister. "I want some lessons."

"Do you promise never to eat or puke in front of me? I just don't think I could handle it. You feel me?" Astrid bargained.

"Promise," Tiara answered as she gently wiped the blood from Astrid's face and reset the broken arm she'd caused.

"Are you done?" I inquired with a raised brow.

They looked at each other and giggled.

"We are," Astrid confirmed, quickly pulling a dagger out of Tiara's thigh that she'd recently placed there and put it back in her purse. "Did you find anything interesting?"

"No," I told them as I picked up a hardback copy of my tome from a large table filled with my books. My agent and Hemingway had certainly worked fast. "Who chose the title?"

"No clue," Astrid said, glancing at the book. "But it's fitting."

"You think *Fashionably Flawed* is fitting?" I questioned. "I was thinking more along the lines of *The Bible Part Two—the Real Story* or *Hotter Than Hell in August* or possibly *So Many Women, So Little Time.*"

"Then it's a good thing you didn't name it," Astrid commented dryly. "Those titles suck ass."

"Thank you," I replied.

"Welcome," she shot back with a grin.

"Umm… guys? Is there a reason that there are a bunch of half naked Eunuchs frozen in compromising poses with the ladies over here?" Tiara called out sounding perplexed.

"Bingo," I muttered, dropping the book and making my way through the motionless crowd to the newest wrinkle.

Tiara was correct, but she hadn't done the description justice. The Eunuchs were clad in what could only be labeled gold lame boxer briefs. It was terrifyingly metrosexual, but from their bored, stock-still expressions, they seemed to be handling the unfortunate fashion choice quite well.

Women were obscenely draped all over the well-oiled men. However, the most interesting part of the lewd display was the large banner next to the table filled with brochures and bowls of candy in the shape of tiny cameras. In fancy lavender script, the words *Adrielle Rinoa—Photographer to the Stars of Romance—*was displayed. The banner was filled with book covers of sexy men and on each cover was one of the Eunuchs—on a motorcycle, pirating a ship, holding a puppy, sporting fake fangs, in military garb, clad in a fireman's uniform... and it went on and on. The only similarity of the woefully ridiculous covers was that the men were all showing copious amounts of skin and looked like they'd just come off a sexual bender. Of course that was impossible, since the bastards had no balls, but my little Elle was good at creating the illusion of sex.

She should be—she was a Siren.

The only thing missing now was the Siren herself. But if her *men* were here, she had to be close by. She'd probably donned another disguise, but I'd find her. I had to.

"Are these the same Eunuchs?" Astrid asked.

"Yes, they are," Dino said as he, Dagwood and Darby appeared in an impressive blast of black smoke and glitter.

The three Demons were dressed head to toe in black combat gear with questionably fashionable berets on their heads. I almost commented on their headwear, but decided to let it slide, along with the embarrassing names they'd chosen. Hell on Earth, it was difficult letting my people express themselves creatively. It gave me hives. Whatever.

"Where have you been?" I demanded. "I was almost neutered by unbalanced women."

"Umm... sorry boss," Dagwood said, taking in the frozen landscape with a bewildered expression. "Do you want us to kill them?"

"No," I snapped. "I don't want you to *kill* them. They can't help themselves. I'm Satan—everyone wants me. I could have just used a bit of extra protection to keep me from blowing up a building of innocent, horny women."

"Got it," Darby said. "Don't kill the hookers."

"They're not hookers," I told him and then paused. "Wait. Are they?" I asked Astrid.

"No, not hookers," she replied with a snort. "They're romance readers. They like hot guys, strong heroines and happily ever afters—but mostly hot guys and well written sex without the use of the word bosom."

Clearly I was never going to live down my usage of the term bosom.

Dino bobbed his head enthusiastically and his beret fell jauntily to the left making him look farcical—nothing like the trained killer he was. "I'm partial to the stories where the heroine gets knocked up and the hero doesn't know and he leaves town for a job or some bullshit like that. Then there are all these fabulous misunderstandings when he sees his little doppelgänger—so thrilling and sexy," Dino, my deadly Demon from Hell announced with a shudder of delight.

What in the name of all that was evil was happening here?

"Lots of hot make up sex in those," Dagwood agreed with a serious nod. "Although I really get my rocks off reading the ones where the hired help with triple D tits accidently drops a tray of steaming hot food on the billionaire's crotch which leads to a round of dry humping which then degenerates into sex with nipple clamps and butt plugs."

"I love those," Darby added with a squeal that *did not* belong in the repertoire of a Demon. "However, I'm quite fond of paranormal romance. Love me some over-sexed werewolves who have to kill other werewolves and then have sex with the entire pack."

"Male and female?" Tiara asked, confused.

"Werewolves tend to be tri-sexual," Darby explained. "So yes. Male, female and other."

"What the Hell is *other*?" I asked, feeling the beginnings of a headache crawling into my overloaded brain. "WAIT. Do not answer that. Ever. Did you idiots happen to leave your man cards in Hell?" I snapped in disbelief at the way the conversation was going. "Because if you have them, you need to hand them over. Now."

"Umm..." Astrid gaped at the three romance novel loving Demons in disbelief. "Not sure what you guys have been reading, but if you'd like I could make some suggestions of actual books—ones that make sense."

"With nipple clamps?" Dino inquired.

"Millionaires?" Dagwood added.

"And secret babies?" Darby finished off.

"Enough," I shouted. "Your reading choices are appalling. I would have thought Steven King would be on your bedside table. Not millionaires, babies, and mammilla clamps."

"Uncle Fucker?" Tiara said, with her hand raised politely.

"Yes?" I hissed, ready to behead them all.

"*Mammilla* belongs in the same trash heap as bosom. Never use that one again—unless you need to cock block."

"She's right, my liege," Darby concurred, bowing his head to me in respect.

Closing my eyes and letting my head fall back for a moment, I gathered myself. It would be wrong to incinerate my men and my favorite nieces in a blazing inferno. I was better than that—kind of. Maybe if I just zapped the Hell out of them I'd feel better.

"I'm trying very hard here not to reduce all of you to ash. I feel that I'm doing well with that goal at the moment. However, if anyone says anything that annoys, confuses or insults me I shall be forced to cremate you. Am I clear?"

In unison they nodded.

"Very well then, I'm going to lift the spell from the Eunuchs. I want all of you to be ready to kill if they don't cooperate. Eunuchs are murder machines. I haven't had the pleasure of fighting one in ages. I thought they'd gone the way of the Sirens. However, I was wrong about the Sirens. I fucking hate being wrong," I growled.

"Are you going to reanimate all twelve?" Dino asked, pulling a mean looking sword from his scabbard and moving the immobile Eunuchs into a group.

"Don't hurt the readers," Astrid instructed as she pried a few off of the Eunuchs and gently put them on the nearby tables. "They're innocent. And let's move this away from Charlaine Harris. I'd be royally pissed if anything happened to her. Everything I know about Vamps I learned from *True Blood*."

"Dude," Tiara commented with a grunt of laughter. "That's fucked up."

"I know that *now*," Astrid said with a lopsided grin as she lifted the Harris woman and cradled her in her arms. "But Eric was dang hot."

"Word," Dino said as he moved the frozen Molly Harper and Darynda Jones to safety as well.

"Wait," Tiara called out in a panic. "Is Janie Erompokitch here? We should probably move her too. Astrid loves her and she *is* the second highest paid romance author in the world. It would be terrible if she lost her head in the shitshow that's about to go down."

Astrid's agonized groan bounced off the walls of the ballroom. "It's Janet *fucking* Evanovich. I know I said I was going to stab you in the head if you desecrate her name again. However, I'm going to give you a pass since we'll probably need you to fight the Eunuchs, but it's very difficult for me."

"I appreciate that," Tiara said. "But is the author whose name I keep screwing up here?"

"No," Dagwood assured everyone. "I perused the list of signing authors and she wasn't on it. We're all clear. However, Robyn Peterman is here."

"Move her too. Love her stuff," Astrid said.

"On it," Dagwood replied.

"Are we ready?" I inquired through gritted teeth.

"Yep," Tiara said with a thumbs up.

Just as I was about to lift the enchantment a warm sensual

breeze blew through the ballroom, giving me pause and a painful erection. Books scattered and tables upended. A smile pulled at my lips. The game was on and definitely about to become more fun.

The air around us changed dramatically from sensually warm to orgasmically hot and I quickly conjured the protective sunglasses for my men and Tiara. The temperature rose even higher as sparkling amethyst crystals rained down from the ceiling and covered everything in sight. Absolutely delightful. Everyone pulled their weapons except me. I didn't have to. I was a weapon —the deadliest fucking weapon in the Universe—pun very much intended.

Maybe I wouldn't have to kill the Eunuchs for information about the whereabouts of Elle Rinoa. I do believe the lady—a loose use of the word—was now in the room.

"Well, if it's not Douche Von Idiotbag," she purred as she took in the scene, standing a relatively safe distance away from me. Her hair blew wildly around her face and her sheer purple robe barely covered her otherworldly beauty.

Little did she know there was no safe distance from me.

The air around the Siren literally shimmered. Her power was enormous and wielded with expertise. Astrid and Tiara hissed and moved in to flank me on either side, but my Demons groaned in male appreciation and fell to their knees.

Adrielle Rinoa was a sensually evil masterpiece.

"That's not a very nice name to call someone you barely know," I said and gave her my wonderfully perfected pout.

"I'm not nice," she snapped. "At all."

"I'd have to agree with that," I replied casually. "Only a horrid piece of work would insist her men wear gold lame booty shorts."

"Yet your men are wearing *berets*," she pointed out with a raised brow. "That's a bit cheesy."

"And the point goes to Elle," I said with a careless shrug, not bothering to explain I had nothing to do with the chagrin worthy headwear. "However, it's far more tasteful than the sparkling banana sacks you've chosen for your men."

"I'd wear those metrosexual ball squeezers for you, Elle Rinoa," Dino volunteered in a dreamy voice, clearly falling deeper under the spell of the Siren.

Her laugh was pure magic and my pants grew uncomfortably tight. Amazing. She was a walking, talking sex bomb.

With a flick of my wrist, I sent my Demons back to Hell. I told myself it was for their protection, but I knew better. I wanted to be the only man with a functioning dick in the room. I wanted no competition for my prize. Ever.

Wait. Adrielle Rinoa was no prize and she wasn't mine. She was a Siren who was selling souls. The woman needed to be eliminated. That was the rule.

But weren't rules made to be broken?

"Unfreeze my men and I'll let you live, *Blade Inferno*," she said with an amused sneer as she crossed her arms over her ample chest and raised her chin defiantly.

My laughter rang out and her amethyst eyes narrowed dangerously making my custom Armani pants feel like they were choking my dick. "That's a goal that can't be reached," I explained. "However, I'm willing to make a deal."

"I don't make deals."

"Dude, what are you doing?" Tiara whispered. "Just blow her up and let's get the Hell out."

"Can't do that," Astrid hissed under her breath. "She hasn't done anything wrong—yet. We just need the soul she's selling before all of us explode into a gob of green goopy orgasm."

"Wrong is such a relative word," I muttered to my nieces while keeping my eyes glued to my quest. "Just don't let her get away."

"Make sure you're thinking with your big head—not your little one," Tiara insisted.

"They're both big," I replied with no humility whatsoever and then focused all my attention back on the Siren.

Glancing down at her diamond encrusted watch and tapping her Manalo Blahnik shod foot impatiently, Elle blew out an annoyed breath causing a delicious cinnamon scented wind to waft around the vast room. "I'm a busy woman. Lift the spell from my men or prepare to die... whatever you are."

"My dear woman," I said, approaching her as she eyed me with distrust and curiosity. "I'm simply a man in the business of pleasure and I'd like to make you an offer you can't refuse."

She considered me for so long it was positively rude. I hadn't been turned on like this in centuries.

"Does that line actually work for you?" she asked with a raised and wildly disrespectful brow that made my pants even tighter and more uncomfortable.

"It has," I answered vaguely. Honestly, I had no recollection of having used that one. It was somewhat lame, but at least I hadn't said bosom *or* mammilla. I was Satan. I could do or say anything I wanted and get away with it—or at the very least get laid for it.

"Not interested, *Blade Inferno*."

With her full lips pursed and a contemptuous nod of her head, she dismissed me almost bringing me to my knees my dick was so hard. Her ass was a fucking symphony as she turned and walked over to her frozen men.

"Oh and just a little advice, Big Guy. Your lines suck. I'd suggest getting some new ones."

"My lines do not suck," I snapped. "I've been very successful over the years for your information."

She paused and glared. Holy Hell on fire, it was hot.

"Where did you buy your ego? Or was it given free and you overdosed?" Elle inquired as she stopped and looked me up and down. Her heat was addictive.

Astrid barked out a laugh and I shot her a look of death. My niece quickly glanced down, but she and her sister continued to giggle—at my expense. Unacceptable.

Elle smiled and continued on to her men. This was not going my way. I hated when things didn't go my way.

"Is she serious?" I demanded aloud.

"Looks that way," Astrid said with a smirk so wide I felt my headache coming back.

"You just got dissed," Tiara whispered.

"She's bluffing," I said. "She wants me."

"Good luck with that," Astrid said, biting back her laugh with effort. "Kinda looks to me like she could eat your balls for breakfast."

Why was I letting a woman throw me off my game? Women fell at my feet, for the love of everything evil. What the Hell was this one's problem? She was a Siren. I was Satan. We were two wrongs that would make an outstanding right.

"Here's the deal, Miss Rinoa," I went on as if I hadn't just had my painfully blue balls just handed to me. "I will lift the spell if you photograph me."

"No," she said, not even sparing me a glance.

"Wonderful," I said as my fingers began to spark. "What time and where?"

"Are you always this daft? Or is today a special occasion?" she inquired.

"You take umbrage at the thought of photographing me?" I asked.

"More like *umbitch*," Astrid muttered.

"I heard that," Elle said, turning her focus to Astrid. "I'm blonde, what's your excuse?"

"That was awesome," Astrid congratulated the Siren with a laugh.

"Thank you," Elle said with her first genuine smile.

I was furious it wasn't directed at me. What was going on here?

"Welcome. Look, Miss Rinoa, Blade Inferno isn't really all bad. He's just a bit egotistical."

"Umm… a lot egotistical. In fact, I'd say he's an egotistical pig from Hell," Tiara added unhelpfully.

Astrid nodded in agreement and went on. "You're kind of in a shitload of trouble for selling souls and all, so I'd have to recommend taking the pig's deal. He can be a real buttbag if he doesn't get his way."

"Did you just call me a *buttbag*?" I growled.

"Yep, and shut it. I think it's working," Astrid muttered under her breath.

Elle froze and then glanced wildly around the room.

"Unfreeze my men now," she demanded as she began backing away with her eyes still darting around nervously.

"Take the deal," I countered, searching the ballroom for what had unnerved her.

"Fine," she hissed. "I'll take the picture. Tomorrow. I have to leave. NOW."

"Shit on a sharp pointy stick," Tiara shouted causing all the windows in the room to explode. "In coming."

With a wave of my hand, I lifted the spell. The Eunuchs sprinted to Elle and produced vicious looking weapons from thin air. Three hideous, ten foot tall Trolls stormed the room and began moving toward my Siren.

Unacceptable.

As she raised her arms to disappear, I grabbed her.

"Tell me how to find you or I'll feed you to the Trolls," I hissed.

"The glasses. Use the glasses," she said, trying to pull away. "You be able to see the portal. I will meet you. You have my word."

"Is your word any good?"

"No. Is yours?" she countered.

"Absolutely not, but if you're lying, you'll pay. I swear on everything evil that I'm far worse than the Trolls."

"This time I'm telling the truth," she insisted as her entire body trembled in fear. "Please. Let me go."

I did. And in an explosive blast of magic she and her Eunuchs vanished. However, the Trolls did not.

I despised Trolls. The King of the smelly bastards pissed me off repeatedly. There were so many times I'd been tempted to off the entire species, but that was a fucking no-no—balance and all that ridiculous shit.

If the Trolls were gone, we'd have problems with the Gnomes— if the Gnomes were gone—the Mermaids would wreak havoc and on and on and on. It was all I could do to police my own Demons. If I had to add man eating Mermaids to the list I'd lose my mind. Normally, I liked the violent ones, but not these ten-foot fuckers.

"To kill them you need to pierce the left side of the neck. Go clean through with your sword. Magic won't work," I instructed as the Trolls realized the Siren was gone and figured we were the next best bet.

"Do we want them dead?" Astrid asked as she centered herself and waved her menacing and fiery hands in the air.

She let out an impressive scream that I felt all the way to the bottom of my toes. Astrid's magic was brightly colored and very powerful. The black and pink crystals of her enchantment gently wrapped around every innocent being in the ballroom.

I watched as the horny women and the favored authors Darynda, Charlaine, Molly and Robyn were elevated high in the air above the fray. My Astrid had a very soft spot for innocents. It was tiresome at times, but I agreed with this particular move. It was going to get ugly.

"Kill two. Incapacitate one. I need information."

And the fight began.

CHAPTER TWELVE

THE TROLLS COULDN'T KILL ME, BUT THAT DIDN'T MEAN THE UGLY bastards couldn't do damage. They were enormous killing machines. I was certain they were *not* my fated darkness—however, *I* was about to be theirs. I'd heal immediately and they would not when I was done with them.

I was getting my picture made tomorrow—needed to be at my best—plus I really liked the custom Armani suit I was wearing—one of a kind. It simply wouldn't do to have it destroyed by Trolls.

"I could blow up the building and solve this quickly," I pointed out as I called to my Fire Sword and stepped out in front of my nieces.

"No can do," Astrid said. "This room is full of blameless humans."

"The hookers?" I inquired with a naughty grin.

"They are *not hookers,* you asshat. They're the readers who will be buying your piece of shit book," Astrid shot back with a grin of her own. "I want the Troll on the left."

"I'll take the right," Tiara called out as the Trolls paused and winced in pain and confusion from the shrill tone her voice.

Bingo. This was going to be far less messy than I'd thought. I could have dead Trolls, a pristine suit and unharmed nieces. The day was taking a turn for the better.

"How about this?" I suggested, hatching a plan so horrifying it made me happy. "Tiara, do you know the lyrics to *Lovin, Touchin', Squeezin*?"

"I know every single word to every song on every album Journey ever recorded," she informed me with pride.

"That's my girl," I said, snapping my fingers and producing earplugs for Astrid and myself. "On three, sing as loud as you can."

"Seriously?" Astrid screeched in terror. "I'm not sure that's a good plan."

Tossing Astrid a set of earplugs, I laughed. "Watch and learn, child. Violence doesn't always need weapons made of silver, steel or fire."

"But I thought you liked the violent stuff," Astrid said, still clearly appalled at my idea.

"Oh, but I do," I replied with a grin. "I just like my suit more."

The three soon to be dead Trolls charged at us like freight trains from the bowels of Hell. The speed was impressive for something their size. But speed would not be a determining factor in this exchange.

"One. Two. Three," I yelled and then slammed the plugs into my ears and watched Astrid do the same.

It was a beautiful sight. Tiara started in the key of Z and hit every other nonexistent musical note known to man or immortal. She was destroying one of the best songs ever written. It was delightfully revolting. I was sure Steve Perry would be proud —or deaf.

The first Troll screamed in agony right before his head blew up, spattering the room in thick green blood. The second roared in shock and disintegrated into a pile of oozing black and green sludge.

I immediately waved my hand and muted Tiara before she imploded the third. I needed him alive for a few minutes. He was severely damaged, but still breathing—growling and gnashing his razor sharp teeth. Pulling on a magic as old as time, I sighed in contentment as the dark enchantment roared through me and encased my body in red flame. As gorgeous as I was, this was one of my more frightening looks. Even Astrid and Tiara stepped back in fear.

With a wink to the girls to assure them this was quite normal—for me—I approached the hissing and spitting monstrosity. He no longer appeared quite as brave and cocky. No, he now was quite cognizant that he'd messed with the wrong people.

"Hi there," I said as I took a seat on a pile of books that went up in a small explosion of flames around me. "Would you be so kind to answer a few little questions I have for you?"

"Go to Hell," he snarled.

"Actually, I live there and it's fabulous. That threat is kind of moot, if you know what I mean," I replied calmly.

His eyes grew wide with real fear when the pea-brained idiot finally recognized who he was dealing with.

"So here's how this is going to play out," I continued, moving a little closer so he could feel the Hell Fire that was very much a part of me. "I ask a question. You answer. If I like the answer, you die quickly, and if I don't…"

I left the alternative up to the abomination. I thought that was a nice change from my usual modis operandi.

"Over my dead body," he shouted, shaking the walls of the large room.

"Well, that's already a given," I told him with a shrug and a wink. "The conundrum is only how painfully you want to die."

I took his silence as acquiescence—or stupidity.

"Why are you after the Siren?" I demanded.

He eyed me with such vicious hatred it was almost startling. "I don't know."

"Whoops, wrong answer," I said and pointed at him with my blazing hand. "That's going to cost you a leg."

With a flick of my fingers, his leg was gone. All that was left was a bloody green stump. His roar rocked the room. I smiled.

"Look, you can make this difficult or simple. I know who you are and *clearly* you know who I am."

"You don't know me," he bellowed.

"Ahh, but that's where you're incorrect, *Donald*," I replied, as I let my power reach out and touch his brain and memories.

He screamed in tormented anguish as I searched his dark and unsavory past. I was going to need a shower after this disgusting field trip into the Troll's mind.

"You've been a *very* bad boy," I chided, as my blood began to boil at the atrocities this particular Troll had committed. I had to remind myself I needed him even though I wanted to torture him to death. *Donald* deserved to be in the basement of Hell for his sins —he'd be going there quite soon.

"Fuck you, Satan," he hissed.

"Sorry, you're not my type," I told him. "Sooo, let's see... You have quite a varied list of offenses, Donald—cold blooded murder of thousands of innocents over your life, pillaging, rape, mass destruction. I could go on, but I might then have to skin you alive, reanimate you and do it again. People like you really piss me off. I really don't have time for this right now, but if you insist..."

"The Troll King wants her," Donald growled, realizing I was deadly serious.

"Why?"

"Wants her soul to put with the rest."

"What rest?" I demanded. And what kind of fucked up game was the Troll King playing collecting souls?

"The other."

I waved my hand and removed another leg. "Wasn't quite specific enough for me, *Donald*." Damn it, the Troll was fading fast and I didn't have what I wanted. "What's he doing with the souls?"

"Power," the Troll choked out as green gooey blood began to pour from his mouth. "He wants the power of the Sirens to destroy Fate—wants to control all."

"That's quite a stretch considering there's only one Siren," I mused aloud.

"More. He has one Siren soul already. He needs a two... Fate makes a trinity."

Interesting. The power of three... the Creator, Redeemer and the Sustainer... or in some beliefs the omniscience, omnipresence and omnipotence.

Could the power of two Sirens do that? And how exactly could that destroy Fate?

And had that bitch, Fate set me up to do her dirty work to save her own ass?

"Explain," I hissed, blowing fire into him so he lasted a few more minutes—or seconds.

"The souls of the winged Sirens can control Fate," he whispered as he took his last few breaths.

"Says who?" I shouted. If this was so, why didn't I know it?

He looked at me in confusion as his eyes rolled in their sockets and he left the mortal plane. He most definitely had a one-way ticket to my neighborhood and I would make damned sure he got very special treatment.

I stood in silence and let my fire recede as I stared at the Troll and wondered if the story he told had any merit. Fate had existed before any of us, as far as I was aware. Or was it one of those *what came first... the chicken or the egg* riddles?

Astrid and Tiara joined me and stared at the Troll.

"In mythology there are three fates," Tiara said. "The Moirai. Is that what he was referring to?"

Shrugging, I gave the possibility some thought. Trolls weren't the smartest of species. "I don't think so. While mythology is amusing, it's not the way it happened. But my guess is that it's no accident we're after the soul-selling Siren. I'm beginning to believe it was *fated* for the convenience of Fate."

"How?" Astrid asked.

"Don't know," I replied honestly instead of lying. "But I shall find out."

Waving my hand I restored the ballroom to its former book loving glory. The hookers—or readers—and authors slowly descended from their perches high in the air and landed gently where they had been before I froze them. The remains of the Trolls vanished and the destruction created by Tiara's voice was repaired. I was at loathe to remove the amethyst crystals, but they had to go as well.

Picking up a handful, I put them into my pocket and also pilfered a few copies of my book. Quickly signing two of them, I gave them to the girls.

"These are priceless. Put them in a safe," I said with a cocky smirk.

"So are we going to the Siren now?" Astrid asked, tucking my masterpiece into her purse.

"*We* are not," I replied. "I am."

"Whoa, Uncle Fucker," Tiara countered. "We're with you all the way. We're the Three Musketeers or some weird inbred immortal version of them."

Glancing up at the ceiling and finding my courage, I prepared to do something I'd never done in my millions of years—at least not with any sincerity. I was surprised I didn't break out in hives or go up in flames, but sometimes doing the right thing was... right.

"Thank you," I choked out on a whisper—actually meaning it. Even though it was right, it wasn't easy, not for someone like me.

"Wait. *What?*" Astrid asked, shocked.

"You heard me," I snapped. "I won't repeat myself and I'll deny it if you tell anyone."

"So, umm…" Tiara simply stood in front of me looking dumbfounded. "Do we say you're welcome?"

I pondered for a moment. I wasn't sure. This was incredibly new territory for me.

"We do," Astrid confirmed. "Uncle Fucker, you're welcome. However, I don't think you should go to the Siren alone. Are you sure you don't need us?"

Was I sure? No. I wasn't quite sure of anything right now, but it felt right. I would face my fate alone. If I were to die, everyone would follow in death, but my girls would not go before me because I was selfish. I mean, I *was* selfish—totally selfish—but occasionally I was a little bit nice. This was one of those unsettling times.

"I'm sure," I replied curtly.

"Can we hug it out?" Tiara suggested with a wide smile and a giggle.

"We most certainly can not," I shot back with a raised brow. "Go home. Now. I will call on you if I need you."

"We're gonna stay for a bit," Astrid said grabbing a pile of books she wanted signed by her favorite authors.

"We are?" Tiara questioned.

"We are," she told her sister.

"Suit yourselves," I said. "I've got a few things to do."

"Have fun," Astrid called out as a cloud of black glitter consumed me.

Fun was a relative word—meant different things to different beings. Where I was headed was not going to be *fun*—at least not for the piece of shit I was going to pay a visit to…

Twice in a week was too much for any sane person to withstand. I supposed it was a good thing I was fairly insane. I almost looked forward to the expression on her face when I showed up. Almost.

Fate wasn't going to know what hit her. She might be the premiere bitch, but I was the original bastard.

CHAPTER THIRTEEN

"The question was simple, Mother," I repeated myself—again. "Tell me where Fate is."

Mother Nature pinned me with her sharp gaze and stomped her small foot. "Tell me why you want to see her and I shall give you what you want—for a price."

Talking with my mother was similar to conversing with a brick wall—it usually went nowhere. However, when one needed information quickly, she was the go-to gal. It just came with a tremendous amount of annoying bullshit and strings.

"I need to know what she knows about the Sirens," I replied, feeling under duress. I did not enjoy needing others.

We were in Mother Nature's palace although we may as well have been in her gardens. It was impossible to tell the difference as trees and flowering vines covered every available inch of real estate. The only clue that it was the interior of her home was instead of grass being beneath our feet the floors were bright pink marble. The riot of color was enough to give me a headache. Add my mother to the equation and it became a migraine.

"Sirens?" she questioned doubtfully, as she poured us each a glass of what I assumed was lemonade from a large crystal pitcher.

One never knew with my mother. Tasting anything in Nirvana was a risk. She couldn't cook to save her immortal life.

"Yessss, *Sirens*," I hissed. "I've repeated myself three times. Even though I adore the sound of my own voice, I shall not keep reiterating."

"They're extinct," my mother said, taking a tentative sip of the yellow concoction and then spitting it out. "Don't drink that—too much sugar—or maybe I used the wrong fruit."

"They're not extinct," I replied, pushing the glass away. "I found one."

"Where?"

"Chicago. It's the soul seller I'm after."

"Fascinating," she said, petting a monkey that was perched in her lap. "So it wasn't a Mermaid then?"

"No. Not a Mermaid," I said, holding on to my patience with effort. "Tell me where Fate is."

"Give me more of the story and I will," she promised.

With a sigh born of long suffering, I considered my options. I could go back to Hell and have my Demons track down Fate, but that would take time I didn't have. My brother, God, was out of the question, so that left my mother. She kept tabs on *everyone*. Mother Nature was an insufferable gossip and a goddamned GPS for the whereabouts of immortals.

"Fine," I snapped rudely. "The Trolls want the Siren. Apparently the Troll King is collecting the souls of the Sirens to take down Fate and rule the world. It's utter bullshit, but I'm getting my photograph taken by the immortal law-breaking Siren tomorrow and I need to be prepared. I refuse to go in blind."

Her knowing smile made me grind my teeth. "You like the Siren."

"I do *not* like the Siren."

"Yes, you do."

"No, I don't."

"Do."

"Don't. Enough," I shouted, causing the monkeys to scatter in alarm. "I don't even know her. Do I want her? Yes. Will I kill her if I have to? Absolutely."

"You think she's selling her own soul?" my mother questioned.

I was shocked to silence—not an easy feat. Was Adrielle Rinoa selling her own soul? That certainly made the game more dangerous.

"I don't know," I admitted.

"Well, whatever. It can work," my mother said thoughtfully. "*You*, my evil, beautiful child, can withstand the Siren enchantment."

"What the Hell are you talking about and what does that have to do with the whereabouts of Fate?" I demanded, regretting my decision to come here.

"You, my dear son, can bed the Siren without dying. No other mortal or immortal would live after a tryst with a winged one, but you're not at risk."

"While that's interesting, it has nothing to do with why I'm here," I said through gritted teeth. Although, the piece of information was interesting—very interesting.

"Possibly. Possibly not," she shot back, absently taking another sip of her drink and regretting it immediately. With a wiggle of her delicate fingers, the pitcher of whatever she'd concocted blew up. "Word to the wise, Lucifer. It's next to impossible to win the heart of a Siren."

"Is there a reason you're sharing useless knowledge?" I inquired impatiently.

"I just don't want to see you get hurt. I am your mother after all," she replied.

Her behavior suggested we were a normal family with typical values and issues. We were not even remotely ordinary. Our mismatched clan was millions of years old and could barely tolerate each other for more than a few minutes at a time. This very conversation was proof of that indisputable fact… and a monumental waste of my time. However, it was clear she knew the location of Fate, so incinerating a few things, throwing a fit and leaving would be a bad plan—satisfying, but bad.

A humorless laugh escaped my lips and I shook my head. In my experience, sex had nothing to do with love. A woman had never hurt me and never would. My mother must have poisoned her own mind and debatable sanity with her *lemonade*.

"I have no intention of winning a Siren's heart, *Mother*. And if I wanted her heart, I would simply steal it, which is far less messy. Problem solved. Fate's location?" I pressed, grabbing a napkin and dabbing at the stains she'd just put on my suit. Three fucking Trolls hadn't ruined my attire, but my mother's questionable lemonade had.

"In a moment," she replied with a mischievous smile pulling at her lips. "There might be something to what the Troll said. Where did you find the Troll?"

"At a romance readers' convention in Chicago where I was almost neutered by hookers."

For a blessed moment, Mother Nature was rendered silent.

And then the moment was over.

"I'm not going to touch that one, but there is a story about Fate being one of three. Mythology usually has some decent hints to the unknown, but since it's never come to fruition, I believed it false. How many souls does that bastard Troll King have?"

"One."

"And he wants the soul of your Siren?"

"First of all, she's not *my* Siren. And if the Troll I destroyed is correct, then yes, the King wants the soul of Elle," I supplied.

"The power of three," my mother mused, as she grabbed her Prada purse and applied some lipstick. "And I love the name Elle."

"What are you doing?" I asked, not liking her actions—at all.

"I'm coming with you," she answered breezily. "That's the price of the whereabouts of Fate."

"No."

"Yes."

"No."

"Yesssssss," she snapped as a mini tornado whipped through her Palace uprooting some large trees and sending her parrots into a frenzy. "There's something bad brewing and it doesn't bode well. You're so incredibly rude, you'll just piss Fate off. You need me to play good cop. Trust me, darling. Together we're unstoppable."

"Fine," I grumbled, giving in. I wasn't going to get the information without paying the piper—or in this case, my mother. Maybe she would be able to obtain what I needed faster than I could on my own. The looming darkness was so close I could taste it. "You can join me."

"Excellent."

And that was the first of the many mistakes I would make in the next twenty-four hours.

~

"LISTEN TO ME, YOU NASTY BITCH," MOTHER NATURE BELLOWED AS she tackled Fate and put her in a chokehold. "You're going to tell my baby boy what he needs to know or I will pull every single strand of your blonde hair out of your head—individually."

So much for my mother being the good cop.

We found Fate in a posh salon in Los Angeles. The staff had screamed in abject terror and ran for their human lives when Mother Nature dumped a vat of bleach over Fate's head upon our entrance. I'd quickly enclosed the entire building in an enchanted mist—no one could enter and no one could leave. The memories of all would be completely erased after our departure.

Of course, Fate wouldn't have the luxury of forgetting our visit. And it was certain to be a memorable one, if the beginning was anything to go by.

"You're insane," Fate screeched as she expertly escaped the

chokehold and landed an outstanding left hook to my mother's face.

"Your point?" Mother Nature ground out. She kneed the keeper of Destiny in the stomach and then body slammed her into a pyramid display of makeup that collapsed and tumbled all over the floor.

I leaned back against the wall and waited for the violent pleasantries to end. There was no way in Hell I was getting involved in a girl fight with two of the most dominant forces in the Universe. Girls never fought fair—well, neither did I, but then again, I was Satan. I wasn't supposed to fight fair.

"Oh my goodness," Mother Nature yelped as she picked up a tube of rolling lipstick and squealed with delight. "I hadn't realized this was available yet. It's so me!"

"Are we done with the bloody part?" Fate asked as she too examined the tubes of lip color.

"Your call," my mother replied, opening the lipstick and applying it liberally. "Cough up some info and you keep your hair."

"You really are a horrid woman," Fate muttered as she pawed through the pile looking for her perfect shade.

"Yes, well, at least I'm gorgeous. What's your saving grace?"

"I'm really fucking scary," Fate replied, clearly finding what she was searching for as she hopped up, stood in front of the lone mirror they hadn't smashed and tried out the color. "What do you think?" she inquired as she admired herself.

All cuts, bruises and gashes were gone. Immortals are strong so we heal within seconds. She was quite a beautiful sight on the outside. From within she was as black as sin.

"Hmm…" Mother Nature said, examining the hue. "I like it, but I think you need more of bluish undertone. "Try this one"

"Time is ticking," I said with an eye roll of exasperation. "This isn't a social visit."

"Everything is a social visit in my world," Fate contradicted me. "I haven't had a fist fight like that in ages. It was immensely enjoyable. Thank you, Gaia."

"You're most welcome," my mother replied with a giggle. "It's not often I find a worthy adversary that I won't kill by accident. Everyone is so damned fragile."

"Not to mention terrified of you—and me," Fate added with a smirk.

"There is that," my mother agreed. "So what do you know about the Trolls and the Sirens?"

"Sirens are extinct," Fate replied and took a seat on the plush couch in while pocketing a few tubes of the lipstick she'd decided on.

"They most certainly are not extinct," I shot back, wondering what game she was playing.

She paused and stared for a long moment. I was sure I spotted a look of uncertainty in her eyes, but it was gone as quickly as it had appeared.

"You've seen one?" she asked far too casually for my liking.

"Maybe," I shot back. "What's the significance of their souls?"

"I don't know."

"You're supposed to know all, you cagey wench," my mother said, cracking her knuckles and preparing for another smackdown. "Tell us what you know. The fate of the world may hinge on this. Pun not intended."

"That's not how it works," Fate snarled, standing up and pacing the room. "I know the fate of others, but my own is a mystery as much as yours is to you."

"You're connected to the Sirens?" I demanded, wanting the riddles to end and get to the heart of the matter.

"What exactly do you think I am?" she snapped.

"A bitch?" I inquired.

"Touché," she shot back. "That's an acquired personality trait."

"You wear it well," my mother chimed in.

"Thank you, dear."

"Most welcome," Mother Nature replied.

"Answer the question," I growled.

Her eye roll and laugh made me furious. I was done being played with by Fate.

"If you haven't already figured it out, *Lucifer*, I'm not permitted to answer directly. I can't fuck with fate. I just *am* fate. Free will would be hindered if I got too big for my britches and I'd bring on the end of the world quicker than a blink of a human eye. It's a fucking hard job and for some reason it's getting harder."

Shoving my hands into my pockets so I didn't smite the woman where she stood, I decided to try on being reasonable for a change of pace. "Fine," I said, balling my hands to fists. "What exactly can you tell me?"

She pondered for a long moment and then smiled. "You have a soul, Lucifer."

"Lie," I shouted and punched the mirror she'd just admired herself in, shattering it to glittering shards and slicing my knuckles. "If you tell me one more lie, I will kill you and enjoy it."

"She's not lying," my mother backed the crazy woman up. "You have a soul. Everyone has a soul. Yours may be buried deep, but it's there."

"And what the Hell does that have to do with Sirens and Trolls?" I snarled.

Was my anger at the situation? At my mother? At Fate? At the fact I'd just given myself with seven years of bad luck by breaking the mirror? At the unreal possibility that my soul hadn't been taken from me when I fell from the Heavens? Did it even fucking matter?

"Everything and nothing," Fate said in her usual cryptic way with a smile that looked more like a sneer on her lips. "It depends on what you do with the information."

"I hate you," I said flatly.

"Feeling's mutual," she replied. "Did you sign a book for me?"

The abrupt change of subject was jarring and I still didn't know much more than I did when I'd arrived.

"You brought her a book and not me?" my mother asked, throwing her hands in the air and inadvertently causing a monsoon in the salon.

"I didn't bring either of you a book," I said, clapping my hands and ending the storm. "However, it's an enormous hit. I'm the highest paid romance author in the world."

"You wrote a *romance*?" Fate asked, perplexed and amused.

"I did," I said in a deadly quiet voice, wiping the smile from her face. "You have something to say about that?"

"Umm, no..." she replied, trying unsuccessfully to quash her grin. "I think you might have a bit of my magic, Evil One. That's all."

"His name is Lucifer, you old cow," Mother Nature growled, lifting her middle finger at Fate. "You know as well as I do that my baby is not evil—naughty with a capital N maybe—but not evil for the sake of it."

I'd never seen my mother shoot the bird. It was actually funny and I almost forget to cross-examine Fate. "What do you mean I have your magic?" I questioned. "Explain."

She shrugged and sighed right after she'd gifted Mother Nature with her own middle finger. "You shall see. However, the stakes might be far more grave than I was led to believe. Listen to the words, Lucifer... and follow your cold black heart."

"All right, you drunken floozy" Mother Nature yelled, clearly having had enough of Fate's slurs at her son. "You need an ass kicking and I'm just the gal to do it. Apologize to my boy or I'm gonna take you down."

"Try it, you red headed shrew," Fate challenged. "I'll make you eat that lipstick and every tube in here. It has to be better than the casserole you made two hundred years ago."

"Take. That. Back," Mother Nature screamed as she began to glow and levitate.

My cue to leave was quickly arriving.

"Make me," Fate hissed as the eerie winds of change whipped through the room.

"My pleasure," my mother snapped.

And then they went at it.

If I'd had time, I might have stayed. I didn't. So I left them to it and hoped they'd remember to lift the spell I'd put on the salon.

I had things to do and places to be. Fate knew more than she'd let on... or maybe she didn't. That possibility was more alarming than if she was lying.

Whatever. The only thing one couldn't stop was time. It marched on regardless of what havoc it created. Therefore I would do the same.

March on.

Create havoc.

I was very, very good at that.

CHAPTER FOURTEEN

"You're NAKED," Elle said, staring at me with her mouth agape and eyes narrowed in shocked amusement.

Much to my Siren's chagrin, her lovely gold-rimmed, purple eyes kept straying to my impressive package. Of course that only caused said impressive package to grow even more impressive and incredibly painful. I was certain all the blood from my brain was now residing in my dick. Movement could be tricky since my instinct was to lean forward to relieve pressure. A hunched over limp was neither commanding nor sexy. I was nothing if I wasn't commanding and sexy.

"You're observant," I replied casually as I took in my surroundings.

I felt anything but casual. My heart was racing as if I were in a fight for my life. It was unnerving and I didn't like it—at all. I was the Devil. I was the ruler of all evil and Adrielle Rinoa was the most fucking gorgeous evil I'd ever had the pleasure of discovering. She was lovelier than she'd been just yesterday. Her body glowed with some kind of mystical internal light. Her scent was enough to drive me wild.

"I've been called worse," she shot back, eyes still on the engorged part of my spectacular anatomy.

The trip to her hidden plane was swift and smooth. The unattractive glasses had revealed the portal immediately. Of course I'd had to go back to the RRAC convention and brave the rabid female readers that I still suspected might be a delightful pack of hookers. But a famous romance author with a soul-selling Siren problem on his hands did what he had to do.

I'd even signed books for a half hour as Dagwood, Darby and Dino blocked the over stimulated ladies from castrating me. Much to the Demons' joy, I left them there. I was positive all of them would get lucky today—even with the emasculating monikers.

"You *need* to get dressed," Elle instructed with her eyes glued in carnal fascination to my excruciatingly erect cock.

"No can do," I replied with a practiced innocent grin and a shrug. "My clumsy, insane, pain in my ass, whack job of a mother spilled lemonade on my suit. It's at the cleaners."

I inwardly chuckled at the thought of Mother Nature's ears burning at my disrespectful description.

"And I'm supposed to believe that absurd falsehood?" she asked, scrubbing her exquisite hand over her mouth to hide her smile.

"Truth is often stranger than fiction."

"Yes, well, the truth can also hurt or in your case, *Blade Inferno*, get you killed."

With a quick wave of her hand she clothed me in a luxurious velvet black robe. It was exactly my style—expensive. However, even the robe couldn't contain my x-rated appendage. I was goddamned enormous and proud of it.

Elle eyed me for a long moment, rolled her eyes and went to set up her camera. Her fitted black pants, stiletto heels and tight white t-shirt weren't helping with my issue down below. Not to mention her backside made me want to fall to my knees and weep in appreciation.

How odd—my mother had led me to believe I was immune to the Siren's charms—but was I? Wanting her didn't feel simple. If I wasn't mistaken, I'd have to admit I might be a bit obsessed.

I was so screwed.

The woman took my breath and I felt light headed. It could partially be due to blood loss from my brain, but something else was at play. I still believed I wasn't susceptible to her charms, but this was unfamiliar territory. Either her power was stronger on her own turf or I was losing my magic and leaving this world very soon.

C'est la vie. If I was bidding immortality adieu, I might as well enjoy the scenery.

"Nice place," I said, making idle conversation as I tried and failed to quash my desire. Clearly my brain, willpower and blood were all now residing in my dick.

Looking at me askance for a brief moment, she laughed. "Thank you. I'll be ready in a minute. Just relax, Mr. Inferno."

Relax? Not happening. I rolled my eyes at my own idiocy. I was the greatest seducer to ever live. However, my lines were going to Hell—at least I didn't say her *bosom* was nice.

The room was opulent, heavy furniture with sensual lines covered in rich lavender velvets and decadent brocades. Candles flickered on every available surface emitting a citrusy scent. Yet something was off. Putting my finger on it wasn't possible yet, but I would. I adored puzzles and the Siren was an enigma.

Adrielle Rinoa was living on a plane I had no prior knowledge of and my guess was that was no accident. It was a certainty that if I was unaware of this wrinkle in time, others were unaware as well. Her secret hideaway was how she'd survived undetected all these thousands of years, and now I knew her secret.

I wondered if she had any intention of letting me leave alive. She clearly had no clue that wasn't a possibility since I was a True Immortal and the fucking Devil to boot, but she'd let me enter her secret sanctum. Thankfully, the Eunuchs were nowhere in sight, but I was certain they were close by. They were bred to protect and I'd already seen how keen they were on restricting access to the Siren. This was shaping up to be an interesting photo shoot.

"Did you kill the Trolls?" she inquired, not looking up from her camera.

"I did. Did you sell your soul?" I questioned as she glanced up sharply. Her reaction made me think she was indeed selling her own soul. I was so fucking furious it floored me. Why should I give a damn if the Siren wanted to die? Tamping back my ire was difficult, but turning into a raging fireball was not exactly in the norm of acceptable social behavior. Not that I practiced normal very often.

"I owe you," she said, ignoring the soul selling inquiry. "Your headshots shall be free of charge."

With the expertise and ease of an actual photographer, she went about focusing the lights and arranging the backdrop.

"I'm not sure that equates," I said, walking up behind her and breathing in her intoxicating scent. She was as aroused as I was and the scent of her desire almost brought me to my knees. Grabbing the pole of a light stand, I held on and stayed upright. *All* of me was upright at the moment.

"Equations can be sooo difficult. Have you tried a vacuum? It might remove the cobwebs from your brain," she said moving away so quickly I felt the breeze of her departure.

"Really, darling," I said getting wildly turned on by her insolence and the cat and mouse game we were playing. Her avoidance of my question didn't even phase me. I'd get my answers soon enough. "Wouldn't it be better to let the world think you're daft instead of opening your delectable lips to prove it? I can think of far better things to do with your mouth."

"I'll just bet you could, Mr. Inferno. However, I'm not the least bit interested."

"What language are you speaking?" I asked, seating myself on the leather chair she'd placed in front of the black backdrop. "Because it sounds distinctly like bullshit to me."

"Are we going to continue this verbal sparring or do you want your picture taken?" Elle crossed her arms over her chest and pushed her mind-bogglingly perfect breasts higher. A move I was quite sure was done on purpose. "Because I can tell you now, I'll win."

"Will you?" I asked with a delighted laugh.

"Yes. I will," she said with a look so sultry I was glad I was seated. Her glance slayed me. She was spectacular.

"Truth or dare," I replied.

"*Seriously?*" she asked with a groan. "I'm a habitual liar and I like to throw things at people. This will not end well."

"Truth or dare," I repeated letting my eyes travel from the top of her head all the way to her toes—taking my time at her lips, breasts and the special spot between her legs that I wanted to taste more than life itself. It was dangerous using my own powers of seduction on the seductress, but no pain—no gain. And Hell knew I was already in pain. My cock now had its own zip code.

With an involuntary shudder of lust that she quickly hid, she sighed rudely and took a seat on the stool behind her camera.

"Fine," she agreed curtly, wound up and threw the camera at my head narrowly missing by an inch.

I was fairly sure she'd missed on purpose. She had outstanding aim. The last time anyone had dared to throw something at me, they'd been burnt turned to ash. Bizarrely, I had no wish to incinerate the Siren. Adrielle Rinoa was far too much fun to destroy.

She went on as if she hadn't just tried to decapitate me. "I suppose I owe you more than just free shots for the elimination of the Trolls. I will play your game for a bit. However, clothing is not optional—it stays on."

"Come now, that's no fun." I snapped my fingers and the stool flew out from underneath her. She landed in an incredibly sexy heap on the floor and glanced up in complete shock.

Her joyous laugh went straight to my balls. I leaned forward so I didn't implode.

"Nice move," she congratulated me as the light stand next to me exploded and caught the edge of my robe on fire. "And fun is a relative word, Mr. *Inferno*. Your idea of fun could lead quickly to your demise."

"Or yours," I pointed out, waving my hand and extinguishing the fire.

"Doubtful," she replied with a humorless laugh as she reset the fire with a wiggle of her adorable nose. "You intrigue me, Angel.

"The feeling is strangely mutual, Siren," I replied. "However, Angel-Demon would be more accurate, but that's for another conversation with far higher stakes." Again, I doused the fire even though it felt wonderful. I didn't want to freak her out—yet. "Truth or Dare?"

She considered me for a moment and then shrugged. "Truth."

Damn it, I was hoping she'd say dare. As punishment for answering incorrectly, I levitated her and turned her upside down. "Is Adrielle Rinoa your real name?"

"No. Is *Blade Inferno* yours?" she shot back, snapping her fingers and changing the color of the black robe she *insisted* I wear to hot pink with marabou trim.

"No and you're cheating. It's not your turn. And honestly," I huffed, glancing down. "Do you really think this is my color?"

"Yes. Yes, I do. Your point?"

"You lied about your name?"

"Absolutely," she replied with an evil little smirk.

Goddamn, she was perfect—a gorgeous, cheating liar who enjoyed lighting me on fire. How much better could this get?

"No point, *darling*," I replied with a grin that had brought legions of women to their knees—literally. And then just for shits and giggles, I let the robe fall open so my assets could breathe.

Her hissed intake of breath wasn't lost on me. I was beautiful. She was beautiful. She knew it and I knew it. We were a match made in Hell. Now if I could only make my Siren see that.

"Truth or dare?" Elle asked, breaking my levitation spell with a flick of her fingers and dropping to the ground on her feet. Of course, since no good deed goes unpunished, the dangerous woman conjured up a lime green cock sock to embarrass my manhood.

"I prefer black and I'll need a far larger size than this."

"Fine," she purred with an evil glint in her eyes.

With and giggle and a staccato wave of her pinky finger, the emasculating banana hammock went from lime green to some kind of horrifying sequined black stretch material—and it was still too small.

"Beware of what you wish for," she chided with a smile.

"Fine point. Well made. I'll take Truth," I replied, wondering if I could—or would—actually tell the *truth*.

"What are you? Why are you immune to me?" Her eyes were narrowed and she studied me intently.

I craved her eyes on me. However, her body would be far more satisfying.

"You already know what I am, little Siren. I'm a Demon with a little bit of Angel thrown in wearing a glittering embarrassment on my dick. Some might refer to me as your worst nightmare, but I think that's pushing it a bit. And as for my immunity to you, my dick certainly didn't get the memo."

Elle tilted her head and looked for the untruth in what I'd said. She couldn't find one because there wasn't one.

"You work for Satan?"

My name on her lips was delightful. "You could say that. Why? Do you know him?"

She shook her head and I wanted to correct her—she did indeed know him, but I hesitated.

"You're very powerful," she commented as she ramped up her

seduction, letting her sheer white bra strap fall down her shoulder and running her pink tongue over her full lips that I had a burning desire to bite.

Her nipples pebbled and it was difficult to keep my eyes on her face.

I didn't move a muscle. She was testing me. While her game was compelling and making my sequined cock harder than I could recall it ever being, I realized I wanted her regardless of the seductive games she could play. I wanted all of her—her body and her devious soul. Unusual for me...

"Seriously?" she demanded in annoyed shock as she waved her hands and conjured a sheer pale lavender robe for herself that hid *nothing*.

I did nothing except stare—memorizing every glorious curve of her body. Not jumping her was the most difficult thing I'd ever done in my eternal life. Of course the debilitating agony of my rock hard dick and blue balls would have made movement awkward at the very least. I looked far more composed seated with an enormous boner. Her confusion at my lack of male response was amusing. She was getting annoyed and it was mind bogglingly hot.

"Are you gay?" she questioned, still mystified by my lack of reaction to her skill.

"It's not your turn and no. No, I'm not gay. Truth or dare?" I asked.

"Truth," Elle replied grumpily as she snapped her fingers and adorned me with cheap jewelry and headpiece of hideous plastic yellow flowers. She had no clue what to do with a man that didn't fall at her feet.

Ignoring the fact I looked like a drag queen with very little taste, I simply smiled. Hell knows I wanted to fall at her feet, drag her to the ground, and lick every inch of her body, but I'd never taken a woman that wasn't willing and I never would. Oh, I was certain she wanted me, but she was holding back. I wanted all of her. No matter how much she resisted, eventually I'd win. Then again, I wasn't used to a woman that didn't fall at my feet either. These rules were new and I wasn't exactly sure how to play.

"Why are you a photographer? I'd think you'd be quite busy collecting and ruining men to feed your vicious appetite."

"Don't believe everything you hear, Demon," she snapped as her hair began to blow around her head and her eyes blazed. "First off, I'm a very good photographer. Eternity is long. I needed a job. And contrary to popular *myth*, I only need lust to survive—male or female. All I have to do is place myself in a situation where desire is rampant and I absorb it. I don't have to kill to feed. Besides, the body count got tiresome. I stopped that hobby thousands of years ago.'

"Really? Why?" I asked, quite interested. I'd always believed that Sirens drained the lives of their victims.

"Don't you get weary of death, Demon?" she asked, avoiding the question.

"Depends on whose death we're discussing, Siren," I answered, cryptically. "I felt nothing killing the Trolls—they deserved it. So if I'm following your *story*, I'm going to surmise that you subsist on the lust of the grabby hookers at the book conventions."

"Grabby hookers?" she questioned with a confused expression.

"The women at the book signing that tried to neuter me."

"That would have been a shame," she muttered trying not to laugh.

"It most definitely would have," I said in all seriousness. I took my manly attributes very seriously. Now I wanted the Siren to take them seriously as well. "So the hookers?"

"They're not hookers," she replied with a laugh. "And yes, it's a good place to leech off the lust I need without killing anyone. There's quite a bit of desire at romance conventions and my Eunuchs are very popular with the ladies. Win-win."

"However, you almost killed my Demons," I countered.

"*Your* Demons?"

"Figure of speech—my homies—my buddies—my dudes," I lied smoothly.

"They weren't strong enough for what I needed—no one is," she replied, staring at me with curiosity. "How high up on Satan's food chain are you?"

Hell on fire, I was so very tempted to tell her who I was, but for some unexplainable reason I refrained. Sometimes when one knew they were dealing with the Devil things got awkward.

"Very high—very, very high. You might even say the highest."

"And you're really not affected by me?" she questioned, warily.

"Affected is another relative word. Do I want you? Yes. Can you bring me to my knees by putting me under a spell? No."

"Is that a challenge, Demon?" she questioned as she approached me with a look in her eyes that was stupefyingly sexy.

"Possibly. Are you up for it?" I asked, enjoying the sway of her hips under the sheer robe.

"Possibly," she said, mimicking my response. "God knows you certainly are."

Wincing, I held up a hand. "Why don't we leave him out of it—total cock blocker."

"Leave who out?" she asked, perplexed.

"God," I replied tightly. Even saying my brother's name pissed me off.

She paused her advance and searched my face. "You know him?"

"In a manner of speaking, yes—not fun at all. A total bore. You'd hate him. Let's get back to something far more interesting and relevant," I suggested.

"And that would be?"

"Me. Buried to the hilt inside of you."

The Siren froze and an expression of raw naked longing passed over her face, but she shut it down immediately. Quashing anything real she was feeling, she gave me a smile that came nowhere near to reaching her eyes. It was false and I wanted to wipe it from her lips. The tilt of her mouth belied the look of devastation on her face.

"Kiss me," I demanded as I stood and met her in the middle of the room. "Just one kiss."

Shaking her head and backing away, she paced the room and tried to compose herself. Her frustration was evident and she didn't know how to proceed.

"My kiss is a Judas Kiss," she whispered harshly, running her hands through her hair and imploring me to understand with her eyes. "You won't survive it."

"Why don't we try it out and see?" I asked, knowing full well her kiss would do nothing except make my dick harder.

"Are you insane or do you have a death wish? I just told you that kissing me would kill you," she snapped.

With a shrug and a quick removal of the unflattering pink robe, I grinned. "Insane? Absolutely. I come by it naturally and I take it as a compliment. Death wish? Not today. Kiss me Adrielle Rinoa aka Name Withheld for the Moment."

"Full disclosure, *Blade Inferno*. My kiss has killed many."

"How many?" I asked, not because I was in fear for my life. I was fucking jealous of those who had come before me. I wasn't a saint—not even close, but…

"Many," she replied flatly.

"I'll take my chances."

She approached cautiously and stood mere inches from me. Her lips were a breath away from mine and she stared at me with wonder.

"You're just horrible—despicable, rude, vicious—you're perfect," she breathed out on a happy sigh.

"And don't forget—hung like a fucking horse."

"Also exceptionally conceited," she added with an eye roll.

"This is true."

"I kind of like you," she whispered in amazement, staring at my mouth with longing. "I'd feel bad if I killed you, which is very rare for me."

"How long has it been since you were kissed?" I asked.

Raising her amethyst eyes to mine, she shook her head. "Can't remember."

"Sex?"

"I can't remember," she repeated.

I sucked in my breath with a muttered a curse. The feeling of relief mixed with victory washed over me in a rush that left me dizzy. Jealousy was a fabulous trait except when it involved me on the receiving end.

Why I felt like I'd won the lotto of the entire world a million times over was a mystery. But the fact that she'd not been touched in pleasure for countless centuries felt like a tangible victory.

"Kiss me," I repeated.

Tracing my lips with her fingers, she was tempted.

"Or how about I take that decision out of your hands?" I asked and then went in for the metaphorical kill.

How was I to know that a simple kiss could be more intense than the act of sex? Kissing Adrielle Rinoa was beyond my wildest imagination. My open lips captured hers. Anything gentle and seductive I'd had in mind flew out the door. Penetrating her mouth with my hungry tongue, I took as she gave and gave as she took. My erection pushed heavily against her flat stomach.

"So good," she muttered against the invasion of my lips, tongue and teeth.

Our power tangled and filled the room. I felt like I was swimming in it. It kissed my skin like the fire I so adored— exhilarating and addictive. In my arms, she felt like liquid desire.

Fire ripped over my skin and I groaned in pleasure. Her magic and need had overwhelmed her—Elle was unaware of her actions. Black fire sparked from her fingertips and bathed my body in heat.

Imprisoning her wrists, I pushed them over her head and aligned my body to hers. Her unfocused eyes sought mine in question, but before speech was an option I took her mouth again with an urgency of a starving man—biting, sucking, licking. Her taste was something I hadn't known I needed. How had I gone without this for millions of years?

Need coursed through me at a speed that left me breathless. Elle's breathing turned erratic and her body danced a rhythm that was so nakedly erotic I almost came. The ancient sensual rhythm from our bodies coming together was almost combustible. Shifting, I deliberately pressed my hard length against her and slowed her carnal dance. It took everything I had not to use magic to strip her bare and take her like I was meant to.

Fuck. I wanted all of her.

"Stop," she cried out and placed her hands on either side of my face.

Her eyes were wild as she searched my face and pressed her fingers to the pulse in my neck. She hissed out a sign of relief that would have been humorous, if I wasn't about to explode—literally.

"You're alive," she said.

"Looks that way."

"How? What are you?"

"I'm Blade Inferno, the highest paid romance author in the fucking world."

I pressed my forehead to hers and absorbed the searing heat she emitted. I wanted her, but now she was going to have to ask for it.

"I want..." she started only to be cut off by the very inopportune arrival of twelve soon to be very dead Eunuchs. They came crashing through the door with swords drawn.

"My lady, are you all right?"

"Don't hurt him," she screamed and stood in front of me to protect me from her nutfree posse. "He's mine. He can withstand my magic."

My shock at being protected stopped me from incinerating the Eunuchs where they stood—probably a good thing. She'd most

145

likely be pissed if I offed her little army. Not to mention the simple fact she'd called me hers. No one ever protected me. I didn't need protection. I was every kind of evil rolled into one very pretty package.

"The Demon can withstand the enchantment?" one her boys questioned, looking at me like I was an aberration.

"Yes," she said. "Don't touch him or I'll kill you where you stand. I've waited many lifetimes for this Demon. Am I clear?"

The Eunuchs looked crestfallen at her decree, but I just grinned like an idiot.

"As you wish. Will he be coming with us?" the Eunuch inquired. "We need to leave at once. Time is of the essence."

Elle turned and eyed me thoughtfully. Where were they going? And what was my devious Siren up to?

Shaking her head, she waved her hands and trapped me in an amethyst glass cage. The spell was both intricate and well executed. However, I could break it with a nod of my head.

"No. I don't want him harmed. I will do this alone."

"It will be impossible without numbers. If you fail, it's over," the Eunuch in the front insisted. "We will fight at your side."

"We will always be with you, my Lady. You will never have to go it alone," another Eunuch solemnly swore.

"Thank you," she replied with a small bow to her men. "I'm sorry to have threatened your lives. I value you, but so help me God, if anyone touches him, I'll burn you to a crisp."

I laughed and let my head fall back on my shoulders. I wasn't particularly fond of her constant mention of my brother's name, but her vicious streak was so delightful.

And that was yet another mistake…

In my gloating, I didn't notice Elle raise her arms and disappear.

All of them disappeared. Vanished in the blink of a fucking eye.

And I had no clue where they'd gone.

My roar of fury brought the glass cage crashing down around

me. With an angry wave of my hands, I dressed myself in a custom Hugo Boss suit and looked for the glasses I'd used to get here. To my naked eyes, I saw no portal. There had to be one. I'd used it only hours ago.

"Who are you?" a weakened feminine voice demanded.

Glancing up from my search, I froze.

It was another Siren—just as lovely as Elle, but frail and not long for this world in my opinion. She was missing her soul. I was sure of it. This one held the key to what I needed.

"I'm Satan. And you are?"

"Elle's mother."

Bingo. I'd just hit pay dirt.

CHAPTER FIFTEEN

"So you're really Satan?" she asked with skepticism written all over her lovely face while graciously offering me a glass of scotch. "I expected Satan to be more…" She lifted a hand and waved it in my direction.

"More what?" I questioned with narrowed eyes. She was treading on incredibly thin ice here and had no clue. My trigger finger felt itchy…

"More evil. More vicious. More… rude."

There were so many ways to reply. *Just give me time* was on the tip of my tongue, but I refrained. Getting my bearings here was tricky. Trusting a Siren was flat out stupid. I was not stupid—at all.

We'd left Elle's photography studio and ventured down a long ornate hallway to an opulent suite of rooms. The art on the walls was positively obscene, depicting depraved sexual acts and naked bodies of all shapes and sizes. It was lovely and felt like home.

"Well, having the *Devil* for tea is a novel experience."

"Actually, I'm not Satan and I don't drink tea. It's black coffee or scotch, neat. I was just shitting you. Name's Dirk—right hand man to the greatest, most powerful and best looking Demon alive,"

I replied smoothly, not trusting this one at all. I almost winced at having pulled the name out of my ass that Astrid had given me in jest, but it was the first lie that came to me. "Are you really Elle's mother?"

She paused and took a seat across from me. Eyeing me like I was an immortal science experiment, she sighed. "No, not in the normal sense of the word. Why are you here and how did you get here? I was unaware we had visitors—highly unusual."

"I killed a few Trolls and garnered an invite," I said casually.

"You killed Trolls?" she repeated, surprised.

"Are you hard of hearing?"

"Are you a rude asshole?"

"Yes. Yes, I am."

She clasped her hands in her lap and let her chin fall to her chest. Her masses of blonde hair covered her expression, but I could scent her sadness and desperation. Normally, I enjoyed people's sorrows, but for some reason I wasn't pleased.

"Were the Trolls after Elle?" she asked in a whisper.

"Not anymore," I replied curtly. "What's Elle's real name?"

"It's Elle. Adrielle Rinoa."

I laughed and threw back the scotch in a single swallow. Of course... my little Siren had lied to me. Then my smile fell from my lips. Was my Siren lying about other men? The thought made me murderous. Pushing my green-eyed monster away for the moment, I focused on the issue in front of me.

"And *your* name?" I inquired as I politely accepted another scotch.

"You can call me Sadie," she informed me with a smile so alluring, I was instantly reminded that she was a dangerous Siren —a dying Siren—but a Siren nonetheless.

"So *Sadie*, you're looking a bit peaked. Lost your soul?"

Her expression of enraged shock warmed my black heart. Pissing people off was an art form at which I excelled. Sadie was pissed—so pissed that I actually regretted my words. Words had meaning, damn it. I wanted information, not an enemy. Hell knew I had plenty of those.

"Why are you here?" she hissed as black fire and smoke began to crawl up the walls of the room. "Elle would not bring an enemy to our plane. You have a minute to explain yourself, or I will send you packing and you will never see this place or any of us again."

Could she actually do that? I mean, I *was* Satan—not Blade Inferno—and most definitely not Dirk. Who did she think she was —denying the Lord of the Underworld access to her home? I was furious that the Fairies had cut a deal banning me and my people from Zanthia. I'd be damned if another species prohibited me from travelling freely.

"Watch yourself, Siren," I snarled in a voice that made her pause. "I'm fucking Satan and I won't be spoken to like that."

"He's gay?" she asked, confused.

"For the love of everything wicked," I shouted and blew up a naked statue of a half man half eagle—it was ugly and I was seething. Far better the statue than the Siren. "I'm not *literally* fucking myself. It's an anatomical impossibility. I am so sick and tired of being misunderstood."

"Well, I'd suggest you stop saying that you're having sex with yourself then," Sadie said, trying not to laugh.

She failed.

"It's a good point," I conceded with a small smile as I calmed myself and picked up the bottle of scotch. "I'll take it under consideration." Taking a healthy swig, I sat back down and started over. "So I'm Satan. You're *Sadie*. And Elle is in a bit of a pickle for selling souls. Would you like to add anything?"

Her smile was positively one of the sexiest things I'd witnessed to date, but it left me cold. Her expression grew confused and she tried again. Sexier smile. Nothing from me. Odd. I was surprised as well. Normally, that kind of smile ended in an orgasm provided by me. My mother had been correct. I wasn't affected by the Sirens —or at least not this one.

"I'll call you *Satan* if that makes you happy," she said with a rude shrug.

"You don't believe me?" I asked, with a laugh.

"I believe you're a liar," she replied.

"It takes one to spot one," I shot back, liking her despite her appalling manners or maybe because of them. These Sirens were fascinating.

"This is true," she agreed, still perplexed by my lack of reaction to her charms. "But pretending to be people we aren't means some of us might be missing out on a few things in life. Like mainly *a life*," she said in a sensual tone that was in stark contrast to her nasty and somewhat accurate statement.

"Point to Sadie," I said flatly. "About the souls..."

"Elle's not selling souls," she said. "Next question?"

To be an asshole or not to be an asshole? That was the question of the moment. I knew I was dealing with a pathological liar. I was a pathological liar, I could spot them easily. *The words,* my mother had said, *listen to the words.* The Siren was bound to slip up. If she didn't, I'd just pop down to Hell with her and torture it out of her. However, I wasn't sure she'd outlast the conversation we were having now. She was obviously at death's door. No matter, with her past she'd end up in my neck of the woods regardless.

"So are there more than just you and Elle?" I asked, looking for another way in.

"No."

"I'd thought you were extinct," I replied. "Imagine my surprise when I was assigned to collect the soul seller and she turned out to be a Siren."

"Look, *Satan,*" she said with an eye roll and a snort—proof positive that she didn't believe I was indeed the Devil. "There are two of us left because we learned how to feed off sexual desire without killing for the most part. We aren't real popular at dinner parties due to our little issue."

Nodding, I leaned forward and to get closer to the fire still smoldering on the priceless carpet. "I can see how that might not appeal."

"Being an orgasmic harbinger of death is what killed off our kind. I would think that would make sense to someone like you."

"So you believe me?" I asked.

"Does the Pope wear red shoes? I knew who you were before you told me."

My wince of annoyance made her laugh. "Let's leave religion out of it, shall we? Not real fond of my brother's favored pets. Why do you think Elle doesn't recognize me?"

"My Elle has led a more sheltered life. I've kept her from the more unsavory parts," she said referring to me.

"I'd hardly think that killing men for sexual pleasure could be considered savory," I snapped, getting straight to the point. I might not be stellar in the morals department, but she was at the bottom of the barrel.

"Touché," she replied with a tired shrug. "We were given this lot in life. We didn't choose it, Devil. We have done the best we could with a horrendous fate. I would think you could relate to that."

"I might," I said, again wondering why I wasn't as attracted to this particular Siren. "However, soul selling is a big fucking no-no and the reason I found your girl."

"My daughter," she said on a sigh. "Elle is my daughter by blood."

"You lied?" I asked amused.

"Bad habit," she replied with a shrug.

"And her father?"

"Dead, of course. Having intimate relations with a Siren leads to a very pleasurable and untimely demise. Some of the myths are true."

We sat in silence and stared at each other. I was quite pleased with my decision not to drag the woman to Hell. It would have been bad form to kill the mother of the woman I wanted to bed.

"The Trolls have your soul," I stated, wanting all the pieces of the puzzle in place.

"Yes. They stole my soul eons ago. I need it back now. A Siren can exist for only a hundred years without one," she explained.

"So the bastards took your soul a hundred years ago?" I queried, not quite following.

She laughed hollowly. "Thousands," she corrected me.

"You lost me. Explain."

"They stole it thousands of years ago. Every hundred years we switch the souls so we can continue to live."

"Why switch? Why not simply steal it back and keep it."

"Not that simple, Devil," she replied wearily. "It's hard enough going to the mortal plane to feed with the Trolls after us, but they feel confident having at least one of our souls for whatever reason. If we stole back both, we'd never be able to leave this plane and we'd die of starvation."

"Why not steal them back and kill the bastards," I suggested. "I hate those fuckers."

With a humorless chuckle she shook her head and produced another bottle of expensive scotch from thin air. Pouring herself a glass, she sipped it and then placed it on the table. "Two Sirens can't kill an entire species of Trolls."

"So you've spent a lifetime buying time."

"That's one way to put it," she agreed.

"Wait a goddamned minute," I shouted, standing up and putting all the pieces together. "Elle has gone to the Trolls to trade her soul for yours? Unacceptable." This did not please me one little bit.

"Not *trade*," Sadie corrected, looking at me strangely. "Steal and replace. She will steal mine back and leave hers there. I will then steal hers back in a hundred years. It's our way, so stay out of it," she warned as the fire in the room ramped back up.

Something was off. I couldn't get a straight answer out of Elle even if I wanted it. Why was this Siren telling me how they survived?

"Why are you telling me this? I could use all of it against you."

"But you won't," she said with a knowing smirk.

"And why are you so certain, Siren?"

She shrugged and sipped her scotch. Her purple eyes looked straight into my soul. Or my mind, I wasn't yet convinced I had a fucking soul.

"Give me your hand, Devil," she said. "Let me look at the lines."

"Is this a trick? Because if it is, you're going to see Hell far sooner than originally planned," I growled.

"No trick. No lies—*this time*," she assured me.

I crossed the room swiftly and held out my hand. Her touch was alluring when she took my hand in hers, but I felt very little for her sexually speaking. Hell, had I lost my mojo? Was the darkness around the corner? Fuck me, what was I even doing here? I needed to find the damned darkness and destroy it. I knew now that Elle was innocent of the crime I'd thought she'd committed. Leaving this place would be the smartest thing to do, but...

Sadie's gasp brought me back from my dark and introspective thoughts.

"What?" I snapped, done playing games.

"It's fated."

"*What's* fated?" I demanded harshly causing her draw back from me. I was fucking sick and tired of even the word fate.

"I can't say," she whispered, looking at me with an expression I couldn't decipher. "That's not how it works."

My eyes went red and narrowed. Red sparks sizzled at my fingertips. In my angry state, I turned and shot a blistering bolt of lightening at a statue of a ménage I'd admired earlier. Whatever, I wanted to blow up the entire plane we were on. I was clearly maturing because I was blowing up art instead of cities.

"Listen to me, Siren," I said through clenched teeth. "This week I've dealt with the bitch Fate herself, my certifiable mother— Mother Nature—and I was almost castrated by hookers at a romance readers' convention. As you can imagine, that's enough to make a sane man snap. Problem is, I'm not even *close* to sane. So cryptic messages aren't really working for me at the moment. You feel me?"

"You love my daughter," she said, giving in.

"What?" I shouted. "Are you demented? I love no one. NO. ONE. I'm *the* fucking Devil. When will people understand this?"

"Umm... okay," she said, biting her bottom lip and trying not to grin. "Whatever you say."

Staring at the palm of my hand, I tried to see what the crazy woman had seen. Was she a fortune teller? Did she have some kind of screwed up connection to Fate after all? Was that why Fate was so surprised to hear the Sirens weren't extinct?

"What do you know of Fate?" I demanded.

"I hear she's a bitch," Sadie answered. "Never met her and have no desire to."

"If you're lying to me, I swear on all that's despicable I will end you where you sit. I will ask once again and trust me, I'll be able to tell," I said with such calm, she blanched. "Do you know Fate?"

Sadie stared up at the ceiling for a several seconds as I watched her consider her words. With a sigh borne of those who had lived for eternity, she looked me right in the eye. "Fate is a Siren—or rather *was* a Siren," she said.

Damn it to Hell and back, Fate's words came back to me...

"You're connected to the Sirens?" I demanded,

"What exactly do you think I am?" Fate snapped.

"A bitch?" I inquired.

"Touché," she shot back. "That's an acquired personality trait."

I hadn't been listening carefully enough. All of it was there for the taking and I kept missing it. How many times could my carelessness bite me in the ass?

"Go on," I pressed.

"Once—thousands of years ago—I came across her. She was revered by our kind. To be chosen as the holder of destiny was an honor that gave us hope we could change and survive in this world. But alas, she was cold and evil. She pulled from our collective magic and became more powerful herself. Fate did nothing to help our kind—never lifted a finger to aid us. Slowly we all died off."

"Except for you and Elle," I finished. "And Fate."

"Yes."

Pacing the room, I wondered if that bitch Fate had sent me on a wild goose chase to find the Sirens so she could take their power. She was failing on the job—drinking and regularly screwing up. Did she need the lives of my Siren and her mother to survive? And why in the Hell was I mixed up in this shit? I needed to search for the damned darkness headed my way.

"Many times I've wanted to kill Fate with my bare hands for what she did to me, but I've stopped myself every time. With her in charge, at least I knew what I was dealing with—a deranged heartless bitch," I said, speaking truthfully for once. "If she were to be destroyed, what or who would take her place?"

"There are things far worse than a cold bitch," Sadie said.

"Correct," I replied. "And what if nothing was to replace her? Where would we be then?"

"Masters of our own fate?" the Siren suggested.

"Fate is an elusive term," I said dryly. "Fate has a past but very little to show for it. She sees the future, but barely exists in the present as she's a sloppy drunk. Unfortunately, she can't be bribed or swayed. Humans are the only masters of their own fate. My brother's gift of free will gave them that. But the Immortals? I don't know."

"Depressing," Sadie commented.

"Accurate," I countered.

"You kissed her," Sadie said.

"I kissed who?" I asked, knowing full well to whom she was referring.

"You kissed Elle."

"I did."

"And you lived."

"Clearly," I said with an eye roll. "I'm not susceptible to the charms of a Siren. I'm fucking Sa...no, let me rephrase. *I'm Satan*."

Her laugh set my teeth on edge. "I'd beg to differ, *Satan*. But that's for you and my Elle to figure out. As for now, I shall not tell her who you are. It's not my place. But a word to the wise, the longer you lie to her, the less likely the chance to win her."

"Like she hasn't lied to me?" I snapped, throwing my hands up and singing a fiery hole in the ceiling. "Whoops, my bad."

With a wave of my hand I repaired the room—the damage I'd done and the damage she'd done.

"Demons and Sirens are a delicate match," she said, nodding her head in thanks for my nifty clean up magic. "Two wrongs rarely make a right, but even the word *rare* leaves some wiggle room. Good things can happen to bad people and bad things can happen to good."

My head whipped up and I pinned her with my angry gaze. I'd heard those exact words recently from Fate. This puzzle kept getting larger and unfortunately more of the damned pieces were missing.

"I'm leaving," I said tonelessly. "Good things do not happen to all bad people, Siren. I, more than anyone, know this. Hell is simply full of *innocent* people. Just ask them."

"Will you be back?" she asked.

Would I? Yes. I knew I couldn't stay away from my Siren, but if I didn't find the darkness and end it, I wouldn't be alive to find out if good things did happen to bad people—and neither would she —nor would any other living being.

"Possibly," I hedged.

"I'd say it's been delightful meeting you, but I'd be lying," Sadie said.

"Well then, I'll be happy to lie," I said with a grin. "It was a delight meeting you, Siren. Be seeing you soon."

With that I conjured up a blast of black magic and engulfed myself in the glittering enchantment. I disappeared in a cloud of sparkling smoke. There was only one problem. I was still on the same damned plane. Without the glasses, I couldn't find the portal.

Not only was I on the same fucking plane, I was in the same fucking room. Rolling my eyes, I marched over to the dying Siren and waved my hand in front of her face.

Nothing.

Good. She couldn't see me.

It would be wildly embarrassing to have to materialize and explain that the Harbinger of Evil couldn't find the damn door. No worries. I'd go back to the studio and find the glasses.

"Oh God, no," Sadie screamed as an explosion of purple magic tore through the room and Elle and her boys came back.

What the Hell? I stayed cloaked in invisibility as I made my way back and I almost imploded in rage. What the fuck kind of army did Elle have if this was how she came out of battle? The need to kill all of the Eunuchs consumed me, but I knew remaining unseen was more of an advantage at the moment. More truth was apt to be spoken if they thought they were alone. However, the Eunuchs were mine after I had what I needed.

Elle lay bloody and torn up in the arms of one of the Eunuchs who gently laid her on the couch. Sadie, wrapped her arms around her and rocked her as she cried.

"I have your soul," Elle whispered as she held the blindingly bright amethyst orb in her hand. "Open your robe."

Sadie did as she was told and Elle pressed the glowing entity to the woman's chest. It was absorbed immediately and the sick Siren became the picture of health. However, Elle was not.

Unacceptable.

I took a seat on the far side of the room and waited for the information to flow. I was not disappointed.

Impending darkness would have to wait.

CHAPTER SIXTEEN

"WHAT HAPPENED?" SADIE DEMANDED, STILL HOLDING A QUICKLY healing Elle in her arms. "Were you caught in the Troll Palace?"

"No, we weren't," Elle said, sitting up with effort and running her hands through her hair.

Goddamn, she was beautiful. Even torn up and bleeding she was exquisite. I was actually jealous of her hands. I wanted my own fingers tangled in her hair... and all over her body as well.

The Eunuchs kneeled around her with their handsome, wimpy and entirely useless heads bowed. The bastards were supposed to be killing machines. No killing machine worth their salt would let the one they were sworn to protect take on injuries like the ones my Siren had. Fucking worthless. From now on she'd travel with a pack of Demons—female Demons. I could never trust a male Demon as far as I could throw him around the Siren.

"Explain," Sadie said tersely, taking the words from my mouth.

"There's a man—a Demon—absolutely awful. He's rude, narcissistic, profane... just awful. I want him."

"A Demon did this to you?"

"No, a Demon did not do this to me."

I almost materialized I was so pissed. A *Demon* had better not

161

have done this to Elle. He would be a very dead Demon if he'd so much as laid a hand on her.

"Does this side story pertain to why you've been wounded?" Sadie asked, shaking her head in frustration.

"It does. I promise. As I was saying, I want to keep this man."

"You can't have a man," Sadie replied.

"This one I can. He withstood the enchantment when I kissed him."

"*You* kissed him?" Sadie questioned.

"Not exactly," Elle admitted with a delighted grin. "He kissed me, but I swear I warned him. He's clearly unbalanced and insane. There's probably something incredibly wrong with him, but I don't care. He's perfect for me."

"We'll discuss your Demon after you tell me what happened."

"Fine," she said with an annoyed sigh. "I slipped in, stole your soul back, and replaced it with mine without incident. The Troll King was asleep and it was the easiest it's ever been."

"And," Sadie pushed for more.

"Aaaand, then I went back to the romance convention where the disgusting, vile Demon killed the Trolls for me."

I rolled my eyes. She could really cut back on the adjectives and it would be fine...

"I wanted to get his book and read about him. He's such a heinous liar. I was hoping to get some insight into his deranged mind," Elle continued.

"And you were attacked for trying to get the Demon's book?" Sadie asked, confused.

"Umm... no. Unfortunately, the Trolls showed up again."

Son of a bitch. I no longer cared about the balance. The Trolls were now on my To Do list of things to fucking wipe off the face of the Earth.

Sadie stood and paced the room in agitation. She came dangerously close to me and I wondered if she knew I was present.

"Your Demon left," she said.

"Not possible. I locked him in a cage," Elle said looking alarmed and crestfallen at the same time.

"Darling, the way to keep a man doesn't include locking him in a cage."

"Seriously? How was I supposed to know this? I've never met a man I haven't killed," Elle shouted. "What was I supposed to do? Let him follow me and get hurt? I find the one dreadful, immoral, sinful and wicked whack job who can touch me without turning to dust. I want to keep him. What's wrong with that?"

"If this Demon can withstand your magic, I would assume he's fairly hard to kill," Sadie pointed out.

"Not taking any chances. When I find that bastard, I'll handcuff him to me. He will not get away from me so easily again."

Hell in a gasoline brushfire. This woman was sadistically perfect for me.

"Good luck with that," Sadie muttered. "You have a hundred years before we have to get your soul back. Just be very careful."

"Careful is what I've been waiting a lifetime not to do," Elle shot back with a grin. "I feel like I can be semi-normal for the first time in my life and it feels good."

"We can't keep existing like this," Sadie said. "Something has been pulling on both of our powers for centuries. I used to think it was the Trolls, but now I'm not as certain."

"May I be so bold to speak, my lady?" a Eunuch asked.

"You may," Elle said.

"We don't know why the Troll King wants your souls. Wouldn't it behoove us to know why they want them to try and end this deadly game?"

All right. Fine. I wouldn't kill *that* one. He had a brain and had made an excellent point.

Elle nodded and patted his head.

Shit, now I had to kill him.

"If we knew that, we probably wouldn't be in the position we're in," Elle agreed.

"I think it's Fate," Sadie said.

"Isn't everything?" Elle snapped.

"No," Sadie insisted. "I think Fate—the actual woman—has something at stake here."

"What?" Elle asked.

"No clue, but you can bet your life, I'm going to find out."

"I believe I can help you with that," I said materializing in a blast of black glitter much to the shocked surprise of all in the room.

The Eunuchs pulled their swords, but the harsh glance and hiss from Elle made them stand down immediately. Sadie was the only one aware that neither the Eunuchs nor their swords stood a chance against me. For the moment, we would keep it that way.

"Well, look what the cat dragged in," Elle said, crossing her arms over her chest and glaring at me. "You're supposed to be in your cage, Demon."

"Umm... not really the way to greet someone you want to keep," Sadie said under her breath.

"No, trust me. He loves it," Elle whispered back. "He's not right in the head, but he's so beautiful I can overlook that part."

With an eye roll that should have won an Oscar, I crossed the room and examined my Siren. She'd healed nicely. I waved my hand and dressed both women in appropriate attire for what we were about to embark on.

Elle promptly wiggled her nose redressed herself in a far more provocative little number that made my pants tent. It really wouldn't do to be aroused where we were going, but I was quite sure that my erection would deflate at warp speed once we reached our destination.

"I can help you find Fate."

"And what exactly will that cost, Demon?" Elle inquired with a raised brow.

I gave her a lopsided grin that caused her breath to hitch unsteadily. "I'll have to get back to you on that one, Siren."

"You know where Fate is?" Sadie asked, her voice full of suspicion. "Elle and I can't go to the mortal plane together. It's too dangerous."

"Trust me where we're going is far more dangerous than the mortal plane," I replied, unable to pull my eyes from Adrielle.

"And Fate will be at the end of this excursion?" Elle asked, looking me up and down like I was a piece of meat and she was a starving carnivore.

It was so rudely erotic, I was tempted to grab her and take her back to Hell. Screw the impending darkness. If my end was fated, there was very little I could do about it. I might as well be having a world shattering orgasm when the darkness took me.

"No, but where I am taking you will lead us to Fate," I replied, giving her back her own medicine as I undressed her with my eyes.

"Where are we going?" Sadie asked, stepping between us and purposely breaking the spells we were casting on each other.

"To my mother's house."

"Seriously?" Elle asked, wrinkling her nose. "The same one who you referred to as an insane whack job who spilled lemonade on your suit—which caused you to arrive *naked*?"

"The very same," I confirmed, knowing I was opening a massive can of eternal nosiness by taking the Sirens to Nirvana. But all of this was connected somehow. Maybe the darkness was connected as well.

"You showed up here *naked*?" Sadie asked with a burst of laughter.

"He most certainly did," Elle informed her mother with a wide grin.

"Nice move," Sadie congratulated me.

"Thank you."

"And your mother's name?" Sadie changed the subject from my spectacular entrance back to the matter at hand. Of course she knew the answer full well since she was aware of exactly who I was.

"Mother Nature," I replied.

"You have got to fucking kidding me," Elle said, narrowing her eyes dangerously. "Mother Nature is *Blade Inferno's* mother?"

"Yes," I replied, loving her insolence. I just hoped it remained once she knew my true identity. "Blade Inferno is her son amongst a few others."

"I do believe *Blade Inferno* might have some explaining to do," Elle said, going toe to toe with me.

My laugh filled the room and Elle grinned despite herself. "All in good time, little Siren. Are we ready?"

Sadie nodded but Elle just gave me the stink eye, much to my delight.

"Very well then. Hold on. This is going to be a bumpy ride."

Truer words had never been spoken.

CHAPTER SEVENTEEN

My mother had lost her fucking mind.

Within minutes of our arrival, a feast fit for a king was laid out. I felt compelled to warn our guests that the food was inedible and possibly poisonous, but my mother was standing too close. Risking a massive explosion wasn't on the agenda, so I said nothing.

Soft violin music floated on the air and she'd dimmed the lights in her palace with a flick of her fingers. Even her monkeys were on board. The little bastards were wearing formal wear and passing out flutes of champagne.

And I was correct about losing my erection. Mother Nature was the answer to controlling the population.

"I'm just so thrilled. He's never brought a *girl* here before," she squealed as she yanked Elle into her arms and squeezed until my Siren turned an unnatural shade of blue. "And you're so pretty!"

"Enough," I snapped, peeling my mother off of Elle. "Mother, this is not a social call."

"Oh pish," Mother Nature sang, shoving me out of the way. She grabbed Elle and Sadie and tossed them down on an elaborately floral and ultra feminine couch.

Wedging herself between the startled women, she took Elle's hand in hers and smiled like the loon she was.

"I don't have baby pictures because cameras didn't exist back then, but I assure you he was a gorgeous child. Sure, he was a bit of a handful, but what else would one expect of Lucifer?"

The expression on Elle's face went from surprise to shock and then turned to fury in a flash. Her hands immediately began to spark and sizzling black fire spit from her fingertips as her eyes found mine.

"What an asshole," she shouted. "You're the fucking Devil? When were you going to tell me that, *Blade Inferno*?"

"Whoops," Mother Nature said with enormous eyes and a joyous cackle. She hopped up and placed herself where she would have the best vantage point of the showdown about to occur.

"You never asked my real name," I replied, walking closer to the black flames. "You simply asked if Blade Inferno was my real name."

"It's not," my mother volunteered unhelpfully while grinning from ear to ear. "I have far better taste than that. I'd never give any child of mine a male stripper name."

The statement was absurd coming from a woman who spent a great deal of time dancing on a pole.

"Blade Inferno is *not* a male stripper name," I snapped, glaring at my mother. "It's the name of the highest paid fucking romance author in the world."

"Total stripper name," Elle said, siding with my deranged mother.

"I'd have to agree," Sadie added, moving to sit with Mother Nature. "You wrote a *romance*?"

"Yesssssss... I dictated my supremely engrossing life story to my niece, then she slapped a bullshit happy ending on it. Research shows that romance is the highest paying and most disrespected genre, so it's a perfect fit for me. Is there anything *else* you'd like to know?" I shouted.

What did I have to do to get some goddamned respect?

"Umm… no," Sadie said, pressing a napkin to her mouth to hide her grin.

"So you think happy endings are bullshit?" Elle inquired with a look on her face that made me think there must be a correct answer to the question.

Hell, what was the right answer? In my experience, women changed their minds like the winds changed direction. What was correct one minute was incorrect in the next. Damn it, all I wanted was to get her naked and underneath me. How fucking hard could that possibly be? Screw this. We were all most likely going to die in the very near future, so I may as well start telling the truth.

"There is no such thing as a happy ending," I said.

The blast of searing hot fire that came hurtling at me was a shock. However, it was a shockingly welcome surprise.

"Ouch, that's gotta hurt," I heard my mother say as the black flames of my Siren's wrath bathed me from head to toe.

It was glorious. I felt my pain and sins dissipate and fall away. As the black flames danced and licked at my skin, I let my head fall back and profound relief washed over me. The intensity of the blaze bit at me, but I was still far stronger than my Siren's glorious weapon of destruction because I was destruction.

With a wave of my hand, I doused the flames even though I wanted to spend eternity lost in them. The silence in the room was heavy as my mother and Sadie waited with baited breath to see how I would handle being set ablaze.

Elle simply stood there with her brow raised and arms crossed over her chest. She was ready to do it again if I gave her an answer she didn't like. She was insane. She was volatile. She was beautiful. She was a pyromaniac.

She was *mine*.

I checked my suit and smiled when I saw that it had come through the fire as intact as I had. I was a resilient handsome bastard.

"Well, *that* was a bit unexpected," I said, to the relieved sighs of Mother Nature and Sadie.

"Watch yourself, *Satan*," Elle snapped, unrepentant. "I'll do it again if you displease me."

"I certainly hope so," I replied.

"My goodness," Mother Nature announced, giggling with delight. "They're such a violent pairing. I love it! I've been telling Lucifer for centuries he just needs to find a nice girl and settle down. Might keep him out of trouble."

"I'd hardly say a pairing with my daughter would keep anyone out of trouble," Sadie told Mother Nature with a chuckle.

"I meant *nice girl* in a very broad definition of the term," Mother Nature clarified herself.

My Siren's eye roll matched my own and pleased me greatly. I didn't believe in happily ever afters or even love, but I'd never been so taken with a woman. She was just terrible in every sense of the word.

"I'd suggest you rethink your ways," Elle said as the tux-clad monkeys danced around her, hanging on her every word.

"Too old," I replied, wanting to piss her off again so she'd blast me with fire. However, I was also telling the truth, and the truth was turning out to hurt so good.

"This is not going to work," she muttered unhappily and went for the food table.

"What's not going to work?" I asked, cutting her off from the feast and moving her expertly away.

"This. *Us*," she said, waving her hands in the air. "I mean I was so excited that you didn't keel over dead when we kissed, but I didn't think it through."

"Think what through?" I demanded, not liking the direction of the conversation.

True, I didn't want love, nor did I even know what it truly meant. Another truth... happily ever afters were not meant for people like me. Yet the most horrifying truth of all was that I didn't want Elle to walk away from me. Ever.

What the Hell was happening? I could only attribute it to the darkness drawing near. Why else would a weakness like this grip me? Thousands of women wanted me. If this one didn't, so be it.

Okay. Even I didn't buy that one...

"I don't really know you," she said, eyeing me with distrust.

"What would you like to know?" Mother Nature asked hurriedly, jumping up and taking a firm grip on Elle's hand so she didn't disappear in a huff. "I'll tell you everything."

"*No, you won't,*" I informed my mother rudely. "I will tell her what she wants to know."

"But you'll lie," my mother stated the indisputable fact.

"Your point?" I hissed as my eyes turned red and a menacing wind whipped up, blowing the food off the table.

One problem solved. At least the Sirens wouldn't leave Nirvana with food poisoning.

"It's fine if he lies," Elle reassured my mother. "I do it all the time."

"Well that's certainly... umm... alarming and fitting," Mother Nature said.

My mother clapped her hands and the music took on a new flavor. If I was correct—and I was—it was *Toxic* by Brittany Spears. I loved that song—wonderful theme.

"What do you want to know?" I asked, warily. The truth had gotten me burned which was fabulous, but I was fairly certain lies might be far worse.

She turned and moved away. While her backside was a work of art, it disturbed me to see her walk away from me. I didn't like it one bit.

"Favorite color?" Elle asked.

"Black. Yours?"

"Purple."

"Food?" I inquired.

"Sushi. Yours?"

"Eggplant Parmesan."

"Ohhhhh, I can make that," my mother chimed in with unabashed excitement. "I'll bake you a large pan next Tuesday."

"Please don't," I muttered with a slight gag as Elle giggled. "Favorite pastime?"

"Porn. Yours?"

"I'd have to say I'm with you on that—although I prefer performing rather than watching. Any other hobbies?"

"Photography, burning buildings to the ground, and bubble baths. Yours?" Elle asked with a laugh, enjoying herself.

"I'm quite partial to fire in any form. I greatly enjoy cheating at cards and watching Wheel of Fortune."

"I can work with that," she replied.

"Dear Heaven and Hell on fire," Mother Nature muttered. "This is going to be interesting."

"And destructive," Sadie added with a laugh.

"Favorite band?" Elle asked with a look on her face that told me I'd better get this one correct.

She wasn't the only one with that look. We'd entered into some very serious territory here. As far as I was concerned there was only one band in existence that deserved the word *favorite* attached to it.

"What's yours?" I shot back, praying to all that was depraved that she would get this right.

"You first," she challenged.

I noticed Mother Nature and Sadie backing away from the potential line of explosive fire. Smart women.

"Together," I replied. "We will reveal the best band of all time together.

I knew there was little chance that we would be obsessed with the same band, but everything else about my Siren was absolutely perfect.

"On three," Elle instructed. "One. Two. Three."

"Journey," we shouted in unison.

My knees felt like jelly and I almost dropped to the floor while Elle squealed with delight. I hadn't thought that there was any way I could want her more. Clearly, I'd been mistaken.

"Karaoke some time?" I suggested with a lopsided grin.

Elle looked shocked and truly alarmed by my question. "Umm... no. Very bad idea."

"I often go karaoke bar hopping with Frank Sinatra, Elvis and Mr. Rogers. Good times."

"You're serious?" Elle asked squinting in terror.

Could my ballsy Siren have stage fright? Did she not like Sinatra? Impossible. Everyone loved Sinatra. It had to be that sweater changing Rogers she was petrified of. Hades knew he still scared me occasionally.

"Absolutely. Singing in public is wildly liberating. You should try it," I insisted.

My mother shot me a look I didn't even remotely understand so I ignored her and decided to drop the real bomb. "I know Steve Perry. He's a Unicorn," I bragged as Elle's eyes grew wide with admiration.

"You kidnapped him," my mother reminded me. "He has a restraining order against you,"

"I didn't *kidnap* him. My daughters did... as a surprise gift," I snapped. "And we've worked out the restraining order issue. As long as I don't sing with him, I'm allowed to sit within twenty feet."

"I'm impressed," Elle said, her eyes lit with amusement. "You're tone deaf?"

"Completely," Mother Nature confirmed with a wince. "Are you?" she asked Elle suspiciously.

Elle and Sadie traded glances and both shook their heads slowly.

"Trust me," Elle said. "You don't ever want to hear us sing."

"Ever," Sadie added with a small shudder.

"Can't be good at everything," I replied with a shrug. "However, I may not be able to sing like Steve Perry, but I'm hung like a horse."

"Yes, I know," Elle said with a grin that made me feel unsteady. "Next question?"

"Favorite sexual position?" I inquired, thinking of the thousands I planned to share with her.

"None," she replied firmly. "I don't have sex. It kills."

I felt as if I'd been doused in ice water. This was not going to work for me.

"Umm…" I said, trying to phrase it correctly so she didn't set me on fire again. As much as I would have loved being incinerated once more, we didn't have a tremendous amount of time. "I didn't die from your kiss. I'm quite sure sex will be fine."

"No can do, Big Boy," she snapped. "We can kiss, burn cities together and lie, cheat and steal our way through Vegas, but I will not risk your evil life for an orgasm."

"Pretty sure *he* would," my mother chimed in. "From all the gossip, I hear he's quite the tiger in the sack. Thousands of women can't *all* be wrong. You really should give him a test drive, Elle. It will be fine—and I'm his mother. I should know these things."

With a furious snap of my fingers, I gagged my mother with duct tape and glanced over at Elle to see her reaction to my being outed as a man whore. Her eyes had narrowed, her fingers were smoldering and she didn't look happy.

"I will tell you this and I will say it once. If you so much as look at another woman with lust in your eyes, I will remove that particular piece of anatomy you're so proud of. Am I clear?" she ground out in a hostile tone that made my dick stand at attention.

"Right back at you, Siren," I said. "Not only will I lock you in a dungeon, I will kill whomever you show favor to—and I'll do in front of you."

My crazy Siren shuddered with delight. She was a dastardly piece of work.

"Dear Heaven and Hell," Mother Nature screeched as she ripped the duct tape from her overly busy mouth. "Maybe this isn't such a great plan."

"I feel you," Sadie whispered, watching the insanity tournament with a wary expression.

"We *will* have sex. Of that, I'm quite sure," I told my Siren.

"Are you now?" she shot back, as a delicious scented wind blew up and her eyes blazed so bright, I felt light headed.

"Yes," I replied with a cocky grin and a painfully growing erection.

"Over my dead body."

"I'm really not into necrophilia," I shot back. "Some things are too taboo even for me."

"You're an idiot," she yelled with a small grin pulling at her delectable lips.

"Your point?" I asked, moving slowly toward her as if she was my prey.

"You really want to have sex and die?" she demanded, standing her ground as I stalked her.

"Yes. I do. And we will. And I won't—die, that is."

"Pretty sure he's serious," my mother added. She zipped it when I shot her a look that had withered some of the most powerful immortals alive.

"Fine," Elle shouted, throwing her hands in the air and creating a hailstorm of amethyst crystal ice. "Let's have sex, you stupid man."

"Now?" I asked, completely taken by surprise.

"Yes. Now," she said, still yelling. "Let's get the Devil's demise over with. And don't say I didn't tell you so when you figure out you're freakin' dead."

My dick was so hard at this point I wasn't sure I'd last even thirty seconds when I got her naked. Whatever. I had a point to prove and a Siren to bring to mind shattering orgasm.

"You can use the guest room on the second floor," my mother

volunteered hastily. "It's sound proof, fire proof, and the mattress is triple re-enforced. It's my favorite room to shag your father in."

"For the love of everything vile," I bellowed as red lightening blasted through the room and sent monkeys diving for cover. "I'm pretty sure your statement just made my balls retreat back up into my stomach, *Mother*."

"That's awful," Mother Nature said with great concern. "Should I call a doctor?"

"No," I said, stomping my foot and stopping myself just short of having a fit that would cause years of reconstruction to Nirvana. "You just need to stop talking. If you keep going, there's a fine chance my dick will never work again."

"That's not a nice thing to say to your mother," she chided— her red curls bouncing as she shook her head in disappointment. "Your dick is just fine. When you were born the voodoo doctor congratulated me on the size. I'm very proud of your dick, son."

"This is all kinds of wrong," I hissed, running my hands through my hair and trying not to laugh or blow Nirvana off the map of the immortal Universe.

"It's kind of sweet in a wildly inappropriate, over-sharing kind of way," Elle commented.

"No. No, it's not," I replied. "It's mortifying. I'm fucking Satan. I should not have to deal with embarrassment like this."

"Darling, you know you can't fuck yourself," Mother Nature reminded me with a loving pat on my back. "You really need a new catch phrase. You don't want people to think you're a contortionist."

With a sigh, I gave up. I let my head fall to my hands and laughter overtook me. There was no winning with my mother— not today, not tomorrow, not ever.

"May I ask a question?" Mother Nature inquired.

"Does it have anything to do with my dick?" I asked through splayed fingers as I looked up at the certifiable woman who bore me.

"No, but I'm sure I could come up with a dick question if it would make you happy."

"No, please don't. I've had all the dick observations from you that I can take. What is the question," I asked, glancing over at my smiling Siren.

Elle's sheer beauty and obnoxious character took my breath.

"Why exactly did you come here?" my mother asked, pulling my focus away from my Siren.

Why had we come here? For the life of me, I couldn't remember. All the dick talk had thrown me off my game.

"To find Fate," Sadie reminded me, stepping up next to Mother Nature.

And Fate was the other sadistic form of birth control. My pride and joy deflated instantly.

"Why? Why do you need her whereabouts again?" my mother asked with a worried expression on her exquisite face.

"I think she's far more involved than she wants anyone to believe," I replied tersely.

"You think she's the darkness coming for you?"

"What darkness coming for you?" Elle demanded as her entire upper body began to shoot black sparks of anger. "Is Fate trying to kill you?"

"No. That's against the rules," I replied dryly. "However, I'm certain she's orchestrating something nefarious. Mother, did you know Fate was a Siren?"

Mother Nature's expression would have been comical if the situation wasn't so dire.

"Shut the front door," my mother said, seating herself on a chair made of roses. "Tell me everything. Right. Now."

My mother was no longer the flighty idiot I most often encountered. She turned into a deadly badass on a dime. Even Elle and Sadie were slightly scared of her. Without missing a detail, I got her up to speed right down to the Trolls and everything I knew of Fate's past.

"The trinity," Mother Nature replied absently staring at Elle and Sadie. "There really are three Fates."

"Explain," Sadie said in a clipped tone as her hair began to float around her head and her eyes burned a bright purple.

"I'm not quite sure, but I think you might have been screwed out of a job" my mother said. "I'm only guessing. But you say you've felt a pull on your magic for centuries?"

Both Elle and Sadie nodded.

"And the Trolls clearly know something the rest of us don't," I added. "Amazing since they're so lacking in the brains department."

"Maybe they're not," Elle said. "Maybe they're not as stupid as they've led us to believe."

"Possible—but that's a reach." I shrugged and took Elle's hand in mine. Her body temperature ran high and it felt like a security blanket I'd denied myself for millions of years.

"And they have your soul?" Mother Nature directed her question to Elle.

"Yes."

"And what of this darkness?" Sadie asked. "Is it connected?"

"Don't know," I admitted. "However, if I were a gambling man —which I am, albeit I cheat... a lot—I'd have to say yes. Definitely connected. And when I find the darkness, I will destroy it, and then I'll go after Fate."

"Umm... nope," Elle corrected me, with a vicious expression on her gorgeous face. "The darkness is mine. Anything that comes for you will have to get by me first. And trust me... *nothing* is going to get by me."

I was shocked to silence. And my mother's mouth was a perfect O as she gaped at Elle in delighted surprise. My Siren was truly nuts. I was far more powerful than everyone in the room. Hell, everyone in the Universe. I didn't need Elle to fight my battles. I was a rock, a goddamn island. It had been working fine for millions of years. Or had it? The feeling that washed over me at hearing her words was similar to her fire that burned away my pain and sins. What was this woman doing to me?

"Fate first or the Trolls?" Mother Nature asked, still staring at Elle.

Yanking my mind from concepts I couldn't comprehend, I made a decision. "Trolls first. Fate second. I want Elle's soul back."

"And I want yours," she said quietly.

For the first time in my life I was sad—not angry—that I didn't have a soul to give her.

"I don't have one."

She tilted her head and smiled. "You most certainly do, Lucifer."

My given name on her lips slayed me.

"I'm sorry, Adrielle, but I don't."

"What a silly bad man you are," she admonished me. "Your soul is actually quite beautiful—little dark around the edges—but it's a blinding gold."

Too overwhelmed to speak, I simply nodded. I had no soul, but if it made her feel happy to think I did, so be it.

"Mother, you and Sadie will stay here. We can't have both the Sirens in the same place—too dangerous. Elle, do you know where your soul is kept?"

"In a locket around the Troll King's neck."

"How inconvenient," I muttered and ran my hand through my hair. Whatever. It would give me insane pleasure to remove the bastard's head to retrieve my Siren's soul.

"I know the entire layout of the Troll Palace. Unfortunately. I've visited many times over the last thousand years," Elle added. "We'll get in and out quickly."

I doubted that since I wasn't going to leave any Troll alive that could come after my Siren. But she didn't need to know that yet.

"Shall I alert backup?" my mother asked.

"I'm the Lord of Darkness, Mother. I'm all the backup we need."

CHAPTER EIGHTEEN

"This isn't the Troll King's Palace, *Lucifer*," Elle said, with a grin and a suspicious expression on her lovely face.

Her delight and distrust made my pants uncomfortably tight. Hell, everything she did made my pants uncomfortably tight. Thankfully, my balls were still functioning after the horrifying visit to my mother's abode.

"No. It's definitely not the Troll King's Palace, *Adrielle*," I agreed and impatiently pulled her through an intricately carved teak door into a suite of rooms I'd never taken another woman to.

My Siren walked around the sinful suite and ran her hands over the black silk duvet on the enormous bed. "Very masculine and dark. If I were to take a guess, I'd have to say you Steve Perry-ed me."

"Interesting conjecture," I replied as I removed my suit coat and tossed it on the sleek black leather couch.

"From the look of the décor, I'd surmise that I'm standing in the bedroom of the one and only Harbinger of Evil. I might have to get a restraining order…"

"You're such a smart-mouthed little Siren," I said as I yanked her close and buried my face in her blonde hair. "Look at us."

I turned so we faced the decadent floor to ceiling mirror, but kept a tight hold on her so she wouldn't slip away. The contrast in our coloring was striking. She was the perfect light to my dark. Her luminous skin glowed against the olive complexion of my own.

"Beautiful," I murmured. "Mine."

"Not yet I'm not," she replied dreamily, staring at our reflection.

"Of course you are," I said.

She said nothing as she pulled away and examined the priceless artifacts scattered around the room. Her movement was practiced, but her true sensuality was bone deep. I knew I would never tire of staring at her—sparring with her—being set ablaze by her.

Now I just wanted to be inside her.

"I want you."

"I know," she said, turning to me.

"Is that all you have to say?" I asked with an amused smirk.

"No, but you seem to go deaf when we discuss this little issue."

"There is *nothing* little about it," I said referring to the very large erection tenting my custom Hugo Boss pants.

She shook her head and rolled her eyes. "It's a very *big* and potentially *life ending* risk."

"Very big? Yes. Potentially life ending? Absolutely not. Besides, I'd rather end my life in your arms than live another moment not inside you."

"Very poetic, Devil."

"I try, Siren."

"Not sure I want to be responsible for the death of the Lord of Darkness," she said. "I'm unpopular enough for being what I am."

Shrugging, I loosened my tie and stepped out of my shoes. "According to my mother, I'm the only immortal being that can have you. We were apparently made for each other."

"And this is the same batshit crazy mother who lives with

monkeys and likes to wax poetic about your pride and joy?" she asked with her brow raised high.

My grin was wide and all I wanted to do was grab her and kiss her senseless. "Yes, the very same one who controls the weather, pole dances, pours vats of bleach over Fate's head and puts her in a choke hold."

"Hmm... I think I like your mother. She hugs kind of hard, but she did produce a very handsome and dishonorable son."

"And we mustn't forget—one hung like a horse," I added, taking off my belt and unbuttoning my pants.

"Right," she purred. "Confirmed by the voodoo doctor."

"Come here, Adrielle."

She paused and glared at me, but her expression was filled with a longing so intense I forgot to breathe.

"This is wrong, Lucifer."

"Everything about me is wrong. Hasn't seemed to bother you yet," I reminded her.

"Too many wrongs do not add up to a right," she said a tone so sultry I had to hold on to the chair I was standing next to. "They can add up to death."

Slowly and methodically, I slid my shirt from my body and dropped it to the floor with unsteady hands. Her eyes went wide as she admired me.

"Beautiful," she whispered. Elle's eyes blazed a bright amethyst and the gold rings around them sparkled. "But we can't do this. Didn't you hear a word I said?"

"I did. Doesn't apply to me so I'm ignoring it. Come."

"I can't," she whispered as her feet involuntarily began to move toward me.

"You can," I coaxed her with my voice. "You will. I'll make sure of it."

"Devil, if you die, I swear on everything unholy I will chase down your soul and kill it again," she threatened as her hands tentatively discovered my chest and shoulders.

"Good luck with that."

Snapping my fingers, I removed what was left of our clothing and kissed her like there was no tomorrow. The thought occurred to me that there might not be a tomorrow. Not because our union would kill me, but because the darkness felt closer than it had ever been.

If it were tangible, I would destroy it, but it was elusive and untouchable.

"Here's the thing," she muttered against my lips as my hands found her full breasts I ran my thumbs over her gorgeous dusky pink nipples. "I really can't think when you do that," she gasped out and let her head fall back on her shoulders.

"I've found that thinking is highly overrated," I replied as my open mouth slid from her lips to her neck.

Elle jerked and shuddered in my arms making my dick pulse with a desire so potent I felt dizzy. I'd barely touched her and was so close to coming it was absurd.

"Just let me pleasure you. I don't need sex. I've gone thousands of years without it—no biggie," she begged, running all her words together in her distress. "I can't lose you. I'm terrified of losing you."

Her words gave me pause along with a feeling I was unfamiliar with—hope. A very strange sensation indeed. What was this woman doing to me? I actually half believed I had a soul.

"Do you really think I would do this if I truly thought I would die?" I asked as my hungry mouth replaced my hands on her breasts—not her *bosom*—her *breasts*.

"No, but everyone has an off day. I'm pretty irresistible," she pointed out with a moan of pleasure as my lips and tongue tasted her body.

I stopped—to both her dismay and mine. Raising her chin so our eyes met, I tilted my head and stared hard. "That you are, my beauty. Why not try this idea on for size? Don't you find it odd that

I have no attraction to your mother at all and yet she too is a Siren?"

My greedy hands found her perfect rounded ass and squeezed, to her gasping delight.

"You don't feel *anything*?" she asked, shocked as her delicate fingers moved down my body with lightning speed and introduced themselves to my pride and joy.

"No. Nothing at all," I confirmed as I watched her hands wrap provocatively around me. It was all I could do to make intelligent sound, but I had more to say. "Our attraction has nothing to do with your magical charms or mine, and everything to do with simply who we are and what's happening between us. Which leads me to assume that *this* is *our fate*."

"Never assume, Devil. It always makes an ass out of you and me, but especially you," she said, stroking me and watching for my reaction.

I didn't disappoint.

Growling with desire, I scooped my seductress off her feet and tossed her gorgeous body on the bed. Her laughter filled the cavernous room and I grinned. Her blonde hair and pale skin on the black duvet were the most beautiful sight I'd seen.

"You lie," she announced, pointing a lovely finger at me as mirth danced in her eyes.

"As do you."

"Guilty as charged," Elle replied, sitting up and patting the space next to her. "We're going to have to make a pact."

"A pact?" I questioned, moving to her and gathering her in my arms.

She nodded and rested her head on my chest. It felt like home —another first for me.

"We have to have a secret signal that means we *must* tell the truth. Of course not all the time. That would be horrible."

"Not to mention impossible," I added.

"Right. But *occasionally* we have to be honest."

"How about Tuesdays?" I suggested.

"Umm… no," she said with a giggle as she slapped my arm. "There's no way in Hell I can be honest for twenty four hours straight."

"Fine point. Well made," I said as I eased her back on the mountain of goose down pillows and lay beside her. "What did you have in mind?"

"Hand to the heart means honesty," she replied, taking my face in her warm hands and searching my eyes for assent.

"My heart is cold and black," I told her. "Not sure you'd want to bet on it."

"Oh, I'll bet on your heart because I shall have it soon enough," she informed me smugly as I let her push me to my back and straddle me. "Question is… will you win mine?"

"I'll steal it—don't have to win it," I told her with a bark of laughter that changed immediately to a groan of satisfaction as she slid down my body and got up close and personal with my very excited dick.

"Please try," she said peeking up at me through the golden strands of her hair.

She wasn't joking. She wasn't lying. She was very serious and I wasn't sure how to respond. This woman undid me and threw me for loops I wasn't aware existed.

"Adrielle," I said, putting my hands under her arms and pulling her up so we were face to face. "I'm Satan. I'm not capable of love. When I fell from the Heavens, that luxury was stolen from me. If my love is what you want, you'll be fighting a battle that can't be won."

She stared at me for a long moment as she considered her next move. "Let me ask you this. How does it make you feel to know that I could disappear and you would never see me again?" she questioned, gently tracing my lips as she watched my face intently.

It was if the wind had been violently punched from my lungs.

My hands tightened on her body and there wasn't a breath of space between us.

"I forbid you to leave," I ground out through clenched teeth. My eyes went red and my hands grew hot with flame.

Elle's delighted laugh slightly eased my tension, but I still didn't trust her not to disappear. She was probably correct in that she could elude me for eternity. Clearly Sirens could create wrinkles in time that were undetectable. The thought of it was unacceptable. She was mine.

"I'm serious," I hissed as I wound her thick hair in my hands and brought her lips to mine. "Tell me you won't disappear on me. Ever. I will come after you and drag you back."

"That's not very nice."

"I'm not a nice man—at all."

"Tell me you'll try." She pushed up, placed her hand on her heart and waited.

My stomach plunged. She wanted the truth. I didn't even know what the fucking truth meant. Would I try? Yes. If that's what it would take to keep her, I would try. But I could also guarantee that the chances of it working were slim to none.

Slowly I put my hand on my chest and nodded. Her sigh of relief pierced my dead heart and made me feel like a scoundrel. I knew I couldn't love her. I could want her and need her, but love her? No.

"Ready to die, Devil?" she asked with a devious little smile on her lips.

"Ready to have a long overdue orgasm, Siren?" I shot back as my body tingled with lust and a need so great I was concerned both of us would end up engulfed in flame.

"Yes, I am. You're sure about this?"

"Never been more sure of anything in my life."

Elle leaned down and pressed her open mouth to mine. Slowly our tongues tangled in a carnal rhythm. Our bodies aligned and rubbed together sinfully, causing sparks. Flames—hers black and mine orange—mixed and danced over our heated bodies. It was surreal and like nothing I'd ever known.

Her desire for me matched mine for her. I was so hard from wanting my Siren that I was in exquisite pain. Flipping her to her back, I moved down her body, tasting every inch. She was slick with moisture when I arrived at the place I most desired to be, and my cock—heavy with need—throbbed for her.

"I'm going to fuck you with my tongue until you beg for mercy."

Her whimper was all the encouragement I needed.

My Siren's legs wrapped around my neck and her amethyst eyes grew wide as a gorgeous groan left her lips. I lowered my head and continued my quest, licking, sucking and nipping with an appetite borne of sheer greed for her. I took her in my mouth as she mumbled unintelligible words of lust. Her body bucked and shuddered as she rode out orgasm after orgasm.

"If anything seems off, you have to stop," she cried out as she twisted and arched with the pleasure spiraling through her.

It was the most glorious sight. Sweat glistened on her luminous body and the light from her eyes bathed the room in a purple glow. She looked like a fucking Angel.

"If you feel like you're going to die, stop or I'll kill you," she hissed as yet another orgasm took her.

"Are you threatening me as I go down on you?" I asked with a chuckle as I went back in for another taste.

"I think you might be killing *me* and I'm pretty sure we just burnt the Hell out of your bedspread."

She swallowed any other inane comment she had and instead gasped as I pushed two fingers inside her. I happily and hungrily went back to one of my all time favorite pastimes. I sucked until she screamed for mercy.

When I was bad, I was very, very bad, but when I was good? I was fucking awesome.

Pausing for a moment, I watched her orgasm with conceit and masculine pride. She was gorgeous and she was mine.

"Are you dead?" she asked in a shaky voice, sitting up and checking my pulse. "Did we burn the Palace down?"

"Palace is still standing and I'm *definitely* not dead," I promised, moving up her body and parting her trembling legs. "Not even close."

"I want you, Lucifer. Now," she insisted, writhing beneath me.

She didn't have to ask twice.

Unable to control my frenzied need, I lunged down on her and took her mouth as she guided me into her. There was nothing slow —nothing gentle. Her teeth grazed my neck as I slammed into her and heaved out huge gusts of air as my entire body tightened to the point of agony. Nothing had ever felt so good—so fucking right.

Throwing every technique I'd learned in my time to the wind, I discovered what sex was meant to be—humbling, raw and explosive.

Elle shrieked at my entry and her nails raked my back as she met each violent thrust with abandon. Wrapping my hand around the back of her neck, I took her like a wild man. My vision blurred and the tightness in my balls was painfully perfect.

"More, Devil. Harder," she begged in a musical tone that I felt from the tip of my toes to the top of my head. Her back arched and the muscles in her neck distended.

"With pleasure, Siren," I growled and did as requested.

When we came, we came together. Flames of orange and black fire licked at our skin as the most massive orgasm I'd known raged through my wicked body. Giving her everything I had, I almost passed out.

Unheard of for the Master of Seduction—but then again, I'd never met my match until now.

~

"ARE WE DEAD?" ELLE ASKED AS SHE LAY DRAPED OVER MY BODY LIMP and breathless.

"If this is dead, sign me up," I replied gruffly. I would never get enough of my Siren. Never.

"I think I want to do that again," Elle whispered on a giggle, her hands coaxing me back to life.

I needed no coaxing. All she had to do was be near me. My need for her was almost unbearable.

"I think that could be arranged."

I flipped her over to her stomach and took a brief second to admire the shape of her ass—absolute perfection.

"Can you really go again?" she asked, looking over her shoulder at me with a smile so seductive I almost came right that second.

"I can go for an eternity with you, Adrielle Rinoa. I'm the goddamned Devil."

"I'm so glad I found you and didn't kill you," she said as she arched her back and pushed back against me.

"I am too," I whispered.

As she turned away from me and let her head drop between her arms, I placed my hand on my heart…

"I am too."

CHAPTER NINETEEN

"You will lead me to the Troll King's chamber and then you will transport yourself away. You can go to Nirvana or come back to the Dark Palace. Either of those locations will be safe," I instructed, sliding my arms into a black Armani sport coat and checking my reflection in the mirror. Smiling, I straightened my collar and chose a tie. Hell, I was such a handsome bastard.

"Whatever you say," Elle answered vaguely.

I'd heard that kind of non-answer before. I used the technique often myself. It wasn't going to fly today—or ever.

"Look at me," I said, taking her arm and roughly turning her to her face me. "You just recently returned from a battle with the Trolls all torn up and bloody and near fucking death. You might be immortal, but you can definitely be killed. That's unacceptable to me. You following my train of thought here, Siren?"

"Yep, I hear you, asshole," she replied, pulling away and moving back to the mirror. Elle finished touching up her blood red lipstick while ignoring me completely.

No one ignored me. For the love of everything malicious, I was *Satan*—people bowed to me. What the Hell was she thinking?

With Herculean effort, I held my composure. I'd already done quite a bit of damage for one day.

The sex had made me a little crazy. I'd never experienced anything like it—and I'd experienced *a lot* in my many debased centuries. When my Siren had informed me that she was going home to change her clothes and get ready to go after her soul, I got so furious at the thought of her leaving me that I blew out the back wall of the Dark Palace. My entire staff was now busy repairing the results of my tantrum.

Not to be outdone by my bad behavior, Elle then proceeded to douse me in fire and call me all sorts of wonderfully horrifying names for telling her what she could and couldn't do. In order to make amends, I might have gone a little over board.

Hell, I was drowning.

With detailed instruction sent to Darby, Dino and Dagwood along with my own special brand of over the top materialistic magic, everything Elle could want or need was produced within minutes—including a closet equal in size to my own. Suffice it to say my closet was enormous. I was a clothes whore.

"No. I don't think you *did* hear me," I replied tersely, as I watched her with greedy eyes. I wanted to get the Troll fiasco over with immediately. All I could think about was taking her back to my bed.

"You're bossy and rude," she said, pointing her finger and shooting a single flame of black fire at me. "While the closet and the clothes are cute, I don't live here."

I caught the flame in my hand and reveled in the cleansing burn. "Yessss, you do," I snapped. "I want you with me. Period. The easiest way to make that happen is for you to relocate to Hell. I happen to have a very important job... just in case you missed that minor fact."

Rolling her eyes and selecting a vintage low-cut lavender Halston from the dresses I'd chosen for her, she made a derisive noise. "I understand your career is rather all consuming. I have no issue with that. I just won't live here."

"And why not?" I demanded, losing patience quickly. I could give her the damned world and she seemed to care less.

"You know why," she said without making eye contact.

I did know why. She wanted my love. What she didn't realize was that my love would destroy her—I was evil—I was death. Nothing of who I was connoted love or anything close to that weak emotion. My heart was black... and the soul she *insisted* I had didn't exist.

What I could give her were jewels, clothing, protection, sex and anything else her heart desired. What I couldn't give was the one thing she seemed to want above all else.

"Elle, I..." I ran my hands through my hair and tried to come up with a spin that she might buy.

"Stop, Lucifer." She crossed the room and took my hand in hers. "Sometimes things simply are what they are. You say you can't love me and I can't live without love. I've waited so many years that I can't even count them to love someone and be loved back. A Siren who exists with unrequited love will eventually wither away and die—immortal or not."

"You *love* me?" I asked, frustrated, annoyed, and for the first time in my existence, scared.

She nodded slowly. "I think I do. You're the most despicable being I've ever come across. You lie, you cheat, you steal... but there's something more."

"You're forgetting that I punish and destroy. There's not a being alive that doesn't live in mortal fear of me. I'm what nightmares are made of," I shot back in a flat tone. She may as well know all if she truly thought she loved me. I wasn't worth the wasted emotion.

"I'm no prize," she reminded me in a harsh voice. "My list of sins is long. I have to live with my monstrous past. I killed with no remorse for a long time. You punish evil—your methods might not be conventional according to polite society standards, but I *am* evil—or I was. The Devil may be nightmare inducing, but I'm the real nightmare—not you."

"I call bullshit. You haven't killed in thousands of years. You chose a different way to feed and go on. You're far more noble than me."

"Noble is a relative word—aristocratic, high-born, splendid, righteous, honorable and good," she said with a sad sigh. "I'm neither honorable nor good. The fact that I think I could love you is beyond what I deserve in this long wicked life of mine, but I feel *something*. It's unfamiliar and frightening, but I like it."

Dropping her hand and pacing the room like a caged tiger, I fought to put a logical case together. "If you've never known love, how are you so certain *love* is what you're feeling?" I snapped, wanting to win the exchange, but knew the possibility was slim.

Her hand went to her heart and I froze as if I'd been threatened with my immortal life. The truth was such a dangerous thing.

"I'm not sure," she admitted.

I wanted to set my Palace on fire at her answer. It made no sense whatsoever, but being reasonable wasn't exactly my forte. Why did I fucking care if she only *thought* she loved me. I didn't want her to love me at all. I didn't want to love her either—I just wanted to keep her.

"Then this conversation is moot. It's simple. Don't love me and all our issues are solved. We'll live in sin and I will bed you *constantly* in between ruling the Underworld. You have my word that I'll kill anything that looks at you sideways. You will never want for anything and you'll always be safe with me. As for your soul, it will be returned to you shortly. Then you can redecorate the Dark Palace to your liking—purple goes wonderfully with black. Hell can look like a massive bruise for all I care. All I care about is you being here with me. What is mine shall be yours. Problem solved," I said in a no-nonsense tone.

If I couldn't win completely, I wasn't going to play. Her laugh, while delightful, was also incredibly confusing. Had I done something right or wrong? Women were so damned hard to figure out. My Siren was almost impossible to gauge.

"Oh, Lucifer," she said still smiling wide. "It's difficult when you have no control, isn't it?"

"I have no idea what you mean."

Elle twisted her blonde hair into a sexy knot on the top of her head and pinned it with a diamond clasp as she continued to watch me with amusement. I had no clue what was happening here, but I wasn't on fire so I assumed it was fine.

"You *are* feeling things," she said, picking up the Hermes bag I'd given her. "And you hate it."

"I beg to differ. I feel nothing," I lied. "Nothing."

"Whatever you say, O Great Deceiver," she replied smoothly. "Are you ready to leave?"

"Are you going to transport once we find the Troll King?" I shot back.

"Sure."

Her smile looked so sincere I was tempted to believe her. But I knew better. Her assurance was as deceitful as my saying I felt nothing. Elle was almost as good a liar as I was. Almost. I was a difficult act to beat, but my Siren came close.

If I weren't so concerned about her being harmed, I would have enjoyed her disrespectful insolence. But her death was not on any agenda I had or ever would have.

Nodding, I pretended to buy the bridge she was selling. However, a change of subject was in order or I'd keep pushing her until we both ended up ablaze and the Dark Palace lay in ruins.

"How do you remove your soul?" I asked.

She glanced up sharply and squinted her eyes at me. "Why? Why do you want to know that? I thought you didn't have a soul."

"I don't," I said. "Just curious."

She placed her hand over her heart. "Like this."

"You chose our signal of truth to be the same as the act of removing a soul?" I asked, perplexed.

"I did. I simply place my hand on my heart and call forth my soul."

"That's it?"

"Yes. That's it."

I grabbed a sword and sheathed it in my belt. I didn't need conventional weapons, but I enjoyed the look. Elle might think she was going to stay while I retrieved her soul, but she was wrong. I had the power to send her away and I planned to use it. She'd be angry, but her anger was something I realized I needed...

Wait a goddamned minute...

Her fire was doing what mine failed to do anymore. I needed her to burn away the sins and pain. I was no longer an island.

Unsure what I thought about this new wrinkle, I decided to ignore it. One thing at a time.

First my Siren's soul needed to be stolen back. Then I needed to find and demolish the fucking darkness, and only then I would deal with what this confounding woman truly meant to me.

"Take my hand," I instructed. "Which Troll compound are we transporting to?"

"Disney World," she said with a wrinkled nose.

"Repeat," I said, closing my eyes and groaning.

"Disney. World."

"I hate Disney World—too damned touristy. And the humans are far too happy there."

"Yes, well, we're talking about the Trolls. Their taste has always been appalling."

"Are you ready to go to the *Happiest Place on Earth*?" I said with an eye roll that rivaled my mother's.

"Devil, I was born ready," Elle replied so seductively I almost forgot what I was doing.

I laughed and gathered my wits. "That you were, my Siren— that you definitely were."

CHAPTER TWENTY

"Do you *know* these women?" Elle hissed as we stood at the gates of the Magic Kingdom and watched the humans exit while screaming for their lives.

"Unfortunately, I do," I said, eyeing the impressive army of female immortals standing beautifully motionless amidst the throngs of fleeing mortals. They were armed and very, very dangerous.

"Are they past lovers?" she growled as her fingers began shooting black sparks.

"Absolutely not," I insisted with my hand on my heart, enjoying her jealousy tremendously. Besides, they were most certainly *not* past lovers. I was related to a good portion of them.

Apparently, my mother had disobeyed me and called for back up. At least she'd had the wherewithal to only call females. Males would have been useless in the presence of my Siren. Plus any ogling of my Siren would have pissed me off. And even *I* knew it was terrible form to kill people who were trying to lend a deadly hand.

"Hi Dad," my daughter Dixie called out, walking over with an enormous grin on her lovely face. "Got anyone you want to introduce me to?"

Elle stiffened beside me, quickly removed some of her lipstick, and yanked the neckline of her dress up. I watched in amusement as she fidgeted uncomfortably. It didn't matter what she did. Makeup or no, my Siren was the most alluring women in the Universe. She could wear a garbage bag and make it look sexy.

For the first time since I'd known her, Elle was nervous and unsure. Dixie was a Demon, but she was far different than most. She was good-ish and it was clear that Elle sensed this anomaly. Hell knows I'd tried to encourage Dixie to embrace her dark side, but my favorite daughter lived with only one foot in that world. The only bad thing she had going for her is that she was mated to the Angel of Death. I hated the bastard, but as long as he made her happy he could keep breathing another day.

"Dixie," I said, giving her a look that was supposed to quash her grin. It didn't. All the most important women in my life had no fear of me, which was frustrating yet fabulous.

"This is Adrielle Rinoa, my..." I struggled to find a word that wouldn't get me set on fire.

"I'm his temporary plaything," Elle supplied and then shook my daughter's hand.

"You are *not* temporary," I hissed.

"That's up to you, *jackass*," she shot back and gave Dixie a tight smile.

Dixie's delighted laugh alerted the others of our arrival and they all flew over. Literally.

"Temporary or not, it's nice to meet you, Adrielle Rinoa. I'm Dixie, the only normal offspring of my father."

"Normal is a word that belongs in *none* of our vocabularies," my daughter Sloth said, eyeing Elle with curiosity. "Are you knocked up?"

"She is *not* knocked up," I snapped. "She's mine."

Sloth took a few steps back, but laughed at my ire. "Oookay, Daddio. Just wondering."

"Stop wondering. I don't want to have to smite you in public," I told Sloth as I sidestepped a pack of humans running like the Devil was on their heels. Of course the Devil wasn't because I was standing right here. "Would anyone like to explain why the mortals are leaving the happiest fucking place on Earth?"

I glanced around at the group of female insanity and catalogued who was present. Clearly my mother was taking no chances. There was enough magic here to end time. Hopefully that wasn't what was about to go down.

My nieces, Astrid and Tiara, were at the head of the group with my daughter, Dixie. My other daughters, The Seven Deadly Sins, stood to the side and whispered amongst themselves. They were a nasty little group, but were loyal to me and fought like the deadly Demons they were raised to be.

Pam, the profane and ridiculously formidable Angel, whose misuse of the English language constantly left me with my mouth agape, stood next to the delightfully vicious Vamp, Paris Hilton. Venus and Raquel rounded out the Vampyres along with Claudia —Tiara's mate. However, a few other impressive immortals were present—Gemma, the soon to be Queen of the Fairies, and Lucy, the shifter who was also a True Immortal.

In fact, there were three True Immortals here other than me— Astrid, Lucy, and Dixie—Compassion, Temptation and Balance. And of course I rounded it out as Evil. This pleased me. If Elle refused to leave she could be protected by those who could not be killed.

"The humans?" I asked again.

"I made it rain snakes," Gemma volunteered sheepishly.

Gemma was a wildly powerful entity—untrained, but quite gifted. Unfortunately, she was also good, as in not an evil bone in her entire body.

"Well, that would certainly do it," I muttered.

"Not poisonous," she assured me. "I just wanted them to leave so they wouldn't get caught in the shitshow about to occur."

"Good fuckin' thinkin' there," Pam said with a curt nod of approval and a loving slap to Gemma's back that sent her lurching ungracefully forward. "So what in the Hell are we doing? I was eating cookies and watching my programs, and next thing I knew I was sucked into some kind of fucked up tornado and my ass suddenly landed in Disney World."

"Mother Nature is playing games," I said. "I don't need you. I can retrieve my Siren's soul alone."

"You're a Siren?" Envy asked. "A *real* one? I thought they were extinct."

"Clearly not. There are two of us left—me and my mother," Elle replied.

"Three," I corrected her. "Fate is a Siren."

"Shut the front freakin' door," Astrid yelled. "That wankhole is a Siren?"

"Was," I replied.

"She's dead?" Tiara asked in alarm.

"Nope," Pam chimed in. "We'd know if she was a goner—trust me. However, you can't change species. That bitch is still a Siren."

"Whatever," I said. "I'm not here to discuss the drunken keeper of destiny. I'm after the Troll King. I'm going to guess the snakes will have alerted the bastard that something is up."

"Sorry," Gemma said with an apologetic shrug. "Wasn't sure why we were here. Just wanted the coast cleared of innocent humans. I assumed it was something ugly when I saw who was gathered."

"Well, the men not being invited makes sense now," Venus said, taking my Siren's hand in hers. "It's a pleasure to meet you."

Elle nodded. She was at a loss for words. I was fairly sure that not many in her experience were happy to meet her—especially women. Maybe having this insane bunch here wasn't such a bad call on my mother's part.

One by one, the women introduced themselves and either shook my Siren's hand or hugged her. She was mute as she accepted the warm greetings.

"You okay?" Astrid asked Elle.

"I'm fine," she assured her and then turned and faced the group. "I don't want any of you here."

"Trust me," Pam chimed in with a cackle, giving Elle the eyeball. "If you're worried about any of us comin' on to your man, you can relax your crack. Ain't nobody wants a piece of that evil ass. He's all yours."

Breathing in through my nose and blowing it slowly out through my lips, I reminded myself that it would be inappropriate to zap an Angel no matter how obnoxious she was.

"*Pam*," I said, grinding my teeth. "While that was colorful, it was crude."

"Since when did crude upset your ugly ass?" she demanded with a mischievous grin pulling at her lips.

"First of all, my ass not ugly," I ground out. "And secondly— damn it—I lost my train of thought."

"I want all of you to go," Elle repeated.

The shocked silence of the women was long and a bit menacing.

"You think we can't handle this?" Astrid asked, insulted as her hands began to glow and shoot little sparks.

Elle shook her head hastily, but stood her ground. "I don't want anyone hurt—or killed at my expense. I have more than enough death on my conscience. Go. All of you go."

My Siren was serious and clearly insane. She too was beginning to spark and the others watched her with distrust. What I really didn't need was a violent immortal female smack down—at all. There were Trolls to kill and a soul to steal. And more importantly, I needed to get laid again. A deadly girl fight was not on the agenda today.

"No can do," Tiara replied with a smile as she crossed to Elle and took her fiery hand in her own. "You need to calm down, Adrielle. You might be a badass who happens to be banging an insane badass, but even badasses need help from other badasses. Badass plus *insane* badass plus more badasses equals *total badassery*. You feel me?"

"Did anyone actually follow that?" Astrid asked, giving her sister an eye roll.

"Umm... kind of," Dixie said with a laugh.

Tiara grunted and flipped Astrid the middle finger. "Fine, I'll simplify. We might be pretty, but we're a tough bunch. Clearly, you're a badass, Elle. Uncle Fucker is also a badass—albeit an insane one, but everyone can use a little help."

"Uncle *Fucker*?" Elle questioned, trying not to smile.

"It's an endearment," I supplied, giving Tiara a glare.

"Besides, most of us owe the Devil, so this will repay our debts," Raquel, the Vampyre Princess of the European Dominion added. "Not to mention, I *despise* the Trolls. This will be fun."

"Your idea of fun is a bit strange," Elle said, staring in wonder at the *badass* women who refused to leave.

"Yep. Being dead kind of warps a person," Astrid explained with a laugh and a shrug. "And those stinky bastards want my son, not to mention they've tried to kill me a few times."

"And me," Raquel said, raising her hand.

"And me," Venus added.

"And most of the rest of us," Pam finished to off before everyone chimed in with a Troll story. "So what's the plaaaan, Sayyy-taaaan?"

Rolling my eyes, I pretended I wasn't dealing with older than dirt immortals who had the maturity levels of fifth grade human males. "We go in. I steal back Elle's soul from the Troll King and you will kill any Troll that tries to stop me," I instructed. "Astrid, Lucy, and Dixie, you three will keep watch over Elle. I don't want anything happening to her."

"Umm... call me *batshit crazy*, but why are we protecting a

Siren? Shouldn't that be the other way around?" Pam asked, confused.

I'd had enough of being questioned. For being as old as she was, Pam was lacking quite a bit of knowledge. Stomping my foot and causing a large split in the Earth made me feel a little more in charge.

"Fine," I ground out. "*Batshit Crazy*, I'm making the rules here. If you don't like them, you can leave. Under no circumstance will a Troll come within a hundred feet of my Siren. They want Elle's and her mother's soul for some unknown reason. The last time Elle battled with them she came back a bloody mess. I want her protected."

Pam and Elle exchanged a covert look and mouthed something to each other. Pam nodded in understanding and gave my Siren a thumbs up and a wide grin.

I had no time to play games with a bunch of stark raving mad immortals. First off, they all knew that I cheated and I'd probably lose. I hated losing. Whatever they'd said I would find out later.

"That's kind of a loose plan," Astrid pointed out unhelpfully.

With a wave of my hands I struck the gates of the happiest place on Earth with a massive bolt of lighting. It blew up sky high and came back down in a fiery explosion.

"Who do you people think I am?" I shouted.

"You're fucking Satan," Astrid shouted back in answer to my question.

"That's right," I bellowed. "*I'm fucking Satan.*"

I froze and closed my eyes. Taking a deep breath so I wouldn't blast Florida—or Astrid—to Kingdom Come, I expelled it on a growl. All of my daughters, the rest of the motely crew, and even my Siren began to laugh. Astrid had just earned my attendance for Christmas for eternity. Not only would I be attending her celebrations, I would be profanely *enhancing* every single ornament she had. It would not be pretty.

"That's quite a talent, Lucifer," Pam announced to the laughing crowd. "I'm surprised you come out of Hell if you can do that."

"Enough," I hissed. The lack of respect shown by these women was appalling. If I were being honest—which gave me hives—I'd have to admit it was also refreshing. It was rare indeed to get busted on by anyone. However, showing my pleasure would be counter productive to my authority, which seem tenuous at best right now.

"So basically we're gonna storm Disney World and then wing it?" Tiara asked, biting on her lips to keep from giggling.

"Yes," I snapped, grabbing Elle by the hand. "We're going to wing it. Anyone have a problem with that?"

No one said a word. That was good. I was on the verge of a massive temper tantrum. Throwing a fit would not further my agenda.

"Umm… does anyone think it's odd that we've been standing here for a while and haven't been attacked?" Gemma pointed out.

She was correct. It *was* strange—alarmingly strange. The Trolls had to know we were here. I'd cracked the Earth and blown up the entrance. Not to mention the park was crawling with snakes.

With a wave of my hand, I called to my army in Hell. In a blast of glittering black magic two hundred well-armed Demons appeared—female Demons. Males would be useless. And my females were far more deadly than my males.

Tiara raised her hand politely. "Should I sing?"

The idea had occurred to me, but there was no way her singing could take down an entire army of Trolls. As ear splitting and deadly as it was, it wouldn't work. No one was that powerful.

"While I appreciate the offer, the answer is no," I told her. "This will be hand to hand and magic. The singing will harm our own and won't be strong enough to take down the enemy."

Tiara nodded and checked her weapons. "Got it."

"The Troll King is mine," I yelled to be heard by all. "No one is to touch him. He has the soul I'm after, and if he's destroyed, the soul will be destroyed with him. That is unacceptable and cannot happen under any circumstances. Am I clear?"

Satisfied with the murmurs of assent, I took Elle's hand and approached the blown out entrance. "You will lead me to the King, and then go with Astrid, Dixie and Lucy," I told her firmly. "Do not disobey me. I can't lose you."

"Why?" she demanded, stopping and glaring at me. She put her hand on her heart and waited.

Damn it to Hell, this was not the time.

"Answer me," she pressed.

Everyone around us stopped as well and watched in with rabid curiosity. *I* was even curious how I would respond…

Placing my hand on my heart, I looked down at the beautiful woman who in a very short time I knew that I couldn't live without. I was still unsure if I could love her. The meaning of love was a mystery to me, but…

"I think I might be feeling things… possibly… maybe. I'm not sure. Although highly doubtful," I mumbled, telling the only truth I knew. "I'm not sure what it is, but I feel something unfamiliar and somewhat alarming."

Her sad smile slayed me and for a moment I forgot to breathe. It wasn't the answer she wanted, but it was all I had. I wanted to wrap her in my arms and take her away from whatever ugliness was about to happen, but that was a dream—an unrealistic dream. There would always be evil and violence. I would always be a part of it. But this woman was well aware of that and seemed to want me regardless.

"That will do for now," she said on a resigned sigh. "Let's do this."

"We're gonna kick ass," Astrid shouted as my army of women descended on the happiest fucking place on Earth.

Today might just be a good day after all.

CHAPTER TWENTY-ONE

THE BLINDINGLY COLORFUL STREETS OF DISNEY WORLD WERE TEEMING with slithering, hissing snakes. It was an impressive sight. However, the Trolls were nowhere to be seen.

"Something is *very* wrong," Astrid said, scanning the area. "Where in the Hell are the bad dudes?"

"Cinderella's Castle," Elle said. "The Troll King resides in the Castle."

"Seriously?" Dixie asked. "How do they get away with that? This place is loaded with humans all the time."

"Keeps them safe. They live behind the mosaics," Elle explained with a disgusted expression marring her lovely features. "Immortals won't risk the lives of humans to go after them."

"Trolls are smarter than I'd thought," Pam said, clapping her hands and sending the snakes back to wherever Gemma had summoned them from.

"Surround the castle," I commanded my troops. "The cowards are inside. The King is mine."

Silently and faster than the human eye could follow, my Demon army obeyed my order. Only the original women who had come at my mother's beckoning remained with me.

"You're positive your soul is in the locket?" I asked Elle.

She nodded and pulled me to a stop. "Just get the soul and leave. I want none of your people to die. This should not be their battle."

Without answering her, I resumed my walk toward the palace. It was getting difficult to lie to her even without my hand on my heart. I had no intention of leaving any Trolls alive. They would keep coming after her until she was broken and dead. I was walking a precarious line by destroying all that were here, but I knew more of the species were elsewhere. I wouldn't be making the Trolls extinct by ending the life of their King and those who protected the bastard. So while I was fucking with the natural order, I wasn't exactly fucking it up completely.

"Cover me," I told Astrid and the others. "And keep Elle the Hell out of this. If she fights you, someone transport out with her."

"You gonna let that man talk to you like that?" Pam asked a clearly seething Elle.

"Let him have his fun. I'll have mine shortly," she hissed.

"That's my girl." Pam cackled as she levitated and prepared to fly toward the castle.

I had an inkling what my Siren was referring to. Her *words* were starting to make sense to me—*listen to the words*. I felt smug in my knowledge. Women weren't as hard to figure out as I'd thought. Of course, I was smart enough not to let on that I knew of her dastardly plan.

Quite certain she'd hatched a scheme to set me on fire in front of everyone, I simply grinned. Little did she know how much I craved and needed her searing magic. Being set aflame by my Siren was a reward—not a punishment.

"Holy shit on a stick," Astrid gasped as the enormous monsters appeared.

The Trolls materialized in the archway of the Castle. There had to be at least fifty and the King stood front and center. They were at least ten feet tall with rotting flesh and a stench that made the Basement of Hell smell like a morning in Springtime on Earth.

My eyes went immediately to the locket at his neck. It was grossly bejeweled—rubies, diamonds, sapphires, emeralds, pearls, onyx. I enjoyed over the top, but this locket was downright garish. But no matter how ugly, I was about to add it to my collection.

"State your complaint, Devil," the Troll King bellowed in a harsh voice that sounded like he'd swallowed massive quantities of glass and his throat was still bleeding profusely. "We have no beef with you."

"Of course you don't," I said with a smile on my face that made the bastard step back behind his men. "It would be *incredibly stupid* for you to challenge me."

"I am aware of this," the King snarled, smoke and fire huffing out of his nose. "Why have you come?"

I'd almost missed what the idiot said due to the gnashing of teeth and the whining and growling of his men. Their skin expanded and contracted with their aggression. The rancid flaps trembled and the odor they emitted was noxious.

"Tell the boys to pipe down. They're giving me a headache," I said. "And Hell's been known to break loose when I have a headache."

With a grunt and an eerie scream that bounced off the walls of the castle, the Troll King silenced his men.

"You have something that belongs to me," I said in a friendly conversational tone that made him even more wary than he already was. Of course my smile—while devastatingly handsome —came nowhere close to reaching my eyes. "I want it back."

"I have nothing of yours, Devil," the Troll King shouted—his lumpy, hairless body turning a hideous shade of greenish-blue and vibrating with fury. "You will leave or you will be sorry."

"Did that fucker just threaten me?" I asked, shocked as I halted my advance and turned back to my girls.

"I believe he did, Uncle Fucker," Tiara answered with a shit-eating grin.

"Unacceptable," I muttered as I turned my attention back to the Troll. "You just made your first mistake, Troll. The next one will be your last. Give me the locket and what's inside."

"Never," he roared.

"I'm sorry. I must have misunderstood you. I could swear you just said *no*," I replied as I clapped my hands and let my body go to one of its most natural states.

Fire.

Pulling on a magic as old as time, I sighed in contentment as the dark enchantment roared through me and encased my body in blazing red flame. With a snap of my flaming fingers, my body increased to a much larger size then the ten-foot Trolls and my voice was far more menacing and raw than his.

"Give me the locket or you die. It's really quite simple."

"Damn that's some fucked up shit he can do," I heard Pam mutter from behind. "How in the Hell are his clothes not burning off his body and how did they grow with him?"

"Shut your cakehole," Astrid admonished the Angel. "We'll ask him later. I was wondering the same thing."

"The locket is my future and your demise, *Satan*," the Troll King hissed as his men began to keen and quake with the need to kill.

It was uniquely horrifying. Trolls were like ticks. They just latched on and sucked life from those around them. Useless. Diseased. Nothing about them enhanced society—at all. Violent for the sake of it and remorseless. Trust me, I knew. Every Troll that perished lived in the Basement of Hell burning for eternity for sins so vile they gave even me pause.

"Nope," I said baring my teeth at him through my fiery shell. "I do not accept."

"Yesssss," he screamed, his vile spittle spraying his men

standing guard around him. "I'm holding it for the Keeper and she is far more powerful than the likes of you."

"Really?" I asked, with an evil laugh that made him blanch. "Where is this Keeper? She's not here to protect you from me."

"She will come. And you will rue the day you came here."

"Okay, sounds great," I said as my fire danced around me. "I'm rather busy today—tight schedule—need to get home and get laid. I don't have time to hang out and meet your *Keeper*. You feel me, asshole?"

"Do not speak to me that way," the Troll said, shoving his men aside and beginning to lumber toward me. "You will take that back, Dark Angel. *NOW.*"

"Uh oh," Dixie said. "Dude's lost his tiny mind. Is he really coming for my dad?"

"Looks that way," Pam added, slapping her knee and laughing like a loon. "I changed my mind about Trolls being smart. That smelly assmonkey fell out of the stupid tree and hit every branch on the way down."

"Take it back, you evil disgrace," the Troll repeated as he continued to advance.

"Or what?" I demanded. "I'm a little hard to kill, imbecile."

The Troll King smiled. It sent warning chills skittering down my spine. His teeth were razor sharp and hideous. His scaly lips were thin and dripping puss. It occurred to me for a very brief moment that I'd never come across a female Troll... or maybe he was a female. Hell on a bad day, this species was horrifying.

"I'll destroy the soul. There's another I can get to replace it."

No, the bastard wasn't stupid—not at all. He did have the power to kill me, metaphorically speaking, but a death was a death. The walking, talking dead were everywhere and I had no intention of joining their ranks. By destroying Adrielle's soul, she would only exist a hundred more years which was a mere blip in eternity.

Not happening—not on my fucking watch.

"Done here," I roared as the Troll stopped his forward motion and went for the locket on his neck. "GO. NOW."

Without hesitation, my Demons and my girls went like bats out of Hell and attacked. I had eyes for only one and the coward tuned and ran. He could run, but he couldn't outrun the Devil. No one could outrun the Devil.

It was fast and it was bloody. In the end it was completely anticlimactic. I set him on fire as my people went for his protectors —seamless and vicious.

Tearing the smoldering locket from his neck I removed Elle's soul and put it in the left breast pocket of my suit—right next to my wicked heart. I leaned down to his prone, disgusting body and smiled. "You're a very stupid man. It's not nice to fuck with the Devil."

"It's *Mother Nature* you don't fuck with," he snapped as he tried to claw at my burning flesh and steal the soul back from my pocket.

"She's my *mother*, Troll. I'm allowed to use her catch phrase. I have to eat her cooking."

"You think you're funny," the Troll choked out as green and black blood poured from his mouth. "But I will have the last laugh."

"Really?" I asked. "You could have fooled me."

"You might have the soul and I might die, but *she* will come for you."

"Sounds great. I look forward to it," I told him as I prepared to end him once and for all.

But as I tore his head from his hideous body, he did indeed get the last word in. Right before the son of a bitch took his last worthless breath, he called out a spell. I froze in both shock and horror. How did this sub human bastard know how to summon death? The Troll King died with an evil smile on his putrid face.

I'd thought the battle was over. I'd thought I'd won. I was wrong.

The battle had just begun. The dying bastard had unleashed the wraiths. The one dead species I had no jurisdiction over.

All Hell had broken loose and it wasn't set off by me.

CHAPTER TWENTY-TWO

THOUSANDS OF SCREECHING WRAITHS DESCENDED ON THE HAPPIEST fucking place on Earth. Their screams were haunting and unearthly. The abominations had dead eyes and gaunt faces with papery skin and open wounds. Nearly transparent specters wailed and moaned as they flew in frantic circles with no other goal than to create as much pain as they were in. The bone-chilling screeching would stay with me long after the battle was done. Swords and magic were useless on the wraiths as they darted like blood thirsty gnats on speed in and out of the bodies of my army.

The shrieks of my people were more than I could bear and I began to chant counter spells in an ancient language that very few still knew existed. The cries of the wraiths reached ear-splitting decibels and I watched in horror as some of my Demons fell to the ground in agony. My spell was working, but too slowly to stop the death and destruction the wraiths were causing.

"Get Raquel," Astrid shouted above the fray. "Surround her and protect her. She can banish them."

Searching like a man gone mad, I spotted Raquel. She was far too injured to do anything but try to survive the attack. Goddamnit, this was not supposed to be happening.

My eyes were wild as I tried to find Elle in the chaos. She would never live through this. My daughters and nieces stood a good chance of making it out alive, but my Siren... no.

Tearing through the deadly specters without care for myself, I searched—I searched desperately. I barely felt the icy blasts as the wraiths ripped into my skin. The savage ghosts carried a blistering wind with them that shot through me like a frozen dagger.

I would survive this toxic strike. I was a True Immortal, but I realized I didn't want to survive if she didn't. I finally had an answer to her damned question and I needed her alive to hear it.

The attack was a clusterfuck of ghostly execution and there was little to nothing I could do about it.

And then I found her...

Pam and Astrid were at her back holding her upright and Elle was shouting directions. My Siren was calling the murderous apparitions to her and they headed for her so quickly I couldn't see through the billowy fog they created in their wake. In their frantic blitz, they resembled a swarm of bloody bees.

What the fuck was happening? I was so close, but I couldn't reach her. The wraiths were so frenzied I could barely move.

And that's when I went deaf.

I was fairly certain everyone in the battle went deaf. I could vaguely make out my Demons touching their ears and grabbing each other in confusion. I'd never heard of a wraith attack causing loss of hearing. But I'd also never witnessed thousands of wraiths at the same time.

I shouted in warning as they went for Adrielle. I couldn't hear myself, but I felt the vibration all throughout my body. It was the worst moment of my life and I would relive it for the rest of eternity.

And then everything went into slow fucked up motion. The wraiths tore through my Siren as she stood there and took it. Her face was serene and she was bleeding profusely. I swore on everything I was that I would avenge her death. Not a day would go by that I wouldn't hunt down and kill anything or anyone connected to the ghostly abominations. The Trolls would be systematically wiped off the face of the Earth and then I would find their *keeper*.

In helpless horror, I watched as Elle raised her bleeding arms to the sky and her mouth opened. I had no idea what she was saying but her lips moved and something maniacal started happening.

My Siren was singing. She told me she never sang.

The damned words—I hadn't listened to the words... again.

"Karaoke some time?" I suggested with a lopsided grin.

Elle and Sadie traded glances and both shook their heads slowly.

"Trust me," Elle said. "You don't ever want to hear us sing."

"Ever," Sadie added with a small shudder.

She was singing and she'd clearly didn't want us to hear her. She'd used an enchantment to deafen those she wanted to survive the effects of her melody. My negating the value of mythology bit me in the ass once more—the song of the Siren lured men to their deaths... or in this case, the wraiths.

It was like watching the movie Fantasia on crack. The wraiths began exploding in vivid color—red, orange, green, blue, yellow. The colors bled together and erupted, shooting over the spires of the castle and flaring up into neon nuclear bombs. The lethal fireworks shot into the sky, fanned out like macabre flowers, and spilled back down to the ground in dazzling burning embers.

My Siren's eyes were closed and her lips never stopped moving for a second. I let my fire recede and I stood as still as a statue while I watched the most glorious, deadly performance I'd seen to date. Thousands of wraiths were detonating and bursting into colors so bright I had to shield my eyes.

My army huddled together and watched in shocked alarm and admiration as my Siren rid the world of the swarm of death.

As quickly as it started, suddenly it was over. Elle fell to the ground and let her head drop to her hands. She then looked up and our eyes met. With a touch to her ears, my ability to hear returned as did everyone else's.

However, no one spoke. Not a word.

With slow careful steps, my broken Demon army circled my Siren and went to their knees in reverence.

"Well, that was certainly some shit you don't see everyday," Pam grunted as she walked around and checked on her people.

"Roll call," Tiara shouted.

Tiara was missing an arm, but it would grow back. The rest of the main group was alive and healing quickly. Damaged but alive. I stood stock still. My feet felt like lead and I simply watched as the women bowed down to Adrielle Rinoa.

More words raced through my brain.

"You gonna let that man talk to you like that?" Pam asked a clearly seething Elle.

"Let him have his fun. I'll have mine shortly," she hissed.

If this was my Siren's idea of fun, we were definitely going to have to talk. I clearly didn't understand women at all. My smugness at believing I'd known what she meant vanished. I was going to need a damned interpreter to figure my Siren out.

The women parted as I approached her. I reached out and gently pulled her to her feet. Elle's smile was as blinding as the fireworks had been and it was all I could do to stay standing. This woman slayed me and cut me off at the knees at every turn.

"That was a bit unexpected," I said, my voice sounding hoarse to my own ears.

"No one will ever die at my expense if I have anything to say about it. Ever," she replied, still smiling despite her bruised and swollen lips.

I carefully ran my finger over her mouth. What I wanted most was to kiss her, but causing her any kind of pain was abhorrent to me. I knew she would heal—all immortals did. That gave me solace, but I despised seeing her harmed.

"You humble me," I whispered with my hand on my heart. "The answer to your question is yes."

"Which question?" she shot back, narrowing her amethyst eyes at me. "I've asked many."

"The important one."

"Refresh my memory, Devil," she replied.

I closed my eyes and grinned. The woman was going to make me work for it. I deserved nothing less and neither did she. Fine. I would work. The reward was worth any discomfort I had stating my feelings in front of my people and my children.

"That girl has got you by the balls, Lucifer," Pam bellowed joyously. "You had best tell her what she wants to hear. That Siren can blow us all to Kingdom Come if she's pissed. You better watch yourself, boy."

Pam's laugh echoed those around us and I let her irreverence go—mainly because she was correct—rude as Hell, but correct.

Taking a deep breath and letting it out slowly, I bit back my smile and raised an eyebrow at the Siren who had truly made me *feel*. "I'm in love with you, Adrielle Rinoa. You are a dreadful woman and I want to spend every horrible moment for the rest of eternity at your evil side. I love you and I'm not even appalled to admit it."

The intake of breath from the crowd of women was so monstrous that I was certain they were all going to pass out from lack of oxygen.

"Holy shit on fire," Pam squealed, hopping around like her pants were on fire. "I can't believe what I'm hearin'. The Devil is in luuurve. Has Hell frozen over?"

"Don't think so, but I'm not sure using the words appalled, dreadful, horrible and evil in a declaration of love is the smartest way to go," Astrid said sounding a little concerned.

I grinned. My niece should be happy I didn't use the term *bosom*...

"No, it's all good. Trust me," Dixie said with a delighted laugh and her hands clasped together in joy.

"Whatever you say, cousin," Astrid replied, shaking her head.

"And I love you, Harbinger of Evil. You're an asshole with an attitude and I couldn't be happier about that. The simple fact that you came out alive after having sex with me is miraculous, but what I really love is your horrifying ability to lie, cheat and steal. However, if you ever cheat on *me,* I will remove your impressive manhood with a dull butter knife. I will let it grow back and then I will rinse and repeat—for the rest of time."

"That was a little TMI," Tiara announced to the open mouthed crowd. "Is she fucking serious?"

"As a human heart attack," I replied with a laugh that came from low in my gut. "And I'd have it no other way. Besides, I'll do even worse."

"Holy Hell on a bobsled," Pam grunted and slapped her forehead with her hand. "Can't wait for the wedding. Should be a dang violent freak show."

"No wedding," Elle said to Pam with her gold ringed amethyst eyes still glued to me. "We prefer to live in sin—much more fun."

"She is sooooo perfect for you," Dixie squealed, throwing herself at Elle and hugging her hard. "Thank you."

"For what?" Elle asked, surprised by the show of affection.

"For loving him."

"That part is easy," Elle replied with a laugh that made my pants tight. "The living with him part will be interesting."

"Is *interesting* a euphemism for *crime ridded shit show?*" Pam joked.

"Actually, it is," I confirmed as I took Elle into my arms and held her close.

Love felt pretty damned good. Who the Hell knew? Everything about this woman calmed me and made me feel… well, happy.

The lone clapping coming from the damaged entrance to the castle didn't take me by surprise. It was staccato and angry. I'd been expecting a visitor and she didn't disappoint. Of course she was a little late to the show, but I was well aware that she didn't like to get her hands dirty—that was for lesser immortals.

The Keeper had arrived just in time for the final showdown of the day. Her timing was shitty—but then again it always was. However, this time her hands were going to get dirty.

Very dirty.

CHAPTER TWENTY-THREE

"How lovely," she said in a flat toneless voice and continued her disrespectful show of appreciation with her slow insolent clapping. "I see you found your *darkness*."

"*Fate*, always awful to see you," I said, placing Elle behind me and stepping out in front of my people. "What brings you to the happiest fucking place on Earth? I'd think Harry Potter World would be more your speed. I do believe you and the Nagini have *so much* in common."

"Touché," she shot back coldly.

"And where is this *darkness* you speak of?" I asked, scanning the horizon behind her. "I will destroy it. Then you can leave and go terrorize other unsuspecting immortals."

"Is that supposed to be funny, Devil?" she asked.

"Not at all," I replied, holding my temper with enormous effort. The need to take her down was almost a physical pain. "Simply truthful—a rarity for me. Show me the darkness or I will show you no mercy."

"This is rich," she said laughing in a way that made me certain she had lost her mind. "You really don't get it, do you?"

"Get what?" I ground out with my fists clenched at my sides.

It would do me very little good to smite her without all the information I needed. Satisfying? Yes. Smart? Absolutely not.

"The *words*, you stupid evil man. It's in the meaning of the words."

I put my hand up as a signal to my growling Demons to stand down. I could fight this particular battle on my own. Fate was a dangerous woman to start with. Add in her unbalanced insanity and she was a ticking time bomb.

"What words?" I demanded, still not following.

"Is a rose still a rose by any other *name?*" Fate purred with a vicious smile on her face.

"My name," Elle said on a gasp as she stepped forward and took my hand in hers. "I think *I'm* your darkness."

"Explain," I said, but kept my eyes trained on Fate. She was not to be trusted.

"Adrielle means dark one."

"And Rinoa?" I questioned as a profound relief began to wash over me.

"One who is a torch of light in the darkness," she whispered.

My joyous bellow of laughter startled everyone. How in the Hell had I missed it? My *darkness* had been with me all along. How fucking perfect. I pulled my Siren closer and kissed the top of her gorgeous blonde head as I continued to observe Fate.

The bitch's words came flowing back...

"The darkness is coming for you, Lucifer. You will need to embrace it when she arrives," Fate said in the same bland tone one would talk about the weather.

I'd missed the word *she.*

"There's fire in the darkness, Lucifer. A fire that will weaken you, yet make you stronger. A fire that could restore your soul."

"Stop talking nonsense, old woman," I roared as the building trembled in reaction to my ire. She was fucking with me and I wanted to end her with my bare hands. *"I have no soul. It was obliterated when I fell."*

"Is that what you think, Lucifer?" she questioned, examining me with pity.

"It's what I know."

My Siren's fire was my savior and I now believed that something else might be a distinct possibility... "Well, while this has been a ball of fucking laughs, it's time for you to go. I'd say it's been a delight to see your drunken face again but it hasn't. Good day, *Fate*," I said with a dismissive nod to the hateful woman.

"I'm not done here," Fate hissed, causing an ominous wind to blow, knocking my Demons off their feet. Astrid, Tiara and the rest were still standing, but it was anyone's guess how long they could take the unpredictable winds of change.

"I'm done," I snapped back equally as vicious.

Elle squeezed my hand and with a covert wiggle of her fingers, she halted the escalating wind. Fate's glare shot to Elle and she simply stared. She tore her gaze from Elle and paced slowly back and forth in the still smoldering embers of the dead wraiths to gather herself.

Elle's action floored me. It made me consider other *words* that had been imparted to me by my mother. Sometimes mothers might know best, even one as unhinged as mine. This time I wasn't going to miss a beat—far too much was at stake here.

"Imagine my surprise when your darkness turned out to be the very thing I'd been searching for," Fate said in such a deranged and angry voice that the hair on my neck stood up. "It's really just so very convenient. Don't you think so?"

"Not really," I replied sounding unconcerned. It was a lie. I was on hyper alert, but I was an outstanding liar. The direction of this exchange wasn't one I liked.

"The locket. It's mine," she said.

"Here you go," I said flatly, tossing the locket at her feet. "The real question is why are you looking for it?"

"It's empty," she shouted as she threw it to the ground and

zapped it into millions of tiny sparkling pieces. "What was in it belongs to me."

My smile was pure evil and Fate took a few steps back. "Really *Keeper?*" I asked in a tone that had all the immortals present—regardless of species—backing away. Only Elle stayed with me—my darkness. "That's not what I heard."

"You heard wrong," Fate said.

"Explain yourself," I snarled as she blanched, but immediately stepped back up and held her ground.

"I need the soul. It belongs to me. End of story."

"No," Elle said, staring right at Fate. "It does not belong to you. It's mine."

"I should have had the Trolls do away with you and your mother centuries ago—all I need are your souls. The bodies are a turning out to be more trouble than they're worth," she shouted. "But you're a slippery one, *Siren.*"

"Takes one to know one," Elle shot back to the surprise of Fate. "You've been using our power for millions of years, old woman, and today it stops."

"And who are you to tell me what I can and can't do?" Fate snarled, but stayed back as Elle began to spark like a black fiery diamond. "I control fate. I *am* Fate."

"Shit's about to get ugly," I heard Astrid mutter under her breath.

"Damn fuckin' straight," Tiara whispered back.

"Call me silly or rude or evil," I said, while yawning rudely to piss Fate off.

"Or Blade Inferno," Elle added with a smirk.

"Yes. I answer to that one too," I said with a smile to my darkness before I turned my attention back to Fate. "But I was under the impression you were one of the reporters."

"I am," she said, looking addled.

"One of the *reporters*—with an *S?* Those were your *exact words* to me. You're the one who likes to put so much emphasis on the words. Would you like to explain how you can be plural?"

Her purple eyes—eyes that matched Elle's minus the gorgeous golden rings—narrowed dangerously. "Occasionally one misspeaks, Devil. I meant nothing by that. Give me the soul or you will pay the consequences."

"Are you threatening me?" I asked so quietly she dropped eye contact and looked away. "Didn't think that was *allowed*, Fate."

"It's not," Pam said from behind. "And I would have to say there are some other important mother humpin' entities who might be very interested in this fucked up little exchange."

Fate's eyes grew wide as she recognized Pam. As horrifyingly rude and profane as the Angel was, she was also one of my brother's top generals. And she didn't take shit from anyone.

"May I take it from here?" I inquired politely of Pam with a wink.

"Be my guest, O Evil Hot Pants," she replied with an irreverent wink of her own.

"You used my fate for your own means," I said to the horrid woman as she stood mutely and tried to figure out how she was going to win this battle.

She wasn't going to win. I was.

"That's a pretty big fucking *no-no*," I went on. "I'm beginning to believe that the mythology of *three* Fates has merit as well. You've been using the power of the other two to keep them weak and yourself strong."

"Lies," she screamed.

"God in a bikini on a unicycle," Pam grumbled. "That bee-otch is making my dang eardrums bleed. You mind if I help you out a bit here, Lucifer?"

"Be my guest," I said, knowing I was going to owe the Angel big time, but I didn't care—at all. Normally, I never worked alongside celestial beings, but Pam was so disgusting I could make it work.

With an unladylike grunt and a crude swing of her hips, a burst of blinding golden light flew from Pam's hands and wrapped Fate in its goodness. The Heavenly virtue of Pam's magic was almost too much for me to take, but I bit back my ill-mannered quips about my brother and his cherubic followers. The upside was that it gagged Fate and made her immobile.

"So as I was saying," I went on, touching my breast pocket to make sure Elle's soul was safe. "You're supposed to be one of three. You've held down the other two for millennia. You came before all, so we had no way of knowing your treason, but you'd better believe I'm going to study mythology with a much less prejudiced eye from now on."

"Can I cut in here, Big Guy?" Pam asked.

With a curt nod, I stepped back.

"You're in a shitload of trouble right now. Fate, I hereby call an immortal tribunal to discuss your *fate*." Pam slapped her thighs and cackled like a patient in an insane asylum. "Did you guys hear that? How I used fate twice in that sentence? I'm so goooood."

A tribunal was no joke. It was binding and deadly. There hadn't been one in thousands of years. Fate's eye grew wide. She jerked her head back and broke through the Angel's enchantment.

"I'd like to see you try," she snarled as she raised her arms and called to the winds. "I may not have what I came for, but trust me, I will get it and all of you will pay for your contemptuous sins. I'll be seeing you, Elle. Watch your back."

"Get her," I roared as I flew at lightning speed toward the psychotic keeper of destiny.

But I was too late. We were all too late. Fate had turned to mist and blew away on the winds of change.

"She won't get away with this," Pam growled.

"Maybe. Maybe not," Elle said in a tone that made warning bells go off in my head.

Something wasn't right.

"Come home with me," I said, extending my hand to my destined darkness. "Let me take you away from this."

Elle didn't take my hand, but she held hers out. "Give me my soul, Lucifer."

I considered not returning it, but then I would be no better than the Trolls who stole it or Fate who had used it.

Putting my hand on my heart, I stared at her. Her quick intake of breath didn't escape me and my cold, black heart plummeted.

"I love you and I always will," I told her quietly. "Take very good care of this soul. I'm quite partial to it."

She nodded as sparkling amethyst tears ran down her face. I put the soul into her outstretched hand and quickly closed her fingers over it. Without breaking eye contact, she slipped it into the Hermes bag I'd given her.

Pressing a kiss to my lips, she placed her warm hands on either side of my face. "I love you too, Lucifer—more than someone like me deserves to love anyone—and that's why I'm leaving you. This is *my* fight, not yours and I won't see you destroyed by it."

"What's mine is yours and what's yours is mine," I said as I felt something breaking and shattering inside me. "Let me help you."

"Not this time," she said sadly.

"Unacceptable," I growled as I pulled her close and held her tight. "You're mine."

I tried to memorize the feel of her body and the scent of her skin. Her heat was my salvation and my happily ever after. With one last bittersweet kiss to my lips, my Siren disappeared is a mist of amethyst sparkles. It didn't matter how tightly I held on, she slipped through my fingers without a backward glance.

Love was for fools. There was no happy ending for the Devil.

"What the Hell just happened?" Tiara yelled as she tore around the area searching for my Siren.

"She left," I said flatly, staring at the ground where she'd just stood.

"Are you just gonna stand there like a dumbass, staring at your feet?" Astrid demanded, punching me in the arm. "Go get her. NOW. She's a little on the terrifyingly violent side, but she said she loves you. AND you love her. What the Hell are you doing just standing here?"

I glanced up and glared at my niece.

"Listen to me," Astrid insisted, running her hands through her hair and making it stand on end. "I wrote you a happily ever after in your bullshit book. It's happened for real now and you're letting it get away. What is *wrong* with you?"

Looking at the women who had stood by me, I smiled and shrugged. "The Devil doesn't get a happily ever after. Didn't you know that?"

"I call bullshit," Astrid shouted, getting seconds and thirds from the crowd.

"While I appreciate the sentiment, it's moot. The Siren was a passing fancy for me and now it's over. Love is a fallacy that I shall not buy into again. Not a big deal. Tomorrow is a new day and the world is full of women who want me. I'm Satan, the world's greatest lover," I reminded them with my signature smirk.

I didn't believe a goddamned word of what I'd just said, and not one other person present believed me either, but they all had the wherewithal—or instinct for self-preservation—not to contradict me.

Glancing around, I sighed. The park was a fucking disaster, but I didn't have it in me to repair it.

"I need to leave," I said in a bright careless tone that belied how I was feeling. "Would you all mind doing clean up duty here? I'm done for today."

"Not a problem, Dad," Dixie said as she wrapped her arms around me and laid her head on my chest. "You're my world."

"And you're mine," I whispered and then raised my head to the crowd of female warriors. "As much as it's not in my character —and trust me it's *not*—I'd like to thank all of you. I will deny that I said this, so please enjoy it while you can. Good day."

With a wave of my hands, I called to my dark magic and my body was engulfed in billowing black smoke and glitter. The trip back to Hell was a lonely one, but loneliness was something I was very used to. It was nothing new.

It was just a bit more devastating than usual.

EPILOGUE

I PLACED THE AMETHYST ORB ON MY DESK AND STARED IN WONDER. IT sparkled and winked at me as I gazed into its glittery depths. I gently ran my index finger over it—soft, smooth, feminine, and a little bit dangerous. I could feel her. She was still with me in a surreal sense of the word.

"Hello, little soul. You're just as beautiful as your owner."

Of course, the soul didn't answer. It simply continued to shimmer peacefully on the black mahogany desk.

"Won't my Siren be surprised when she takes out the soul I gave her?" I asked with a laugh as I leaned back in my chair with the satisfaction of a job well done.

I didn't need an answer. I already knew it. She would be shocked, appalled and furious. And if she were here, she'd set me ablaze for what I'd done.

The switch had been simple. I'd put my hand on my heart and silently called for my soul. There would never be anyone more surprised than me that I actually had one—and it was just as Elle had described it. My soul was the gorgeous gold of an Angel with the beautiful dark outer rim of a Demon, and it was now in her safekeeping, just as hers was in mine.

Picking up the orb and holding it in my hands, I carefully pressed it to my lips.

"Don't worry, little soul. You'll see your owner very soon. I promise. She can run, but she can't hide—or maybe she can hide, but I have an advantage. I have two things she can't live without."

I tucked Elle's soul safely into my pocket and grinned.

"And what might those two things be, might you ask little soul? The answer is quite simple. You and me. Those are the two things Adrielle Rinoa can't live without."

I'd lied earlier when I'd said there was no happy ending for the Devil. There was no doubt I excelled at lying. I was the master of it, but I was very aware when I told untruths. I'd most definitely and deliberately told an untruth.

I was going to get my happily ever after and so would my Siren. We were just going to go about in in an unconventional way.

Losing wasn't an option. I never lost. I'd lie, cheat and steal until what I wanted was mine. I wanted Adrielle Rinoa. And I knew she wanted me.

Love might not conquer all, but the Devil and his deceitful ways most certainly could. I had an arsenal of devious plans up my Armani sleeves and I would use each and every one until *my darkness* was mine once more.

Tomorrow would be a day like any other. Punishments must be doled out, chaos must be encouraged, and a Siren must be found before Fate got her vicious claws into her.

A vacation would be lovely, but there was no rest for the weary or the evil. Standing up and glancing in the mirror at the image of the exquisitely beautiful man staring back at me, I smiled. I was a fucking handsome son of a bitch.

"It's show time, folks."

— The End (for now) —

PRE-ORDER THE NEXT BOOK IN THE SERIES!

Coming to an e-reader near you, March 12, 2018

Pre-order your copy of <u>Fashionably Forever After</u> and get your next Satan fix!

NOTE FROM THE AUTHOR

Thank you for reading *Fashionably Flawed*!

If you enjoyed this book, please consider leaving a positive review or rating on the site where you purchased it. Reader reviews help my books continue to be valued by resellers and help new readers make decisions about reading them. You are the reason I write these stories and I sincerely appreciate each of you!

Many thanks for your support,
~ Robyn Peterman

Want to hear about my new releases?
Sign-up for my newsletter to be notified.

http://eepurl.com/pTM61

BOOK LISTS

(IN CORRECT READING ORDER)

HOT DAMNED SERIES
Fashionably Dead
Fashionably Dead Down Under
Hell on Heels
Fashionably Dead in Diapers
A Fashionably Dead Christmas
Fashionably Hotter Than Hell
Fashionably Dead And Wed
Fashionable Fanged
Fashionably Flawed
Fashionably Ever After

SHIFT HAPPENS SERIES
Ready to Were
Some Were in Time
No Were To Run
Were Me Out

MAGIC AND MAYHEM SERIES
Switching Hour

Witch Glitch
A Witch In Time
Magically Delicious
A Tale Of Two Witches

HANDCUFFS AND HAPPILY EVER AFTERS SERIES
How Hard Can it Be?
Size Matters
Cop a Feel

If after reading all the above you are still wanting more adventure and zany fun, read *Pirate Dave and His Randy Adventures*, the romance novel budding novelist Rena was helping wicked Evangeline write in *How Hard Can It Be?*

Warning: *Pirate Dave* Contains Romance Satire, Spoofing, and Pirates with Two Pork Swords.

ABOUT THE AUTHOR

Robyn Peterman writes because the people inside her head won't leave her alone until she gives them life on paper.

Her addictions include laughing really hard with friends, shoes (the expensive kind), Target, Coke Zero Cherry with extra ice in a Styrofoam cup, bejeweled reading glasses, her kids, her super hot hubby and collecting stray animals.

A former professional actress with Broadway, film and TV credits, she now lives in the South with her family and too many animals to count.

Writing gives her peace and makes her whole, plus having a job where you can work in your underpants works really well for her. You can leave Robyn a message via the Contact Page and she'll get back to you as soon as her bizarre life permits! She loves to hear from her fans!

Want More Info About Robyn? You can find her here...
www.robynpeterman.com
robyn@robynpeterman.com